THE CURSE OF NONA MAY TAYLOR

JESS K HARDY

Character art: Aljane Compendio

Cover art and design: Katie Golding

Published by Pinkity Publishing LLC

A NOTE TO READERS

Thank you so much for picking up this book. There are so many wonderful stories out there, and the fact that you're taking the time to read one of mine means the world to me.

Please visit jesskhardy.com for content notes.

PRAISE FOR JESS K HARDY

COME AS YOU ARE (Bluebird Basin book 1)

"...the older protagonists are refreshing—and their sex scenes are hot as hell. This is a winner."
- *Publishers Weekly*

"Cozy & sexy. This was a win."
-*KATE CLAYBORN, Author of Love Lettering and Georgie, All Along*

"A charming and heartfelt romance."
-*ALICIA THOMPSON, Author of Love in the Time of Serial Killers*

"…a hot cider, snow, slobbery rescue dog, fireplaces, cabins with rocking chairs, and mix tapes novel."
-*MARIA VALE, author of the Legend of All Wolves series*

"I loved this…A very sweet & steamy romance with a very good dog."
-*ANITA KELLY, author of Love & Other Disasters and Something Wild & Wonderful*

LOVE IN THE TIME OF WORMHOLES

"An enjoyable romp through space with a sizzling love story at its core... Offers irresistible characters and a fast-paced story that deftly balances action and passion."
-KIRKUS REVIEWS

"With all the makings of a cult classic, Love in the Time of Wormholes is a ridiculously funny novel with a surprising amount of heart."
-INDIES TODAY

For my husband, who reads my books and tells me they're wonderful. And for my son, who doesn't read my books, but still tells me they're wonderful.

PART I

LILIES

CHAPTER ONE

BRIGHT MORNING SUN glints over my axe as it slices through the air and drives into a log. The crack when the log splits in two echoes through our quiet valley. My back is sore, there's a burning between my shoulders, and a shaky weakness is building in my arms. I know if I don't stop chopping soon, I'll lose the axe. It's happened before, the axe flew out of my grip at the top of my swing, hitting the ground funny and bouncing back at me. Even though it was still ten feet away, I'd screamed and jumped like I was on fire. When there's an axe coming toward you flying end-over-end and the only soul who could keep you from bleeding out is miles away, ten feet feels a hell of a lot closer than you'd think.

Fresh blisters sting my palms, but when the snow comes it'll come in fast. So I keep chopping. Out of necessity, I've gotten pretty good at reading the skies over the years and I know the signs: the bright grayness swallowing the western sky, the dull headache brewing between my temples, and I haven't heard a bird or seen a squirrel all morning. This storm will be a doozy. Montana NPR predicts over two feet. This far north these early season storms can easily drop that much, and then it's a snow-covered world for months.

I grunt through trip after trip carrying wood from the woodshed to the cabin, cursing at the flat tire on my wheelbarrow with every stumbling step I take past it. No matter how many exercises I do, my balance gets worse every year. I've fallen twice just in the last six months, once slipping on wet tile when I'd tried to get out of the bathtub, and again when I'd tripped on a rug under the kitchen sink that had curled up at a corner. Luckily I didn't break a hip, but both falls terrified me, and everyone I live with.

After an aching eternity, I've stacked enough wood alongside the cabin and in the rack by the stove to last us at least a couple of weeks. I've also turned the skin of my arms into a horror show. It's been five long years since the witch cursed us all and sentenced me to life in this old body because I kissed a boy I hardly remember, and I'm still not used to it. I doubt I ever will be.

Hunched over the kitchen sink, I run my arms under a stream of warm water, washing my skin with this goat's milk soap I bought last fall at the farmer's market in Three Rivers. It's mild, smells like lavender, and doesn't sting the tears I get so often in my tissue-thin skin. After patting my arms dry with a soft cotton dish towel, I wrap them in several layers of gauze.

Clouds thicken outside the window over the sink, wind whipping through the pines surrounding the cabin. Their wild, thrashing limbs remind me of those blow-up tube dancers at car dealerships. Lord, when's the last time I saw one of those?

You'd think I'd miss my life before the curse, my youth, the swelling crowds screaming my name, the rush of writing and performing songs I loved. That warm glow that burst into my chest when my fans sang those same songs back to me. And I do, but not in the ways I'd expected. There's a strange comfort in being old, living out here, being nobody special. My thoughts are calmer, fewer things are worth getting worked up about since getting worked up is so exhausting I have to nap for two hours afterwards, and I'm more substantial, solid. Like an old oak standing on deep roots.

"Hey, girly. What are you looking at?"

Not that solid. "Christ, Wally! You scared the shit out of me." I have no earthly notion how a 500-pound hog sneaks up on a person, but Wally, my stepdad, gets me at least once a week.

He chuckles at me in short, staccato snorts. "So jumpy. I was just out trying to find your momma before the storm."

"Did you?" My quick glance around the cabin then out the window reveals not a single chicken.

"She's in the shed. Said she had to see a man about an egg."

I grimace. The witch's curse didn't spare a single one of us, making me old and turning my family and manager into animals, but Mom may have it the worst. "Poor Mom. I wonder what it feels like, laying an egg."

Wally shudders from snout to tail and suggests, "Girthy?"

I laugh. "That's an understatement."

Hobbling into the front room, I slide the rocking chair closer to the wood stove. While I sit and feed logs into the stove, rolling up strips of *The Daily Moose* for kindling, Wally labors through three full circles before thumping heavily to the ground in front of the couch.

"Have Bridge and Jack come in?" I ask as the fire creeps to life, tiny fingers of orange and red flame tickling the edges of the logs.

"Don't think so, but Fritz has. I'm looking right at him." Wally's head turns so that a blue, thickly lidded eye peers under the couch.

"Hey, Fritzy," I coo to my former manager. The sable-coated ferret scurries to me from the spot where he'd been napping under the couch. He's warm and floppy when I pick him up and pull him into my lap. "Glad you made it in before the storm."

"You and me both. I was freezing my ass off out there. I'm not ready for another winter, Nona. I'm seriously considering hibernation." Fritz nibbles on a strip of the dried venison I keep for him in one of Poppop's old cigar boxes next to the rocking chair. Ferrets are technically supposed to eat kibble, like cat food, but you tell that to a posh foodie like Fritz. Luckily, everyone's stomachs seemed to have been spared by the curse and they can all still eat normal food and, probably more importantly, drink normal drink. I shudder to think where we'd be if they couldn't. 'You can take our humanity, but you'll never take our whiskey!' has become my family motto.

"Ferrets don't hibernate, do they?" I ask.

Fritz sighs, shakes his head, and keeps chewing.

"Did you see Bridge and Jack?" I'm frowning at the fat, drunken snowflakes falling lazily outside the window. Soon they'll blow sideways, flying across the sky like angry hornets.

"No. I've been comatose." He shrugs his narrow shoulders. "Wide awake and thinking about that picture of Shawn Mendes in your gossip mag one minute, then, *poof*, sound asleep the next."

"#FerretLife," I say with a snort, then I set Fritz down on my chair to walk back to the shed and find Mom.

It's not really so much a shed as it is a large room I've added onto the cabin with dirt floors and better ventilation for, well, there's no delicate way to put it, the stinky barnyard animals I live with.

I'm trying not to inhale the musty, earthy scent of the room too deeply into my lungs. The shed's unique aroma tends to stay nestled in a person's nose hairs all day were they to breathe too deeply in here.

"Mom, you finished?" I ask in the general direction of the nesting boxes, pointedly not looking. She says I'm being silly, but the laying of an egg seems like an act that deserves a certain amount of privacy. And before you ask, yes, we do eat them. Food is food up here.

There's a burk-burk-burking sound and a rustling of wings as my mom careens down from her box to land gracefully in the dirt. "All done," she says, fluffing out her feathers. "Get it while it's warm."

"Awkward, Mother," I groan, but I gather the egg anyway and can't deny that a warm egg in hand feels pretty amazing. I'm making a frittata for dinner with elk from earlier in the fall and dried morels from last spring, so the extra egg is appreciated. I toss the egg into the air and catch it with my other hand.

"Watch it, Nona," Mom scolds. "That's my precious near-baby." Then she clucks a laugh, so similar to her lilting human laughter. The sound makes me smile, but it's also a gut punch. I miss her, the human her. I miss her body, her arms, the smell of her perfumed powder. She can still talk, still laugh, everyone can, but it's not the same. Mom's a bit clucky, Wally's a touch snorty. You get the gist.

"Apologies." I bow dramatically then tuck the egg into the front pocket of my coveralls. "Although you will be eating that near-baby for dinner so..."

"True enough," she says, waddling her way back into the cabin. Even though her lot seems the hardest, in true Penny Sheldon fashion she's taken to it like a fish to water. My sister Bridge and I always say Mom would find a way to be happy even during the apocalypse. Even if she was trussed up and spinning over a roaming band of cannibals' fire pit, she'd somehow make the best of it.

In the first couple of years there were so many unknowns about the curse, about our lives, about being old and being animals, that a cold, dull fear was our constant companion. Jack, Bridget's husband, taught us that their lifespans don't seem to follow their animals' trajectories, most rabbits only living a handful of years and Jack still going strong. But I still worry about them, my menagerie. It's dangerous out here for critters. And I know they still worry about me, growing older and weaker every year. Speaking of worry.

"Bridge and Jack haven't come in yet and the snow's started."

Mom halts in her tracks, her beak swiveling back to me. "That's not good."

I open my mouth to agree with her when a mad thrashing and wild scrambling erupts through the side door. Then I see my brother-in-law.

"Jack, what is it?" Wally asks, grunting back up to all fours.

Jack skids to a stop and falls onto his front legs. "It's Bridge," he gasps.

I pick the rabbit up and hold him around his chest so that his nose points to mine and his legs kick out at the air. "Where is she?"

His ears flatten to flop over my fingers as he pants in my grip. "She's found a hiker. He must've fallen. He's unconscious and his head's bleeding. Bridge won't leave him."

I set Jack down on the couch and walk to the closet to pull on my coat, shoving my hat over my ears. "Where?"

"North, about a mile. I'll show you."

"Wally." I nudge my stepdad's ribs with a knee as I walk to the door. "You're coming with."

"Well, of course I am, Nona," Wally snorts testily.

THE SKY HAS TURNED a charcoal gray by the time we reach the drainage basin that sits north of our property. Wally hauls the sled we use to pull downed trees to the cabin for firewood and Jack's riding on top of it, giving directions.

"Bridge! Bridge!" My voice is hoarse from shouting into the woods for my sister.

A barked, "Nona!" echoes from a nearby stand of trees.

Bridge, now a petite red fox, is at my feet a moment later, her amber eyes wide and her furred ears shooting straight up.

"Where is he?" I blink away the snowflakes landing thickly on my lashes as the lazy snowfall transitions into a proper dumping.

Bridge swerves in a darting circle, her full red tail sweeping through the inch of already accumulated snow. "Over here." Then she's off and we do our best to keep up, especially poor Wally who trudges through the wet snow and thick brush like a fat fly through honey.

I shove my hands into my pockets and stomp feeling back into my numb feet once we reach the hiker. He's sprawled in the snow under a steep bank abutting the drainage. His pants are torn and there's a four-inch gash on the side of his thigh. Occasional abrupt snorts interrupt his otherwise shallow breathing.

"Must have been hiking up there and fell," says Jack, shivering and twitching on the front of the sled.

"Hiking? All the way out here, before a storm?" I kneel in the snow at the man's side, placing my fingers on his neck to check for a pulse. There it is, bounding solidly under my fingers like a guitar string being plucked.

"People have done stupider things," offers Wally.

The man is young, maybe in his mid-twenties. He's wearing a red puffy coat over a checked flannel shirt and—bless his heart—blue jeans. I fish a gray knit cap out of the snow beside his head and shove it in my pocket. There's blood in his hair, some wet and crimson, some dried to a deep brick red.

"We have to get him home," Bridge says, hopping onto the sled next to Jack. She shakes snow from her head while Jack nestles his nose deep into the fur of her shoulder.

I nod, wondering what the hell I can do about any of this. Although I realize now that I should have, I've never taken a backcountry safety course or CPR or anything at all helpful. "Wally, please bring the sled."

The man groans as Wally and I push him onto the sled, my back cracking and popping like a campfire with the effort. I slip in the snow while I lift up his heavily booted feet, being as careful as I can with his wounded leg. Bridge hops from the sled to help, grabbing the man's jeans between her teeth and tugging. Once he's fully loaded onto the sled, Wally begins the grueling task of dragging him back to the cabin.

My stepdad is breathing hard when we reach the northern edge of our property.

"You all right, Wally?" I ask through my own ragged breathing.

"Fine, Nona," he grunts while Bridge runs up ahead of us to scratch at the side door, letting everyone know we're back. I push the door open and Wally heaves the sled the last few steps until it sits flush with the door.

"Bring him inside." Mom waves a wing at us. "We have to get him near the fire."

I grab the man by his shoulders and pull him bodily from the sled, sliding him over the threshold and onto the floor in front of the wood stove. Then I stare at him. I have no idea what to do, where to begin. My teeth sink into my lower lip, my brows pressing tight together. Turning around to face the stove, I warm my icy hands over the fire, but really I'm just stalling.

"Nona." Mom's tone slaps with disapproval. "What are you doing?"

"Well, Mother, at the moment I'm kind of freaking out." I rub my hands together, then spin to face everyone. "What am I supposed to be doing?" Jack, Bridge, and Fritz all stare at me with wide, unblinking eyes.

"Nona, you need to get his jeans off so we can see the wound," says Wally after returning from hauling the sled back behind the cabin. He shakes off a heavy layer of snow from his pink and black-spotted skin, sparkling crystals still clinging to the coarse hairs that poke up from his back. "It'll need to be stitched."

"Right, stitched," I whisper, chewing on my lip now. "And I would do that how?"

"Well…I mean…maybe you could…" Bridge stammers, then shakes her head. "This is absurd! This man needs a hospital."

I glare at my sister. "You gonna take him in this weather, Bridge? It's already dumped half a foot. It could be days before the road's passable. We don't have a choice but to try to take care of him here."

She chews on her tail, spitting out a soggy burr she finds there. "Fine, but if he dies in here, I might lose my mind for good this time."

An icy dread runs through me at this reminder of our bleak first year after the witch cursed us, when we all went a hair's breadth shy of bat shit. After the initial terror, a numb confusion gave way to a dark and desperate depression, both of which were ultimately crushed under the boot heel of a near psychotic rage that ran through all of us like dysentery. We were tricked, abused, magically altered and forced to abandon our lives, our hopes and dreams. Jack had to leave his family, and Fritz, who spent the first few months away from us, trying and failing to convince his mother he wasn't some talking-animal sign that she was losing her mind, ultimately had to leave her and come to live with a bunch of crazy white people just to survive in some semblance of peace. We might have all lost it completely if it hadn't been for Mom, somehow immune to the ravages of post-curse psychosis. She kept us together, kept us sane.

I'm staring wide-eyed at the man's leg. "All right, uh, okay. Shit. I need scissors. Where are the scissors? Do we even have scissors?" The word *scissors* starts to sound, in my mind, like an ancient, foreign term I have never said or heard before in my life.

Jack bounds over, dragging a pair between his teeth. "Of course we have scissors, Nona," he slurs, spitting the red-handled shears out at my feet.

After removing the hiker's boots as carefully as I can, I pluck the scissors from the floor and say, "Thanks, Jack," before setting in to snip the man's jeans. "Who the hell hikes all the way out here in jeans, anyway?" I say, cutting away denim to expose the gash in his thigh.

"An idiot," mumbles Fritz, biting the edge of the cut denim flap and pulling it away from the wound.

I swallow suddenly as I stare at the hiker's leg. The skin around his wound is a bright angry red and the blood dribbling from the base of the gash is so dark it's nearly purple. "That doesn't look good," I say absently, then I hear a thump and notice Jack flat on his back with his feet twitching in the air. "And I think Jack just passed out."

Bridge curses and darts to her husband, nudging his belly with her wet, pointy nose.

Jack rolls onto his side, groaning back to consciousness.

Mom stares down at me from her perch on the back of the rocking chair. "That will definitely need stitches."

I rock back onto my heels, defeated. "I can't. I can't do it." My heart thunders against my ribs and I'm breathing so hard and fast each inhale shoots fire into my lungs. My vision blurs and there's a metallic tang on the tip of my tongue. I don't have much stamina for losing my shit anymore. Old ticker. I'm worried I might pass out just like Jack, but then I'm surrounded. Fritz scampers up my back to sit on my shoulder while Jack and Bridge flank me on either side.

Mom flits down from the chair back to stand stalwart above the man's head. "Nona, sweetie, take a breath. It's just like mending a sweater, easy as sin."

"This," I'm pointing hysterically at the hiker's gashed and bleeding leg, "is not a sweater!"

Bridge runs into my bedroom, returning with my sewing kit clenched between her teeth.

My mouth falls open. "I can't stitch up a stranger's leg with a sewing kit."

"He'd look good in red," suggests Fritz, ignoring my protests as he pulls the spool of red thread from my kit.

My laughter is a maniac's laughter and for a moment everyone stares at me with deeply concerned expressions. "I suck at sewing, guys. You know this."

"You'll do just fine," Mom says, calm as a dairy cow. "But do it now while he's still unconscious."

She's got a point. I stumble to the bathroom, pour rubbing alcohol over the needle shaking in my fingers, then wash my hands, begging my heart to stop trying to beat itself to death inside my chest.

I bring a bowl of soapy water back to the hiker and set to washing around his wound. Then I try to thread the needle, but with my trembling hands and squinty eyes, it takes forever. Finally I press the edges of his wound together with one hand, squealing a little at the blood. Then I suck in a breath and whisper, "Wish me luck," as I drive the threaded needle into his thigh.

The hiker's scream as he jerks to life is the most terrifying thing I've ever heard and I nearly shit myself in response. With eyes huge and rolling, he grabs for my shirt while I do everything I can to not push the needle further into his leg. Mom leaps to her feet and pecks ferociously at the man's head. Fritz scampers up the man's arm, biting at his fingers in an effort to free them from my shirt. Then the man releases me and I fall onto my ass as his eyes roll up into his skull, his head thudding heavily against the wood floor.

A profound silence descends, except for the howling wind.

"That was intense," Jack eventually says. His front feet are planted on the man's chest, as if he could have kept him from killing me with his little bunny body.

After a long moment of talking myself down from the edge of an epic, full-on, world-class panic attack, I rock forward into a kneeling position, hissing at the pain biting at my knees and ankles. "Wally, hold him down."

Wally lays the front segment of his body over the man's chest, pinning his arms to the floor. As quickly as I can, gagging a little with every puncture and pull, I stitch the man's wound with the same bright red thread I used to embroider 'I Wanna Hold Your Handle' on my favorite potholder, which I will never look at the same way again. When I'm finished, the unconscious man's wound looks like a hairy red caterpillar crawling chaotically toward his belly.

I ask Wally to stay put while I splint the hiker's thigh in a makeshift brace, wrapping my old copies of *Forager's Monthly* and *Famous Lives, Famous Loves* magazines around his leg, then securing the magazines in place with elastic bandages. I lean over the hiker to brush his blood-crusted hair back from his face. He's pale and burning and I whisper to him, "If you can hear me, please don't die on the floor of my cabin."

CHAPTER TWO

AFTER I WASH the blood from the hiker's hair and clean the small cut on the side of his head, he looks better, still pale and unconscious, but better.

I leave everyone to watch over him as I push myself painfully to my feet and hobble into the kitchen. I flip the radio switch and take a moment to breathe deeply as Neko Case's timeless voice lilts through the speakers. Once again, I thank the bright and shiny lord for NPR.

Frowning at the snow coming down in blinding white sheets through the window and what it likely means for the man on my floor, I pull Mom's forgotten egg from my pocket, absolutely shocked it's still in one piece, and crack it over a pan to start making dinner.

~

"THAT WAS DELICIOUS," Mom warbles after pecking her plate clean. It's always weird to watch her eat her own eggs, but she says she doesn't mind, so I try not to judge.

It's funny, I'd never cooked before the curse. I mean, I'd

boiled water for ramen or thrown the occasional hot pocket into the microwave, but if you'd asked me to poach an egg or sear a flank steak, I would have told you to go fuck yourself. Now, since I'm the only one of us who can still cook, I've had to learn. Not only have I learned to cook fairly well, I've also learned to love it as a way to pass the time and keep us all alive. And cooking reminds me a little of writing songs, simple ingredients combined to make something else, something more. Although no single song I ever wrote earned me anywhere near as much praise as my venison stew.

Our new houseguest sleeps fitfully by the fire, rousing every once in a while, just enough to groan and writhe before passing out again. After I finish doing the dishes, the snow now crowding half-way up the window as it piles against the sill, I wipe my hands on a dish towel and pull on my lower lip, watching him sleep. It's not unusual to run across hikers up here since our property skirts national forest land. What is unusual is finding one this far out, at this time of year, and with a storm coming.

Wally sprawls out on the floor next to the hiker, snoring. I pat his rough head before feeding two more logs into the fire. Mom has retired to the shed, Bridge and Jack are curled into each other on the couch, and I decide to settle onto the rocking chair for the duration. No sooner has my ass hit the cushion, however, than a bounding Fritz scampers up my leg and into my lap.

My voice is tired and gravelly as I ask, "What do you think, Fritz? Will he make it?"

"I don't know, Nona. Maybe, if his leg doesn't get infected." Fritz points his shiny black nose up at me. "Wild night, huh?"

I laugh. This is a Fritzism. He said these same words to me after every show on my last tour. Chicago, Austin, Seattle... "Wild night, huh?" And they were, all of them, wild and ecstatic and beautiful. As Fritz coils himself into a little ball on my lap, growing immediately heavy with sleep, my eyelids droop, my vision swimming. The dry wood snapping in the stove and the wind howling at the doors and windows fade to soft, distant whispers as I fall face-first into a deep and exhausted sleep.

"HOLY SHIT!"

I wake with a start, my heart lurching so wildly and painfully in my chest that I have to clutch at it. I'm too old for this shit.

The hiker is still on his back, but his head is rotated to the side and he stares wide-eyed straight into Wally's glassy blues. Wally snorts, then sticks his muscular snout into the man's shoulder, sniffing at him like a gigantic porcine detective.

"Where am I?" The hiker turns his head to me, moving directly into a shaft of morning sunlight sliding through the window. It casts this warm, muted light over his broad forehead and high cheekbones. "Who are you?"

After his initial shock, the hiker seems absurdly calm considering the massive hog at his side, the fox and rabbit now sitting beside him, and the whole probable broken leg and shoddily applied stitches situation. But he stares at the animals and actually laughs a little.

I notice a flicker of puffed up red tail in the corner of my vision and shoot Bridge a look, warning her not to speak. Her smiling eyes tell me well enough what she's thinking. She likes him already.

"You're..." I try to speak but my throat is dry from sleep and I croak the word. I clear my throat and try again. "You're in my cabin. Just outside the Red Bear Wilderness."

"How did I get here?" He tries to move his legs, then barks, "Jesus!" reaching down to grab at his thigh as if he just now realized it exists. And hurts. A lot.

I take Fritz from my lap and set him back down onto the

cushion, but he scampers off the chair and follows behind me anyway as I walk to the hiker's side. I kneel down and take hold of the man's hand. I'm aiming for a comforting tone. A comforting old lady who lives in the middle of the Montana wilderness with a fox, pig, hen, rabbit, and ferret. I'll be shocked if I come off as anything other than insane. I've seen *Misery*.

"We...I," I stutter to correct, "found you unconscious in the woods. Were you hiking? There's a trail above where you fell. I think you've broken your leg. And you had a wound in your thigh that I had to stitch. You'll have a scar."

He doesn't answer me, instead flipping the blanket covering his left leg to the side. He goes a little pale, then he utters a clipped but profound, "Shit."

Wally heaves himself to his feet and walks into the shed, probably to go wake Mom.

"What were you doing all the way out here? Didn't you know there was a storm coming?"

The man considers this question for a moment, then says, "I got lost."

I wait for more, but he's staring at me so intensely that it makes me blush. I haven't felt blood rush up into these cheeks for years and the sensation is so unfamiliar it's hitting me like a flash bomb. Then I remember who he's staring at and realize he's about to ask me—

"How did you get me in here. You must be..." He lets the thought hang in the air between us and I laugh at the embarrassment on his face. He can't believe he almost told an old lady exactly how old he thought she was.

"I'm eighty-three, thank you very much," I say. "And I'm stronger than I look. I hauled you here on my sled, with some help from the pig."

I stand, bite back a groan, and walk to the door to let Jack, Bridge, and Fritz out. The hiker watches, amused, as Wally waddles back from the shed with Mom perched between his shoulders. Wally lets Mom hop to the couch before he ambles over to the open door, lowering his head into the snow and driving a path through the drifts with his substantial pig weight for everyone else to follow. The wind is quiet and the sky is a crystal-clear blue as I peek out the door behind them, but the snow is outrageous, drifts blown up to block the windows and tree branches swooping to the ground, weighed down by pounds of accumulated powder. It's one of the biggest early season dumps I've ever seen up here. Nobody is going anywhere anytime soon.

I motion for Mom to head outside, but she shakes her beak, giving me the closest approximation to a raised brow a hen can muster. I suppose she's as interested in the stranger on our floor as I am. Fair enough.

I shut the door, shivering as a gust of icy air sneaks through the hinges. The fire fell overnight and the cabin is frigid again, so I step carefully over the hiker's legs and kneel next to the stove. As I start feeding more logs into the stove, I notice the hiker is watching me. I also notice I keep calling him 'the hiker.'

"What is your name, son?" I don't know, seems like something an old lady would say.

"Charlie," he says, and I inhale my own spit.

Charlie? Seriously? My biggest hit, well at least before the witch stole my career and became far more famous than I ever was, was a ballad called *Missing Charlie*. And now there's a super cute guy on my floor that I have to nurse to health, possibly through the entire winter, and his name is Charlie. Is this real life?

"I'm Nona."

Charlie lifts his head to glance out the window, then lowers it back to his pillow with a thump. "No chance of getting me to a doctor, right?"

I shake my head. "Not unless we want to die in the snow."

"How bad is it?" Charlie pushes aside the elastic bandaging to try to see his wound. "My leg?"

"It's not great." I close the door on the stove after heating my hands over the fire again. "The wound was deep and I have no clue if or how badly your leg might be broken. And your stitches are a hot mess."

His eyes find mine and he's looking at me funny, because I am an idiot. Eighty-three-year-olds don't say things like 'hot mess.'

"I have a granddaughter who visits in the summer. She teaches me all the current slang," I say, smiling too wide, honestly wondering if 'hot mess' is even current slang anymore. I point at his leg. "Does it hurt?"

"Like hell. But I think my ass might hurt worse, believe it or not." He props up onto his elbows to reposition his hips on the hard floor.

"Hmm." I'm considering him. "I wonder if I can make you a better splint today so you can at least get up onto the couch." As I think about gathering sticks and twine, I hear squabbling through the window, loud animals speaking English squabbling.

"Excuse me for a moment, Charlie." I pull on my boots, nod to Mom to watch over him, and head outside.

Wally and Jack stand near the sled we used to cart Charlie here, bickering with Bridge who's running in mad circles around them.

"What is going on?" I whisper harshly. "We can hear you inside. *Charlie* can hear you, which is something we don't want to happen, remember?"

Bridge slides to a halt in the snow. "Did you just say Charlie? His name is Charlie?" She cackles. "Seriously?"

I nod, snorting. "I know right? What are the odds? It's the stupidest thing."

Bridge juts her pointy nose at Wally and Jack. "See, this is it. It's happening!"

Wally huffs and Jack replies, "Bridge, that's ridiculous. The man could die if his wound gets infected. We have to get him to a hospital."

"Guys," I hiss, "if you don't shut the hell up, we'll have to get him to the loony bin. I agree he needs a hospital but there is absolutely no way we can get him to Three Rivers right now. I can't walk all the way to Sam's place in this snow." Sam is our closest neighbor and he has a snowmobile, which we don't, but he's miles away. "And what's that supposed to mean, Bridge? What's 'happening'?"

Bridge trots up to me and sits in the snow, her tail wagging. "It's our chance. The curse, Nona. Don't you remember? The witch said the curse could only be broken once you find your own love to lose. This is it. It must be. You have to make him fall in love with you."

I stare at her, my jaw hanging by its hinges, my brows furrowed so tightly a headache forms instantly between them. "Bridge, I'm eighty-three, he looks about twenty-five. You don't see a problem with this plan? Plus, that's the dumbest thing I have ever heard and probably complete witchy bullshit."

Wally and Jack sit staring at us with blank faces. I guess they've decided to let me disabuse Bridge of this nonsense on my own.

Bridge bounces in place like she's on springs. "But you aren't eighty-three, you're twenty-three. You guys are the same age! No offense Nona, but it's not like trying to find men your body's age has worked for you. This may be our only chance."

I sigh loud through my lips, because she's not wrong. Years ago I tried with one of the market vendors in Three Rivers. He was sweet and handsome, and it does get lonely out here. But in the end, it didn't feel right. He was younger than me, than my body is, but still old enough to be my grandfather. I couldn't do it.

I settle my sternest stare on Bridge, or try to because she's still bouncing in the snow like a caffeinated toddler and it's funny. "I am not about to seduce the injured man on my floor to try and break an unbreakable curse. He's young and good looking and probably taken anyway and this is ridiculous and just no. Now shut up, act like the animals you are, and come help me make him a better splint so he can lie on the couch. He says his butt hurts."

Bridge pouts at me and I know this conversation is far from over, but she runs into the trees to gather sticks anyway.

I know how hard this curse has been for them. I may be old, but at least I'm still human. My poor family—and Fritz— weren't even afforded that luxury by the witch. And now I feel like an asshole for not agreeing to try anything to break this curse. What would they do for me if the tables were turned? Everything. Everything and anything, that's what they'd do. My hatred for Rebecca Delanore, the witch who cursed us, soars to heights not previously considered possible as I walk back to the cabin, clutching sticks in my hands so tightly one of them snaps in half.

I find Charlie sitting up, poking curiously at his leg like a child poking at a dead bird.

"Don't touch it," I scold. It's very easy to scold in this body, as natural as dry eyes and a constantly runny nose. "I'm worried it's infected already."

"Sorry." Charlie grimaces guiltily. "If it gets infected, I die, right? No doctors around here, I'm guessing."

"Well, I certainly hope not. But you're right, no doctors. And it'll be a while before I can get you to Three Rivers. I don't have a snowmobile. I don't even have a phone. I usually just hunker down for the winter." This is true and even though it sounds isolating and cramped, it's really not so bad. It's beautiful most of the year and everyone is free to be who they are. So even though the deep winter can be cold and cruel and exceedingly long, I don't hate it.

When Rebecca stole my identity, my career, she also stole most of our money and any chance any of us had to make more. All we had left was my Mimi and Poppop's cabin. So here we are.

"Nona?" Charlie asks and something about his voice saying my name tickles the tiny hairs on the back of my neck.

"Yes," I reply, laying the sticks out in a row beside him and trying very hard to ignore those tickly hairs and the little shivers they're sending down my spine.

"I have to pee."

My hands still on the wood, those little shivers snuffed out like a pissed-on fire. Of course. Of course he'll have to pee. And do other things, too. "Right. Let me, uh, just get a thing."

A thing? What thing? A glass? Will that be big enough? Will I need to watch? Or hold it for him? No, that's ridiculous. There's nothing wrong with his hands. Christ. I glance imploringly at Mom who shakes her bemused beak at me like she doesn't have a clue either. Then Wally ambles back in from the yard and I gesture frantically for him to follow me into the shed.

"Wally," I whisper once I close the shed door behind us, "he has to pee. What do I do?"

Wally's entire body shakes with silent laughter. "Just give him the vase and he should be able to do the rest."

"But that's my favorite vase, our *only* vase," I grumble.

He laugh-shakes even harder. "It'll clean, Nona."

I kiss my fingers and press them onto his snout, then I hustle to the kitchen. After standing on my tiptoes and nearly falling again because standing on tiptoes is shockingly difficult when you're old, I tip the vase out of a high cabinet and rinse it out before bringing it to Charlie.

"Will this do?" I ask him. I'm not sure I have ever felt so awkward, not even when I got that stomach bug years ago and Fritz stayed with me in the bathroom that whole night. Which, objectively, makes no sense since crying on the bathroom floor to a ferret after repeatedly barfing my guts out and, uh, succumbing to other uncontrollable-bodily-function-type things was far more embarrassing.

Charlie laughs, probably at my awkwardness. "Yeah, this'll do. I think I can manage." He starts unbuttoning his jeans which triggers in me a sharp, involuntary need to squeal. I lock my lips between my teeth, stand up, and turn around. The ceiling becomes infinitely fascinating as I try very hard not to listen while he pees into the vase behind me. I fail miserably.

"I'm, uh, done. I guess," he stammers, then produces this adorable, self-conscious type of giggle that makes me bite my lips even harder.

Eyes averted, I take the vase from him and dump it into the toilet. Then, still not looking, I rinse it and leave it in the bathroom sink to dry. With a fire-engine red blush breaking out across my cheeks, I gather twine and scissors from the kitchen. Settling down on my rusty hinges beside Charlie again, I do what I can to construct a more rigid splint. I measure a stick against his leg and break it over my knee to make it the right length, then repeat with the other sticks until I have enough so that when I bind them together with the twine, they should surround his entire leg like a cast.

Carefully, I unwrap his elastic bandages and uncoil the magazines to inspect his wound. Charlie watches me with pursed lips and his brow furrowed deeply into this seriously concerned expression. It's making me feel all kinds of maternal.

The wound doesn't look bad, I don't think. The skin around the wound is red but not as angry as before, and it doesn't smell. He might get lucky. I replace the magazines and bandages and slide my hands above and below his knee, preparing to lift his leg. After stopping just short of asking Mom to help, I'm hit broadside by the terrible realization that as long as Charlie is our guest, I can't ask anyone to help me with anything. "You ready?"

"I can help," offers Charlie like he's reading my mind. "You lift and I'll pull the brace under. But you'll need to lift high."

We wear matching grave expressions now. "Count of three?" I try to keep my voice firm so he thinks I'm calm instead of scared shitless.

He nods and starts counting. On three, I jerk his leg up and he barks, "Shit! I thought we'd do it on 'go'.1, 2, 3, go."

"Sorry," I grunt holding the weight of his leg, "but... please...help."

He sits up, swears again, and pulls the stick brace so it slides underneath his leg. I murmur another apology as I set his leg back down. Mom is at my side now and I wonder if Charlie finds it strange to have a hen staring at him with such compassionate concern. If he does, he doesn't mention it, or doesn't have the presence of mind to care as he groans, fisting his hands and clenching his jaw while I secure the brace around his leg.

"There, there," I console, shrugging to Mom who is looking at me like, *"Did you just say 'there, there'?'"*

When I'm finished, his leg looks absurd. The brace is enormous, but it's sturdy and strong and he can't move his leg inside it, which is the point. "You probably shouldn't put any weight on your leg, in case it's broken. Do you think you can scoot over to the couch if I help?"

He's panting, his face pinched in pain, but he nods.

We move in short bursts. I move his leg a little to the side, then he scoots his hips over an inch or two until he's next to the couch. During our excursion, his shirt falls open at the collar and tiny beads of sweat break out on his brow. Grunting, he pushes his hips up onto the couch while I support his leg. Then it's a quick turn and he's lying down.

"I'm sorry," I repeat, grimacing. "That probably really suc... suffered you." *Suffered you?* I was going to say "sucked" but, again, thought that was something eighty-three-year-olds don't routinely say. But 'that suffered you' is something nobody says. I'm not surprised to hear Mom's burking laughter behind me.

"Yes," he murmurs, dropping his head to the pillow and blowing his bangs out of his eyes. "That suffered me plenty."

"I think I have some Tylenol or something." And why the hell didn't I think of giving him that before I moved him? I am the worst nurse ever.

"Please," is all he says.

I give him an awkward pat on the hand and leave to go rifle through my medicine cabinet. I've got aspirin, but it's the worthless baby shit Mom made me buy because it's supposed to be good for old people's hearts. I can't bring Charlie a stupid baby aspirin. I push aside a box of Preparation H to reveal a small, red-capped bottle of Tylenol. Sounds like there are four or five pills left when I shake the bottle, and that's something at least. Then I frown, scanning dismally over the shelves of the cabinet. They're lined with suppositories, fiber pills, Vaseline, the electric razor I use on my lady beard... all sad, grim reminders of my advanced age. I slam the mirrored door and don't look back.

"Here you go." I hand him two red pills. "Do you need water?"

He nods.

"Are you hungry?" *Hungry, hungry*...shit. My eyes burst open wide as the blood drains from my face. Yes, he is an adult man person. He will get hungry. He will need to eat, a lot. We don't have anywhere near enough food for another human mouth. "I can make you a grilled cheese?" I try hard to keep this knee-buckling worry from my voice.

"It might make me throw up, but I could eat." He manages a smile and reveals adorably crooked front teeth. His brown eyes sparkle like sunlight reflecting off the tips of river waves. He really is cute, so I smile back at him. But inwardly, I'm already hating my life at the idea of hunting in this snow.

CHAPTER THREE

I LEAVE Charlie passed out on the couch after he eats his lunch. I made the grilled cheese on bread I'd baked a few days ago and served it with a side of venison stew from the freezer. I'd spread garlic butter on the bread before grilling and the aroma in the cabin is delectable. It draws Wally, Jack, and Bridge in from the snow and they creep past Charlie, trying not to wake him.

"Can I have some?" whispers Wally, his snout curling at the air. Bridge and Jack nod at me as Mom runs into the kitchen and leaps onto Wally's back.

"Yes." I glance warily at Charlie, still sleeping. "But then I have to hunt. We don't have enough food for all of us."

Jack and Bridge glance nervously at each other as Fritz bounds into the kitchen and slinks around my ankles. "I know, it's not the best time for me to be out there. But what other choice do we have?" Last time I tried to hunt in the snow I nearly died of hypothermia. I get so cold so quickly now. But that was much later in the season and I saw pheasant just the other day not a quarter mile from the cabin. "I'll be fine. Bridge can come with me."

Bridget nods and rubs her nose into Jack's fur where he sits twitching beside her. He's worried about her. He worries about everything. It must be a rabbit thing. Bridge and Jack were childhood sweethearts and married just out of high school. I really don't think most young couples would have survived this curse, and Bridge and Jack have had their struggles. But they have this intense and impenetrable love for each other, like he was made for her and she was made for him.

A gravelly noise like a throat clearing comes from Charlie's general direction, and I look up to find him watching us. I freeze in place, wondering how much he's heard of me talking to my animals. If he's heard anything, he doesn't let on as he rubs his eyes and says around a yawn, "Did you train them all yourself? It's amazing how well behaved they all are. The fox doesn't eat the rest?"

Bridge growls at the insinuation and I nudge her ribs with my foot. "Not yet," I reply while shooing everyone except for Mom back out the door.

"They keep you company though. It must get lonely up here."

I lean over him and place the back of my hand against his forehead. "No fever." I smile. "How do you feel?"

"Tired." He gives Mom a pat on the head after she flies over his legs to perch atop the back of the couch. "What are their names?"

I walk back into the kitchen to make more grilled cheeses and say over my shoulder, "That one is Penny."

He coos, "Hello, Penny," while scratching her beak.

"The pig is Wally, the fox is Bridget, Jack is the rabbit, and the ferret is Fritz." I turn on the radio, fiddle with the antenna, then crank up the volume as Jimmy Rodgers warbles through the speakers. "Do you need anything?"

He laughs. "I could use a drink."

I bet he could. For someone who just fell off a cliff, woke up next to a pig, and is convalescing in a stranger's cabin in the middle of the Montana wilderness, Charlie has been a damned trooper. "I have wine, whiskey, rum, gin, vodka…" I stop talking as his laughter grows.

"You've got it all. Looks like I ended up in the right cabin. I'll take some whiskey, and thank you." He sniffs the air. "Are you making more grilled cheeses? That was seriously the best grilled cheese I've ever had. The stew was delicious too."

I pour two fingers of whiskey into a glass and bring it to him. Then I help him sit up enough so he can drink it without choking. Somehow, despite all his pain-sweating, when I lean in close so I can reposition the couch cushion behind him to keep him propped up, I notice that he smells fantastic, all piney and smoky. Like winter.

He catches my eye and asks, "Have you always been a good cook?"

I clutch at my aching back as I stand back up. "Thank you. And no, I've really only started cooking for myself the last five years. Since I moved out here." I leave him with his drink to finish making lunch for the rest of the crew.

"What brought you out here?"

He's not shy, I'll give him that. "Give me a minute and I'll tell you all about it." I cut the sandwiches up and bring them into the shed, then I open the small door that leads from the shed to the yard and let everyone back in. Whispering their thanks, they set into their lunches as I pat each of their heads. When I return to the kitchen, I pour my own whiskey knowing I'll need the warmth for my hunting trip. I tilt the bottle toward Charlie and he nods, offering his glass to me for a refill. Then I swivel the rocking chair to face him and take a seat.

I've only told the story I'm about to tell him a few times before. Mainly when talking to curious tourists in Three Rivers who find it hard to believe—yet super charming—that an old woman would live out in the woods alone. Although I'm certainly not the only person to live this far out, I am the only one over seventy since the eccentric woman we all called Aunt

Lulu passed away just before we moved up here. I actually have several neighbors within 10 miles, mostly men, all nuttier than fruitcakes and sweeter than molasses. Most of my neighbors have snowmobiles and occasionally they visit in the winter, but usually we're visited only in the summer. I'm hopeful one of my neighbors will stop by this winter and take Charlie to Three Rivers, but I'm not holding my breath.

"I moved out here after my husband died. This was my Poppop's cabin and Harry, my husband, and I spent every summer here. When he died, I came up here to get away and just never left." I shrug. "It's home."

"I'm sorry about your husband," Charlie says.

I give him a grim smile. Poor Harry, my fake husband. He died in a tragic hot air balloon accident. Or maybe a NASCAR crash. Thankfully, nobody has ever asked how Harry died. There is a polite respect of secrets this far away from civilization. You never know what brings a person to this kind of life, and I never ask. Charlie, on the other hand…

"How did Harry die?"

My eyes slide to him as I ready myself to deliver some mild 'I'm older than you' dressing-down about minding one's own business, but his expression is so sincere that I sigh instead and say the first thing that comes to mind. "Heart attack."

"What was he like?"

All right, that's quite enough prodding from the whipper-snapper. "You," I say as I get to my feet, "should probably get some rest. And I should go get a pheasant."

"Is that a euphemism for something?" Charlie asks and I bark out a laugh.

"Yes, it's a euphemism for dinner. I'm going hunting."

His mouth pops open. "You're going hunting? In this?" He points out the window at all the white beyond it.

"Yes, sir!" I yell over my shoulder while stepping into my snowsuit, zipping it up, and pulling my shotgun from the rack.

Even at the height of my fame, I still went to the range as much as I could. I'm a crack shot. My Mimi taught me well.

When I look at him, there's this twinkle in his eyes, like he's impressed but also, strangely, like he's proud. I'm not gonna lie, it's a weird twinkle. But with his sandy-brown hair lying in a scruffy heap on top of his head and sticking straight up on one side, the weirdness melts away in the warmth of his lopsided grin. "Well, good luck then. And, don't die." He points down to his leg and wiggles his toes. "I'll be in a bit of a bind if you do."

My heart does something in my chest as he smiles at me. It's like a fluttering, electric buzzing and I barely recognize the sensation. But recognize it I do—this is crushing. I am crushing, hard, on someone young enough to be my grandson. Or just the right age to be my boyfriend, in a different life. This thought tries to dig its wretched little fingers into me.

"Bridge!" I shout into the shed, shaking off those miserable thought fingers while I grab my pack and snowshoes from the wall.

Bridge comes bounding out to meet me and my eyes flash wide at her. I'm giving her the look we've shared since we were kids. It's a look that says, "I need to talk to you about a boy." Her tail whips in psychotic circles and I can feel her restraint as she remains silent.

Before we walk outside, Bridge stands with her front paws on the couch and licks Charlie full on the face. We leave the cabin to the sound of his laughter.

"Really, Bridge?" I ask while trudging through the snow. "A tongue bath? You hardly know the guy." The snow has melted a bit in the afternoon sun and the going is slow, the snow heavy.

"You like him," she warbles as she trots behind me in the trail my legs make for her.

I hoist my shotgun strap up higher on my shoulder. "I don't like him, Bridge. I don't even know him."

"Yeah, but he's cute right? Those red lips and that hair, lord. Have you noticed the little wisps that curl around his ears?"

I smile, scanning for any thick brush where pheasants might be sitting tight in the snow. "I have. And yes, he's cute. But also sixty years younger than me, and I literally know nothing about him. He could be a serial killer." I turn toward her. "Shit, Bridge. What if he's a serial killer? What if once his leg heals, he kills us all and wears my face skin as a mask and your tail as a shawl?"

She ignores me. "Joke all you want, Nona. But I know you and you were blushing. And you gave me *the look*. I think he might be brushing off some of the cobwebs over your ancient hormones."

"Ugh, I wish. A break from the vaginal dryness alone would be worth it."

"Ew," she says.

"You think that's 'ew', it's nothing compared to the atrophy."

"Atrophy?" She nearly gags. "In your vagina?"

"Yep. You could, like, bowl through it."

"That's so gross."

"That's aging. Do your Kegels. And you're gross."

"Your face is gross," she volleys.

"Your mouth is gross," I return, but then I hear a rustling to our left, and then a twig snap. I hold out my hand signaling Bridge to hold still, and when I squint through the trees, I can't believe my eyes. It's a buck, not fifty yards away. A good sized one too, big enough to feed us for a while, but not so big I won't be able to drag him back to the cabin.

"Holy shit," whispers Bridge. I tell her to hush with a silent "shhh" and a finger over my mouth.

A buck would be a hell of a lot better to bring home than pheasant. Quiet as snowfall, I switch out the birdshot in my rifle for the slug I always carry in my pocket, just in case, swing the shotgun up into my grip, and take aim. One breath in through my nose, slowly releasing it through pursed lips. Then, in rapid succession, I rack the gun and squeeze the trigger, absorbing the kick into my shoulder. My ears ring loud enough to wake the dead, but after a few running steps, the deer falls. It's a clean shot and a good kill.

"Nice shot!" Bridge races through the snow to the spot where the buck landed on his side.

I have no illusions about how hard it's going to be to drag this guy through the snow back to the cabin, but right now I don't even care. This is food and up here in the winter, food is all that matters.

"Nona, he's perfect!" Bridge sniffs at his antlers.

"I know." Looking at him up close, I realize he's bigger than I'd thought. I consider this for a moment. "I'll dress him here, I guess. He'll be lighter at least." Even though I'd rather walk back home naked than dress a deer in deep snow right now. My bones ache and my muscles seize just thinking about it.

"Did you seriously just kill that animal?"

The cool voice behind us raises Bridge's hackles and turns my blood to fire in my veins. I know this voice. I know it as well as my own. Because it is my own.

"Well, what do you know," growls Bridge, teeth bared. "If it isn't the Wicked Bitch of the West."

CHAPTER FOUR

Not many people can say they've stared at someone who looks just like them. Twins, I suppose, but even then there are subtle differences, differently shaped eyes, unique smiles. Staring at Rebecca Delanore leaning against a tree, smiling at me with my pink lips, winking at me with one of my green eyes, is as unsettling as one of those falling dreams where you jerk awake right before your face hits the pavement.

Rebecca is none other than the ultra-famous international pop sensation, Nona. Nona who, five years ago, was me. I never knew Rebecca before she cursed us. But I evidently pissed her off royally when I kissed a boy at one of my concerts. I don't remember much about that night, only a warm breeze blowing over my skin, fireflies floating in the sky above us, and the kiss, which was knee-buckling. I'm guessing the boy was her boyfriend, although she's never told me anything about herself in any great detail. Turns out, she's a bit guarded, a touch sensitive, and a metric fuck-ton vindictive.

Since she cursed us, Rebecca has turned my modest fame as folk singer Nona May Taylor into near icon status as Nona. I followed her at first but bearing witness to my career in her hands felt a bit like slowly sinking in place as waves swept the sand out from under my feet, inevitable and suffocating.

She's changed my hair, my brown waves now an edgy, snow-white bob. She's put tattoos on my body, a dragon on my back and a serpent on my wrist, perhaps others that I can't see. I managed all of this with as much patience as I could muster, but when she remixed all the songs from my first album into EDM versions, I hit my limit. "Missing Charlie" with the incessant *oonts oonts oonts* of techno beats behind the lyrics still makes me want to light myself on fire. I am a fair person, however, and I'll admit that I do like some of her songs. "Flashlight Dancing" is an especially good song, haunting and addictive. But she's still an asshole. An asshole who stops by whenever she damn well pleases to make sure we're all behaving ourselves, or still cursed, or still alive…who could say?

"Rebecca," I grumble by way of hello. "What brings you to our neck of the woods this time? Need help with lyrics? Or fashion perhaps? What the hell was that thing you wore to the Grammys? Looked like Bridge here ate a wedding dress and a bag of skittles and barfed it up all over you."

Bridge cackles behind me. "That wasn't barf."

"Made the worst dressed list for that one," I mock.

At this point, you may be wondering why Bridge and I aren't more scared, or pissed, or maybe even planning to capture Rebecca and force her to remove the curse. All I can say to that is we used to be, we still are, but hide it better, and we've tried, a lot. But Rebecca can disappear whenever she pleases. Learned that one the hard way after spending months contriving an elaborate system of snares that did little more than make her 'poof' into mist. And, yes, before we moved to the woods, I researched everything on magic and witchcraft that I could, but as far as I can tell, the secrets of magic are well hidden from regular humans. At least I couldn't find anything that worked—couldn't light a candle, make a pencil spin, or bend a single spoon. So we have resorted to the only weapon left in our arsenal: biting, unrelenting sarcasm.

Rebecca smiles ruefully. "Just checking in on my favorite grandma and her menagerie."

"Shit, Bridge, did you hear that? I've just become my own grandma."

"Fancy," croons Bridge.

"Well, Rebecca, if you're my granddaughter in this scenario, might I impart some elderly wisdom? Nobody, and I mean *nobody*, can pull off an orange lip."

Rebecca scoffs. "As if you'd know anything about current fashion, Grizzly Adams." She's playing it off, but I can tell my jab hit its mark. She's so vain and insecure that it's incredibly easy to rile her.

For a moment we all just stare at each other as the wind blows obliviously through the pines. Then Rebecca's eyes, my eyes, narrow into slivers. "You look different."

"Yeah, well, age settles harder every year." I open and close my hands, gnarled by huge joints and windswept fingers.

She scowls. "Not what I meant. Something's changed up here." Her eyes dart past us into the woods, toward the cabin.

My heart thumps once, twice. Shit. Does she sense him? Charlie? What would she do to him if she found him? Her nostrils are flaring in and out, like she's smelling him on me.

"Nothing changes up here but the weather," Bridge says while prowling around to stand behind Rebecca. "Why do you ask anyway? Have you finally decided to lift the curse?"

I shake my head at Bridge, warning her not to attempt to bite Rebecca's ankles again.

A breathy laugh comes from the witch. "Not quite." She sniffs the air again. "You're up to something, Nona. I don't know what it is, but I can feel it." She's got a perfectly manicured finger pointed at my face, painted with this sparkly black polish that, honestly, looks amazing and I want it. "Don't get smart.

I've allowed you your peace up here, but I can easily take that from you too."

"Really, Witch? You don't say." And suddenly I'm filled with an angry strength, pumped up with white hot rage adrenaline. Coming up here to threaten us, pointing her finger at me, looking all young and firm. How dare she?

I throw off my gloves, whip my hunting knife from my belt, and stalk over to the downed buck, my eyes never leaving hers.

Rebecca recoils, her face squeezing into a repulsed little fist. "What in the hell are you doing?"

"Preparing dinner," I reply, smiling like a fiend while I start dressing the buck.

"You're really going to eat that?" She's grimacing like she just swallowed rotten garbage. I secretly hope she'll throw up.

I laugh at her, a hearty boom that echoes off the trees. "You haven't really left us much choice. I'm not sure if you've noticed, but there isn't a Taco Bell around here for miles. Now get your flat ass out of my woods you boring, no talent, career stealing hack!" It's okay to insult her ass since it's actually my ass, and I'm old and can say whatever I want.

A shadow passes over her, even though there's not a single cloud in the sky. She's hurt. I've hurt her. As the former owner of those down turned lips and hollow, distant eyes, she can hide nothing from me. But just as this tiny sliver of humanity wriggles out from some chink in her armor, she refortifies.

"Whatever, Life Alert. I'm only leaving because that," she waves her hand over me, disdain and revulsion firmly in possession of her/my face once more, "is disgusting. But I'll be back. I'll always be back. Never forget that."

"How could we?" asks Bridge. "You never fucking leave!"

Bored with us now, she raises her middle finger, which remains hovering in the air a full second longer than the rest of her as she vanishes back to whatever hell-mouth she popped out of.

Sometimes, although I hate to admit it, I do feel bad for her. I've read the stories about her in my gossip mags, the never-ending string of failed relationships, the rumors of an eating disorder, and the constant scrutiny she's under as one of the biggest pop stars on the planet. Would I change places with her now if she offered? I would, if it meant my family and Fritz could be people again. But for myself? I honestly don't know. Besides, she's a witch and can probably just switch bodies with a banker next if she wants a quieter life. Never mind, I don't feel bad for her at all.

Still, every time Rebecca comes, every single time, hearing her speak with my voice ruins me. I'm not sure I'll ever get over it. I miss my voice, so much. The voice that comes from my throat is so different now; it's gruff and it cracks and wavers. I haven't been able to sing a single note since the curse. I shake off my jealousy, rage, misery, you name it, and get back to work.

Even dressed, the buck weighs a ton and the hike back to the cabin dragging the thing by its antlers is grueling. Bridge helps as much as she can, but the lion's share of the work falls on my shoulders. I lose my balance twice, both times landing hard in heavy snow.

By the time we reach the cabin I've almost forgotten we saw Rebecca, my thoughts overwhelmed by a bone-crushing fatigue and throbbing, rubbery muscles. Once I'm in the shed, I tie a rope around the buck's hind legs and loop it over a pulley suspended from the ceiling, then Wally holds the other end of the rope in his teeth and pulls to lift the buck until it's hanging by its haunches. I bend in half, my hands bracing against my knees as I stretch the muscles of my back which have balled up against my spine like knots in a rope.

After a few, heaving moments, the spasms relent enough that I can stand up again. I return to the buck and working quick with my knife, I dissect out its tenderloins through the incision where I dressed him. Holding the soft, red meat in my hands, I smile despite my entire body aching like I might very well die, because tonight, by the grace of all that's holy and unholy, we will have steak.

I notice that Wally's snout is investigating the buck and threaten him within an inch of his life to leave the animal alone. He has been known to gnaw on a leg or two when I'm not around.

Before heading back into the cabin, I shovel a path in the snow toward the greenhouse door. Jack, as he so often does, bounds up behind me. "What are you making?" he asks, his bunny whiskers flicking at the steaks still in my hands.

"It's a surprise," I tell him, pushing open the glass door.

Our greenhouse is a miracle, metaphorically, at least. My Poppop built it years ago by hand. It's fully wired with an insulated irrigation system so that he and Mimi, and now the rest of us, could have veggies year-round.

"I'll need garlic, potatoes, and a bunch of herbs. Basil, rosemary, and thyme."

While Jack jumps away to nibble off the herbs, his twitchy little whiskers etching tiny lines into the dirt, I wonder about him. I wonder if he's happy. It's not like any of us are ecstatically flipping cartwheels, but as the lone introvert stuck with a pack of extroverts, I sometimes worry that he lives in a constant, exasperated state of wishing we'd all shut the hell up every once in a while.

"How you doing, Jack?"

He drops a modest pile of herbs at my feet, then answers, "Good. You?"

"Weird. Things are weird. I hate not being able to talk to you guys whenever I want to."

Rocking back onto his haunches, he rises to his full, unimpressive height, his tiny paws folded down toward his belly. "I hate it, too. But it's also kind of exciting, having someone new in the cabin. Charlie is way more interesting than reading the same ten books over and over. And he seems like a really nice guy, don't you think?"

"Yes, he seems nice," I say with some hesitation, wondering if Bridge has pulled Jack over to the dark side of encouraging old lady seduction as a curse-breaking strategy.

Jack's right ear presses flat, jutting out sideways from his head. "A person could do a lot worse, that's all I'm saying."

"Did Bridge send you in here?" My hand falls onto my hip, one eyebrow arched at him as high as I can lift it.

"No."

"Jack?"

Both of his ears dart back now, plastered guiltily to his head. "Fine. She did. But she has a point, Nona."

"Fredo," I gasp, "you broke my heart!"

"Just think about it, okay. That's all we're asking," he tells me, falling back down onto all fours.

Huffing and with an irritated expedience, I yank up some potatoes and snap free several tomatoes, then I snatch up the herbs Jack's left at my feet.

"I'm sorry. Don't be mad, Nona."

My shoulders droop, my head weighing far too much. "I'm not mad. Not at you, anyway. I just really hate this curse sometimes. And I also really have to pee."

He hops over to stand in front of me again. "I know. I won't bother you again about Charlie, I promise...No matter how dreamy he is."

"Jackson Alexander Robinson!" I shout while he chuckles, ducking away from the tomato I lob in his general direction.

"Whew!" I hoot, exiting the bathroom. "Sometimes I think my bladder might be smaller than Fritz's."

Charlie, giggling from the couch at my overshare, is

surrounded by animals. Penny is nestled above him on the back of the couch while Fritz sleeps curled up into a ball on Charlie's belly. Bridge is leaning hard into the side of the couch and Charlie's scratching her under her chin in a way that makes her poofed-out tail float back and forth. A purring sort of noise I'm not sure I've ever heard her make before is rumbling contentedly from her throat.

I slide my eyes toward Jack who's hopped onto the kitchen counter and is now rather angrily devouring his carrot. Watching a rabbit chew through his jealousy that a human is petting the fox who happens to be his wife makes me keenly aware how strange the world in which I reside has become.

I clear my throat louder than necessary in an attempt to draw Bridge's otherwise rapt attention. Once I have it, her pleasure-heavy eyelids fluttering open, I jerk my head in Jack's direction.

Jack's withering glare snaps her out of her swooning daze and she trots into the kitchen with her tail tucked between her legs. When I hear Jack whisper, "What the hell, Bridge?" I cough and sneeze and might even burp, anything to cover their squabbling as I shoo Jack off the counter and then both of them off to the shed.

"How are you feeling?" I ask Charlie while I get a glass of water from the sink. After the hike, hanging the buck, and trying to prevent the world's first fox/rabbit divorce, I'm parched.

He twists to look over his shoulder at me, the movement cuing Fritz to uncurl from his spot on Charlie's stomach and slink away down the side of the couch. "It hurts," he says. "A lot."

"I should probably check your wound again."

"Probably. But before you do that, what I really need to do is use the bathroom."

"Oh! I'll get the vase for you,"

With his face turned back up to the ceiling, he sighs deeply and says with some reluctance, "I don't think that will do it this time, if you ever want to use that vase again."

The gulp of water I just tried to swallow makes a sharp and burning turn straight into my lungs. I splutter and cough and try not to drown in less than an inch of tap water.

"Nona, are you okay?" Charlie asks. He's swimming through my tear-streaked vision but I can see him trying to get up from the couch, like he wants to come help.

I wave him off, wiping my eyes. "I'm fine," I strain to say. "Just went down the wrong pipe. And no, I'd prefer it if nobody took a shit in my vase. It's the only one I've got."

The awkwardness of helping Charlie to the bathroom is surpassed only by its difficulty. By the time I get him to the toilet, we're both sweating and panting and generally exhausted. I stare dumbly at him for a while, probably too long, but I'm not sure how much help he'll need or how to ask him about it and I'm waiting for him to take mercy on me and just tell me.

Eventually he clears his throat, smiles at me a little, then tilts his head toward the door. "I think I can manage from here."

"Oh, right. Of course. Good, good. Well, the toilet paper is over there and the, uh, the sink is right here." I point to the sink at my side.

"Am I right to assume that the oblong porcelain contraption behind me is the toilet and this receptacle over here is the bathtub?"

He's funny. "That is correct," I tell him, laughing. "If I didn't know better, I'd think that you'd been in a bathroom before."

He smiles at me and while I try not to melt into the tiny dimple that appears in his left cheek, I become aware with a sudden, distressing certainty that my tiny, rustic bathroom smells just like old lady. My eyes scan the room, snagging on the ragged towels dangling from the bar, the opportunistic patches of mildew hugging the corners of the tub, the ancient bath mat that might be older than even me. Would it have killed me to have taken ten minutes to tidy up for him? I'm just not used to anyone other than me ever using the bathroom. And I'm absolute shit at cleaning.

With a peremptory, "Sorry for the mess," I turn on my heel and shut the door firmly behind me, leaving him to do his business without giving him a chance to reply. His business, turns out, takes a jaw-dropping, awe-inspiring scant three minutes. I won't drone on about my jealousy that young Charlie is able to relieve himself so quickly and easily. I'll just say it's been at least two days since I've had a decent BM and leave it at that.

After he's back on the couch and we've both stopped gasping for breath from the trip back from the bathroom, I unwrap his splint again and check his wound. The skin is pink and shiny around the edges and there is no dried blood on the gauze I'd wrapped around it. "You heal quickly," I say.

"Thank you?" he says like he's not sure if the statement was a compliment or not. "I come from a long line of good healers."

I laugh. "Good healing, great hair, superior genes for sure."

He brushes a hand instinctively over his hair, eyes going wide when it runs up against a spiky mass of bedhead. "Oh no, is that?" His grimace is equal parts amused and mortified. It's adorable.

"It's pretty impressive. I'll get you a brush."

I help him sit up but, because I can't resist, instead of handing him the brush, I crawl in behind him so I can brush his hair myself, my knobby fingers running softly through his curls. While there isn't a lengthy list of benefits to being grandmother-age, I am not above taking advantage of the few there are when they present themselves.

A tiny moan sneaks out of him while I'm taming his mane and the sound has little feathers that tickle their way up my slightly hunched spine. I smooth down one last kinked curl by hand and bite my cheek as Charlie reaches up to give me a squeeze. His hand is warm, his fingers long and gentle over mine.

"Thank you," he says and then, saving me from a flustered response, asks, "What's for dinner?"

Dinner, right. He leans forward so I can heave myself up from the couch, using the pillar of his broad and sturdy shoulder for support. "It's a surprise, but you are going to love it."

While slowly floating back down from an absurd high because a cute boy held my hand, I make my way dreamily to the kitchen. After I season the tenderloins in salt and pepper then truss them up in rosemary sprigs, I let them sit for a moment and head back to the shed to see if Mom's laid any eggs today.

I find her sitting in a nesting box, absently humming "Lilies" in her sweet chicken warble. "Lilies" is the most beautiful song I ever had the sheer creative luck of writing and hearing the lilting melody of the verse again makes my eyes mist over.

We listen to the radio nearly all the time up here, but since I can't sing anymore, my family rarely sings, or hums even. I've never asked them to stop singing, but they know how hard it is for me that I can't join them. I lost pieces of my heart when I lost my voice. When I sang, it was like I had a best friend who knew me better than anyone else ever had, or ever would. Who knew exactly what to say when I felt down, or how to push me when I felt uncertain. And this friend lit the world on fire with me when I was feeling good. And then, suddenly, my friend died and took almost everything that made me who I am with them. I still feel lost, even now.

Several years ago, during one of Rebecca's visits, I broke down after hearing "Lilies" on the radio. I fell to my knees in front of her and begged her to give me back my voice. Not my youth, not my family and Fritz returned to their human forms, I begged her selfishly for my voice. I will never forget her eyes, the pure ice in them as she shook her head and vanished, her cold laughter trailing on the wind behind her.

That was the only time I ever asked her for anything, well aside from the first year when I'd begged her to release us from the curse every time she'd showed up—we all had. We'd begged and pleaded and promised to never say anything ever and to let her have my career as long as she'd wanted. I'd offered to let her change me into someone else entirely, or even keep me old. Obviously, she never released the curse. The most I got from her was a horseshit declaration that even if she wanted to release the curse, she couldn't.

That's when she'd told me the curse could only be broken if I found my own true love. I'd laughed in her face then, hysterically. After I could breathe again, I said something along the lines of: "You're turning this into a Beauty and the Beast situation? And I'm the beast? That's not only ridiculous, it's ageist too." Rebecca had been unmoved.

As Mom starts humming the chorus of "Lilies," I ask her, "Why are you humming that one?" wiping away the tears streaming down my cheeks.

Her eyes are wide when she sees me, remorseful. I guess she didn't hear me come in. "Oh, Nona, I'm so sorry, sweetie. I didn't mean to upset you."

And now I'm sobbing. I'm not even sure why. Mothers do that, you know. They pull out the tears you've been too busy or too stubborn to cry. It's only after the tears fall that you realize they've been drowning you.

"Don't be sorry, Mom," I say, sniffling. "I want you to hum. I want you to sing. Just because I can't..." the tears overwhelm me.

She drops from her box and runs over to me. I pick her up, holding her close for a while, until my tears finally dry up. "Even without arms, you still give the best hugs."

She pulls away from my chest to look at me. "I don't know

why I was humming that song, Nona. But something feels different about this winter. It feels...hopeful."

I'd smile at her if I wasn't so busy rolling my eyes. Penny Sheldon is prone to wild fits of grand optimism. In the spring when the flowers push up through the snow, purple and yellow and pink, she becomes possessed by an exuberant type of mania and runs around for days like a literal chicken with its head cut off. She's indomitable, but I try not to get too wrapped up in her enthusiasm. Especially now.

"Did you know Charlie is a musician?" she asks.

"What?" This pulls me up short. "How the hell would you know that?"

"He told me. I suppose he got bored today and I am a phenomenal listener, even as a chicken."

I'm nonplussed. "He talked to a chicken? Out loud? You don't find that slightly odd?"

"No, I do not. And don't change the subject. He said he plays guitar for a wedding band. He also writes songs. You should talk to him about it."

I set her down and point a finger straight at her feathery chest. "And you should mind your own business, Nosey Nellie."

Mom singing is one thing, but a wedding band? I will not abide any jam sessions or soulful renditions of *I Just Died in your Arms Tonight* in this cabin. Wedding bands are the worst. He probably knows all the moves *and* the words to *The Macarena*. Just, no.

"I'm serious, Nona," she says, sashaying around me to the door. "He's got something. You should talk to him."

This time I roll my eyes so hard I get super dizzy and have to grab onto the table next to me so I don't fall. "Not you too, Mom. I am not seducing Charlie. He's young enough to be my grandson."

"Oh, don't be so dramatic," she chirps, a Penny Sheldon-ism if there ever was one. Then she's gone back into the house and

I'm left in the shed, staring at the dirt and thinking thoughts I should not be thinking. Thoughts about long fingers on guitar strings and soft lips and cute bedhead. I shake these thoughts forcefully from my head, then grab Mom's egg and almost trip over Bridge as I stumble back into the house.

Her huge amber eyes are glistening back at me, jubilant. "I just came from the kitchen. Are you making what I think you're making?" Her tail is high and wiggling.

I squat to meet her eyes, then boop her on the nose. "You bet your ass I am, sis."

CHAPTER FIVE

I BOUGHT my sous vide cooker years ago during a rare visit to White Lodge with my neighbor Sam. I was shopping for a new shotgun and better winter boots when I saw the display promising perfectly cooked meat. Much of what we eat up here is meat. The greenhouse keeps us from getting scurvy, but we eat a lot of meat. And fresh venison tenderloin sous vide is so good it makes you hate all other food for weeks.

I sear the seasoned and trussed venison steaks in a hot pan with olive oil and butter, garlic and aromatics. Then I bag it and drop it in the stockpot with the sous vide. Everyone is in the kitchen with me, except for Charlie, who's on the couch shouting, "Holy shit, that smells amazing!"

It makes me like him even more, that he swears. I like the honesty of people who swear. I swear, probably too much, but I come by it naturally. Occasionally Mom will tell me to watch my language, which is some rich irony because you should hear Penny Sheldon during a Cubs game. It makes even me blush. Absolutely fucking filthy.

I peer down at the five sets of ravenous, staring eyes as the animals surround me in a semicircle, waiting for me to drop something. Backing away from the stove to fill a pot with water, I nearly step on Fritz.

"All right, everybody out!" I shout, shooing and kicking everyone from the kitchen. "Outside! And nobody is allowed back in until I'm done!" They leave through the door I open for them, a grumbling, scampering huddle of fur, feathers, and snorts.

I return to the kitchen just in time for the weather report on the radio. "Did you hear that?" I ask Charlie, plopping potatoes into the bubbling water. "More snow."

"Looks like I might as well get comfortable," Charlie says pragmatically, then he sobers. "I'm sorry, Nona. I know having me here makes things harder for you. I wish I could at least help out."

He sounds distraught and I feel this overwhelming urge to sit with him and pat his hand. Console him. So I do, bringing over a second glass of wine along with the one I've been drinking.

"How old are you, Charlie?" I ask, sipping my wine after checking his leg one more time.

"Twenty-four, twenty-five in August."

It's strange how young twenty-five sounds, even though I'm really only twenty-three. But when you don't look your age, you tend to believe your eyes. "I'm sorry I don't have a phone. I'm sure you have people worrying themselves sick over you." This is sneaky. I am a sneak. But it seems rude to just come right out and ask him if he has someone.

"I doubt it," he says with a one shouldered shrug. "My parents are used to me disappearing for months at a time. It's what I've done since I was eighteen. Sometimes I just need to get away, but I'm guessing I don't need to tell you what that's like."

His smile, the way he's looking at me, it's...odd. It's like he's cleared a circle of fog from a window between us, and now, somehow, he's seeing me, the real me, under the wrinkles. It's like he knows.

"Nona, are you all right?" he asks, sliding his hand over mine.

My shoulders are pulled up to my ears and my eyes feel like they're a single sneeze shy of popping straight out of my head. Why is he staring at me like that? Can he see me? Can he see young...No. No, that's ridiculous. "I'm fine. Fine, fine," I lie.

"Do you need to lie down?"

This breaks the spell. "Do you need to lie down" is one hundred percent something young people only ask old people. And an old woman is what Charlie sees when he looks at me, of course. After examining my glass of wine, nearly empty, I realize that instead of sitting with a person who can see through magically induced aging, I'm probably just drunk.

Charlie is still holding my hand and I give his a grandmotherly squeeze before sliding out of his grip. "I'm finer than frog's hair, Charlie." My smile stalls out. What the holy hell did I just say? I have never said "finer than frog's hair" in my entire life. I don't even know what it means. "So," I trill, rendered too embarrassed now to give two shits about being rude, "there's nobody else who'd be worried about you? A girlfriend? Wife? Boyfriend?"

Charlie shakes his head. "No. And you? Any other partners after Harry died?"

I'm strangely touched he remembers the name of my fake dead husband. It's really sweet. "Not really. It's slim pickings up here, I'm afraid."

"I'd imagine." He peers down at his hands. "But, I was almost married, once."

"Almost?"

He starts picking at a hangnail. "She left me, two weeks before our wedding day. I've been single ever since."

This is painful for him, he's sad. I should be sympathetic, but all I hear is "single, single, single," repeating in my mind like a record skipping on the most desperate scratch. "I'm sorry. When did this happen?

"A few years ago. That's why I was out here hiking alone. This weekend would have been our anniversary. It's a hard time for me. I loved her. I loved her more than I ever thought I could love anyone. I still love her."

His eyes are on me now, full of loss and longing and intense as a thunderstorm and it's completely inappropriate how much I want to crawl into his lap and smash my mouth onto his and maybe Mom is right because he really does have something and... "But she left you? Why? Where is she now?"

"I don't know. She never told me why, only that she couldn't stay. I haven't seen or spoken to her since the day she left."

The timer dings for the potatoes. "Charlie," I tell him before I get up, "I'm so sorry she left you. Sometimes young people don't have any idea what they really want. So they end up wanting too much and not appreciating what they have. But you have an old soul. You know what you want and you'll find another partner to give it to you." I give his hand a little pat while I secretly fantasize about sliding my fingers through his hair again.

This is so bad. It's just really, really bad. And wrong. And I suddenly feel, like, gross because he thinks he's letting his guard down in front of a sympathetic old lady when all that old lady can think about is what he looks like without his shirt on. Ugh.

"Thank you, Nona."

I start to stand from the couch but he takes hold of my hand and tugs me gently back down.

"Wait. Um, before you go," he's nervous, avoiding eye contact, "this may seem like a weird question, but do you have any pictures of you, when you were younger?"

I didn't think there was a single thing left in this whole wide world that could shock me anymore. This did the trick. I'm caught so completely off guard by Charlie's question, in fact, that at first I think, of course not. But that's not entirely true.

While I don't have many photographs of pre-curse Nona anymore—in an unfortunate act of righteous but misguided rage, I deleted or burned most of my pictures after aging sixty years with the snap of Rebecca's fingers—I do have several pictures of Rebecca that I've cut out of magazines—also intending to burn them, this time for fun, but never getting around to it.

I could show him those. That would be a fantastic idea. *That's right, Charlie. You've ended up in the cabin of an insane old hag who thinks she was a current international pop sensation when she was younger. And for dinner, we'll be eating the flesh of the men who came to this cabin before you.*

"I don't," I finally answer. "Why do you ask?"

Now he meets my eyes. "You're a very beautiful older woman." My inclination is to burst into hysterical, deranged laughter, but I cough instead as he continues, "I bet you were gorgeous when you were younger."

Bridge has snuck into the room and from the corner of my eye, I can see her peeking at us from the hallway, grinning.

If you've never seen a fox smile, which you probably haven't, I can't begin to describe how delightful it is. Mom can't smile, Wally's smile is terrifying, Fritz and Jack both just show a bunch of teeth when they're happy, but Bridge, her smile is wide and beaming and absolutely adorable. It is also, unfortunately, completely contagious.

I bite my lip to keep from grinning, not only because Bridge is cute as shit, but also because Charlie, young, handsome Charlie, just called me beautiful.

Pulling my eyes from Bridge, who's now feverishly chasing her tail, I wink at Charlie. "You're a charmer Charlie…" I pause. "What's your last name?"

"Brown," he answers, deadpan.

I snort. "Seriously, your name is Charlie Brown?"

"What?" he defends, laughing. "It's a family name."

"I'm so sorry. The playground must have been a nightmare with that name," I tease him. "Well, Charlie Brown, I need to finish dinner. The potatoes might be beyond saving already." I stand up from the couch, surprised by how little my knees are aching, what with more snow on the way.

Charlie's smiling eyes are crinkling at the corners. "You saved me," he says, interlacing his hands behind his head. "I'm certain you can save some potatoes."

I hear a thud and see that in a fit of dramatics, Bridge has fallen onto her back, her paws stiff in the air. I gaze imploringly at the ceiling. She's going to be impossible tonight, but I can't really blame her.

Bridge and Jack were trying to get pregnant before the curse and I know Bridge still wants kids. She's twenty-seven now and must feel the years passing by up here like a door swinging closed on her chance to be a mother. I'd do anything to make sure she has that chance. Anything.

Shit. I have to try harder, don't I? Even if it means being the oldest cougar this side of the Mississippi, if there's a chance, I have to try.

A corner of my mouth kicks up. "If you think you've been saved now, just wait until you eat my steak." It's a terrible line and I feel like a perv even saying it, especially with the smarmy swagger in my voice. But the way to a man's heart is through his stomach, right? Or some bullshit like that?

"Can't wait," he says and the smile he flashes me could melt all the snow.

I return to the kitchen, perma-grinning and sweaty-palmed, to puree the potatoes and make a reduction from a handful of thawed huckleberries I'd picked late last summer. I finish up the sauce just as the timer goes off for the sous vide. This meal will be richer than a bowl of molten chocolate, but the raspberry sorbet I made last week should cut through the heaviness.

It hasn't escaped my attention that my family has returned.

Fritz is circling my feet, Jack and Bridge are on their haunches behind me, and the heat from Wally's mass is fogging the windows in the kitchen. But Mom waits for her dinner, patiently perched on the back of the couch, looking downright indecent as Charlie pets her, head to tail feathers.

Wally rolls his eyes, then snorts loud enough to wake the dead. Mom jumps from her spot and dashes off the couch, careening to the floor with her wings flapping like sheets on the line caught in a tornado. Poor Mom, it's so easy to startle a chicken.

I plate the food, place the plates and bowls of wine onto the ground for the animals, then fill our wine glasses again and bring Charlie his dinner. I'd sliced the tenderloins into medallions, arranged them on top of the puree, and finished them with the huckleberry reduction. The meat and sauce, ruby red against the whiteness of the potatoes, remind me of mountain-ash berries cradling snow.

"Hard to believe, but this looks even better than it smells," Charlie says after I help him sit up and set a tray out in front of him with his wine and steak.

"And it tastes better than both," I boast, settling onto the rocking chair to dig in.

The meat is tender and juicy, and that mild gaminess only helps to temper the tang of the reduction. Eating fresh meat, especially from an animal I killed myself, is an intimate experience. There is an appreciation, a gratitude, and, for me anyway, a lot of sadness. Although I could shoot as soon as I could walk, I'd never actually hunted until I moved up here and had to. I don't love it, but I understand it in a way I never thought I would. Even though a small corner of my mind always wonders if this deer or that elk could really be a person, fumbling through their own curse. There was a time, around the second year of our lives up here, when we all nearly starved because this wondering morphed into a bone-deep certainty and I refused to hunt. Everyone begged me to reconsider, their hollowed eyes and protruding bones still not enough to make me change my mind. In the end, it was Wally, a veteran of battling through unrelenting, paralyzing dark fears, who turned me around.

So I hunted, and we lived. And the meat is so insanely good, like eat it until you're sick good. Which we all do tonight. The sorbet helps a little, but not enough to keep us from lounging like sloths after we've stuffed ourselves.

Eventually, Wally and Mom retire to the shed. Charlie wishes them sweet dreams—no really, he wishes my pig and hen sweet dreams, out loud—as they totter off, Mom perched on Wally's back, Wally staggering like a drunken sailor after two bowls of wine. I step outside with Bridge, Jack, and Fritz to have the talk I can tell they've been itching to have with me since snooping Bridge eavesdropped on Charlie and me earlier.

I can taste snow in the air, crisp and clean even though above us there's a clear, star-filled sky. I'd better keep this meeting short so I can get the fire started because believe me, this conversation could go all night. The second I turn around, laughter bursts out of me. Jack, Bridge, and Fritz are sitting shoulder to shoulder on the woodpile, staring at me like they're expecting me to give a speech. "What?" I ask.

"*What*, Nona?" Bridge blurts quietly, mindful of Charlie. "That's all you have to say?"

My head tilts. "What is it exactly that you want me to say?"

"Don't play games with us, Nona." The tone of Jack's voice, the grave, desperate tone of it settles the weight of this meeting firmly over my shoulders.

I come to my senses. "Shit. I'm sorry, Jack, all of you. I know how hard this is for you, and I shouldn't joke." This is the honest truth because even in my worst days up here, even with my joints grinding in a mortar, my hair falling out handfuls at a time, and my back slowly hunching and twisting, I don't hate this life. I don't hate being old. Not that I would ever tell my family this. *I'm sorry you now have only one hole you poop, pee, and lay eggs from, Mom. I'm sorry you can't have sex with your husband anymore, Bridge. But I'm just ducky as an old hag.* Nope, not saying that, not ever.

Knowing full well what needs to be said, what needs to be done, I admit, "I get it, guys. I do. I understand the once in a cursed lifetime chance we all have with Charlie being here. And even though it skeeves me out to no end, I will do whatever I can to free us, to free you all. Even if it means pulling a reverse Lolita. But, fuck it," I throw my hands up, "older men do this all the time, right?" I might be trying to convince myself more than them at this point.

"Are you sure?" Fritz asks. He's always calm, always cool. Except for now.

I nod at the three of them. "I'm sure. I love you guys. I love you all so much. Of course I'll do it. I'd do anything for you, all of you. Anything I possibly can."

Bridge and Jack wrap their bodies around each other and Fritz scuttles from the wood to stand with his front paws on my feet. I pick him up.

"Thank you, Nona," he whispers in my ear. "Thank you from the bottom of my tiny mustelid heart."

I kiss him on the nose before setting him down into one of my footprints in the snow. "But listen," I tell them, "none of you, not one of you, and I'm dead serious, can make fun of me while I try to…seduce Charlie." I choke on the word. "Because I just tried a little already and it sucked. I felt super gross."

Bridge trots over to me, staring up at me with her round, sincere eyes. "You are not this body. You are not your age. You are Nona May Taylor, and you are a goddess."

"The goddess of daily fiber and bunion pads," I mutter, driving a line through the snow with the toe of my boot.

"Not true, Nona," says Bridge. "You don't see yourself the

way we do. You are still stunning and strong and you can do this. He doesn't stand a chance, sis."

I'm smiling at her, but I'm feeling suddenly impossibly heavy. I'm not sure I have this in me. And as much as I love my family, I can only do so much. I refuse to do anything that might hurt Charlie, because he seems like a kind man, and he's charming, and cute. And dammit, fine, he's hot. He's super hot.

"All right, cupids, I need to go start the fire, in more ways than one I guess."

Fritz waggles the white tufts of hair over his black eyes and starts to say, "Hubba hub—"

"Nope. Stop," I cut him off, making myself scowl so that I don't laugh at him. "Y'all need to go to bed and stay out of sight. I can't come on to Charlie with any of you watching. It's way too embarrassing."

"You're right. Of course, Nona. Of course we'll stay in the shed." Jack's voice is practically trembling with this pure, unadulterated hope. Jack always holds his cards close and seeing him now, barely able to contain his excitement, it's like a shot in the arm.

I take the deepest breath my lungs are capable of and say, "Well, wish me luck," thinking I'm going to need a hell of a lot more than that.

CHAPTER SIX

I'M KNEELING next to the stove, building up the fire and my nerve. Now that I've decided to flirt with Charlie, I feel too obvious, like he's on to me, and it's making me clam up. I do need to say something to him. A word, preferably more than one. That's kind of how this whole flirting thing works. I think. Mom said he was a musician; I'll ask him about that.

The fire roars to life, like even the flames are rooting for me. While the wood pops and cracks like my mummified hormones crawling out from their tomb, my new mantra repeats itself in my mind: *I can do this. I can do this. I can do this.*

I sit next to Charlie on the couch and check his wound again. "It looks really good," I tell him. Then, completely forgetting whatever young Nona might have known about the art of seduction, I sniff it. "Smells good, too."

He laughs at me. "That's good, right?"

"It is. Means it probably isn't infected." I touch the back of my hand to his forehead. "And no fever."

We stare at each other, smiling, for an awkward amount of time and my armpits are perspiring all of the sudden. *I can do this. I can do this.* Just...not yet. I slide back over to my rocking chair. "So Charlie, what's your story?"

He laces his fingers behind his head and settles his head back onto his pillow. "Well, as much as I wish it were, it's not very exciting. I grew up in a small western suburb of Chicago, solidly middle class and an only child to my folks, James and Janey. I'm fortunate, my parents are...were," he corrects, "really phenomenal people. My dad's retired from the Forest Service and my mom," he pauses, "she died several years ago."

"I'm sorry."

"Me too," he admits quietly. "Anyway, when I was growing up, my family spent every summer traveling to national parks for my dad's work, so I got used to wandering through the woods alone. Although I never thought it would lead me here." He's smiling and there is a glimmer in his eyes. A shining, adorable, glimmer and it smushes my heart into a throbbing little blob. I'm caught in this truly unfortunate internal struggle between wanting to kiss him but also wanting to pat his hand, ruffle his hair, and bring him sweets.

"Life takes us in strange directions sometimes," I reply. An understatement in the extreme. "What do you do for a living?"

He's squinting at me, considering, like he's trying to decide how much to tell me. "I teach middle-school chemistry," he finally says. "And I play in a band."

I notice he doesn't admit to it being a wedding band. Smart man. "A teacher. That's wonderful!" Christ, I sound old. "And a musician! What do you play?"

"Guitar. Sometimes keyboards, but mostly guitar. And I sing."

He sings. I used to love singing with other musicians. I'd love to sing with Charlie. I'd love to just sing. Just one note.

"I have a guitar," I say. "I can't play it anymore, though." I show him my hands, knuckles knobbed like tree roots, fingertips darting at odd angles. "I miss it though. My fingers always want to play."

"I know that feeling," he says, and I believe that he does.

I steel my nerves. "Charlie, would you play me something, if I brought you my guitar?"

His cheeks turn a dusty pink, the color blooming into a bright crimson that crawls sweetly up into his hairline. "I'd love to. I don't think I've ever performed for only one person though. I'm nervous." His laughter is unbearably charming. Like the sound angels must make when they're playing with puppies.

Ignoring the warm, fluttering thing in my chest that I'm pretty certain isn't an impending coronary, I stand and walk to the pantry where I've stowed my guitar. Her case is covered in years of dust. I trace a swirling line through the thick motes with my finger before laying the case carefully on the floor and flipping open the latches.

She's holding her own, my beautiful girl. Her wood still shines and although she's horribly out of tune, her strings still hum under my strumming fingers. Tears burn my eyes, blurring my vision as one slips off my nose, splashing onto her neck. I miss her.

I wipe away the tears from my cheeks before I bring the guitar to Charlie. After helping him sit up, I hand him my guitar and watch him while he tunes her. This act, his breath brushing over her neck, his fingers winding her pegs and grazing softly over her strings, is intimate, erotic even. I wouldn't mind switching places with my guitar right now.

The stove has filled the living room with that glowing sort of warmth that radiates deeply into your bones. Fire warmth. Through the window, fat snowflakes fall in slow motion.

He strums a few chords. "This is an old one from your namesake," he says, then he starts to play. His voice is soft and clear, but it's what he's singing that forms a lump in my throat the size of Texas.

"You were mine, and I was yours
One summer 'neath the willows
When we met, when we danced
With the sun sinking low

You took my hand, like taking sand
And let me fall through your fingers
Only to snatch me from the sky
And never let me go

Bring me the lilies of the valley
Sing to me a song about love
If you kneel in the grass and tell me you love me
I will sing you to sleep as the stars shine above"

It's "Lilies". My "Lilies".

He's stopped singing. "Nona, are you okay? I'm sorry. It's been a while and I probably should have warmed up."

He's rubbing his throat and I'm staring at him with my mouth hanging open, tears streaming down my cheeks. He thinks I didn't like it, that I didn't like his singing. Nothing could be further from the truth.

But how could he know? How could he possibly comprehend what I'm feeling, what that song means to me? I barely have a handle on it myself. "I'm sorry, Charlie." My voice is thick. "Lilies" is one of my favorite songs, but I haven't heard it in a very long time. And you have a lovely voice."

Something like anguish flashes over Charlie's face, but in a blink, it's gone. Considering my eyes are just as old as the rest of me, it's entirely possible it was never there to begin with.

"You like Nona May?" he asks.

A deranged cackle bursts out of me. "I do," I answer after catching my breath. "I really do. Please, play me some more."

And so he does.

~

THAT NIGHT as I'm curled up in bed, I think about Charlie, his voice still ringing through me, the memory of it stirring the hairs on my arms and neck. He sang to me for nearly an hour, wedding bands know lots of songs evidently. When I begged, he sang "Missing Charlie" for me, which he also knew word-for-word.

I wanted to sing again, with him. My voice kept trying to rise up in my throat, the harmonies singing themselves in my mind. But I didn't. I didn't even try. I was too scared.

When he finally put the guitar down, I set her back in her case, and then I kissed him on the forehead, thanking him for the show. His fingers brushed over my cheek and it was like tiny flames licking my skin. He curled a loose wisp of my hair around his finger and tucked it gently behind my ear. "Good night, Nona," he whispered.

I can still feel his fingers sliding over my skin, soft and warm. I also feel something else. Something deep and needy. Something I haven't felt in a very long time.

My heart is rising up into my throat and I swallow hard to push it back down. I scan the room to make sure Fritz hasn't already crawled in under the door to sleep with me. When I'm certain I'm all alone, I slip a slightly trembling hand under my blankets. It's been years and I feel an awkward unfamiliarity with this part of my body, like shaking a stranger's hand when you're pretty sure you've met before. But after several hesitant, then familiar, then glorious minutes, I stare at the ceiling with a smile cracking my face. I am completely shocked things still work down there. Shocked and delighted, and then shrieking when Fritz bounces onto my chest.

He leaps in place, beeping, his tail bottle-brushing even more than that summer a feral cat took up residence under our porch, its sharp claws grabbing for him whenever he walked out the front door.

"Jesus, Nona. What's gotten into you?" he asks, curling up next to me.

My heart lurches, stumbling, tripping over itself like a newborn colt. What did he see? What does he know? "Nothing, you just scared me."

He snuggles into himself, wrapping his tail tightly around his front paws. "Masturbation makes you jumpy, I guess."

"Oh my god," I groan, red faced and intolerably embarrassed as I shove my pillow over a snickering Fritz.

CHAPTER SEVEN

"You look different. You're glowing. Did something happen last night?" Bridget's mouth perks up in the corners.

For a mortifying second I'm terrified that she, too, knows what I did in my room. Did Fritz tell her? No, he wouldn't do that to me. Was I loud? I don't think I was loud, but what if I was? What if the bed was squeaking? What if Charlie heard me! No. That's ridiculous. I was cool, super cool. Cool as a cucumber.

"You're blushing," Bridge says, giggling.

I'm shoveling the new snow, another foot that fell overnight, from the path leading from the shed and feeling frisky as a foal. I heave massive shovelfuls over my shoulder and I'm a little concerned I might give myself a heart attack with all this unbridled vigor.

"You looooove him," Bridge croons until I smother her under ten pounds of snow. She pops up through the powder, shakes a coating of snow from her head, and repeats, "loooooovve..."

I laugh at her. "I am not in love with him. But I do like him. Did you hear him last night?"

She shakes her head. "Jack and I crashed hard. Too much meat."

"He sang for me."

"He did?"

"He did. For like an hour."

Bridge gazes up to the pink and vanilla dawn sky. "Was he amazing?"

"He sang me "Lilies", Bridge."

She snaps her head back to me. "Really?"

I nod.

"Shit, Nona. Is he any good?"

"He's really good. Like, he's beautiful. His voice is sweet like honey, but also deep as an ocean. I wanted to sing with him, Bridge. So much."

"Oh, Nona. You've got it so bad you're making similes. Did you try? To sing?" She's careful with this question. She knows how devastated I am that I can't sing.

"No. But I wanted to. I wanted to try."

She sits in the snow. "I wasn't kidding, Nona. You really are glowing today. I think it's working."

I huff at her, my breath clouding in the chilled morning air. "What's working?"

"You look younger today. Clearer. I think he's weakening the curse."

My loud laughter makes Bridge pull her tail between her legs and flatten her ears to the sides of her head.

"Sorry, Bridge, but don't hold your breath. I'm still old as the hills and it's going to take a lot more than one night of guitar serenades to make him overlook that tiny detail."

Her ears perk back up, one and then the other. "Whatever you say, sis. But I think you should look in the mirror before resigning yourself to Crypt Keeper status."

"Bridget, what's gotten into you? Nona does not look like the Crypt Keeper. What an awful thing to say to your sister." Mom hops out of the shed, fluffs her feathers, stretches up as tall as she can and flaps her wings, fine swirlings of snow gathering around her feet.

"Bridge is trying to convince me I'm aging in reverse because Charlie is a magical, curse-breaking, heartthrob. Good morning, Mother."

"Really?" Mom waddles through my shoveled path. "Let me see about that."

I stand at a self-conscious attention as Mom looks me up and down, and up again. "Interesting," is all she says. It's difficult to decipher a chicken's expression, but hers is even more cryptic than usual.

Desperate to change the topic, I open my mouth to ask what they want for breakfast when Fritz darts around Mom and slips between my legs to bound and disappear into a pile of snow.

"What on earth's gotten into you?" I shout.

He leaps back up to the snow's surface, turns back to face us, and says, "I have a private matter to attend to." Then he scampers away, occasionally falling through the surface, cursing, and climbing back up again. And then he's gone into the trees.

"He's a strange man," Mom says.

"Yeah, but he's a good one." I smile after him.

"One of the best," agrees Bridge.

CHARLIE IS awake and idly petting Wally's head as I stride into the kitchen. It's cute. Everything about Charlie is cute. And now I can think of no other word besides 'cute.'

"Good morning," he says to me, sitting up to lower both of his legs slowly off the couch so that his feet rest on the floor beside Wally.

"You're moving much better today. How's the leg?"

"Still hurts." He pulls on his brace, sliding it gingerly up his thigh. "But I feel better. Clearer."

This was the exact word Bridge used earlier, *clearer*, and hearing it from Charlie's mouth slows me down. There is something strange about this morning that I can't seem to put my finger on. The cabin smells mustier, the fire smokier, the venison from last night hanging rich and heavy in the air. Sounds have even changed. The crackling of the fire is crisp and brittle, and Wally's heavy breathing resonates, roaring through my ears like the tides. It's like I've been wearing earmuffs and just now decided to take them off. Everything *is* clearer.

Charlie is clearer too, big black pupils swimming in pools of whiskey, sandy strands streaking his mussy honeyed mop, full red lips surrounded by a dusting of golden stubble. I'm openly staring at him now, like a psycho. "I should probably check your wound again."

"Checked it myself when I woke up. It still looks good." His lopsided grin wobbles my arthritic knees as he quirks a brow and says, "Smells good, too. When do you think I can try to stand on it?"

I'm sniffing, inhaling, marveling at how phenomenal wood smoke smells. "I have no earthly notion," I answer while I let Wally outside, then make my way to the kitchen to heat water for coffee. "Maybe a couple of weeks?" I shrug. "Or less? Or longer? Or you could try now."

He laughs at me. "Solidly uncertain, got it."

Unfolding the tabs on the sides, I stick my face deep into the bag and breathe in the coffee grounds. I'd happily get my morning caffeine today by sniffing them directly up my nose they smell so good. I check the bag, same old coffee. But coffee doesn't smell this good. Does it? My brain is a kid in a candy store in the midst of this colossal sensory processing meltdown. The sounds, the smells, the Charlie. It's a lot.

I bring him a cup of coffee after narrowly avoiding a fit of uncontrollable sobbing in the fetal position over how amazing mine tastes. When he takes it, he's staring at me, frowning.

"What is it? Is there something on my face?"

"Did you do something different to your hair?" he asks.

My hand runs over the coarse length of my braid. "Same as always. Why?"

"I don't know," he says, squinting. "Something's different. Maybe you just got a good night's sleep."

"Charlie, will you excuse me for a moment?" I don't wait for his reply, instead bolting to the bathroom. I've had enough of being told I look different today, never mind how different I *feel* today. I need to see for myself.

At first, my reflection in the mirror is the same wrinkled version of my real face, the version I've never gotten used to seeing even after the few instances where I've bothered to stare at it for any length of time. But after closer examination, I see it. It's subtle, but it's there. A change.

The coarse kinks of my hair have smoothed into waves, a whisper of brown peeking through the silver strands. My cheeks are fuller, and a pink blush sits high over my cheekbones. There's a shape to my lips, a puffiness like I've been making out with someone all night. I look...younger. How did I not see it right away? I look substantially younger.

Bracing my hands on the sink, every molecule of oxygen vanishes. The room swirls and I very nearly vomit. Then, after trying to take a deep and slow breath, I do vomit, barely making it to the toilet in time.

What the actual fuck? Is Bridge right? Is this what will break the curse, flirting with Charlie? Or is there something else happening? Am I finally just going insane? None of my family members are changing, they're just as furry and stinky as ever. Because that would be the worst thing I could imagine, if I was freed from the curse and they weren't, the absolute worst. My reflection warps in the mirror as tears pool in my eyes. I blink them free and I don't even know if I'm crying because I'm ecstatic or because I'm terrified. Probably both.

"Nona!" Charlie yells and I'm so panicked that I scream, then cover my mouth with my hand and try not to freak out even more about how absurdly pouty my lips feel against my palm. I rush from the bathroom, panting when I reach him. "What? What happened?"

"I think something's burning." He points a finger toward the kitchen.

"Oh, shit!" The coffee cake. I'd made coffee cake this morning after I'd started the fire, while Charlie had slept peacefully on the couch like the world's most adorable man-baby—not that I'd watched him for at least half an hour or anything. But in the midst of my Benjamin Button crisis, I'd forgotten all about the coffee cake and now smoke billows from my oven to the wood beams crossing the kitchen ceiling. Breakfast is ruined. I turn the oven off and don't even bother opening it to look inside, just crack the window to let the smoke slip out.

"Everything all right?" asks Charlie.

"No. I burned breakfast. Want an egg instead?" Eggs are always a good choice and sometimes I wonder why I ever cook anything else for breakfast. They're easy, delicious, filling, perfect. And Mom makes them. From her body. Good Christ, I have got to get out of this cabin. I'm losing it.

"An egg would be perfect." Charlie's smile calms me down. "I can play while you cook. If you want."

I very much want. He chooses James Taylor's "Something in the Way She Moves". He is perfect singing this perfect song. With his voice floating into the kitchen, I feel less like I'm spinning out of control. My hands stop trembling. I'm not breathing hard anymore. I could almost pretend to forget about my reversal of aging as I crack three eggs and pour them into the skillet.

As Charlie's fingers strum over the strings, I feel them

strumming over my skin. His breath between each line of the song whispers across the back of my neck. When it happens, I barely notice it at first, the notes rising from me like mist off a lake. I've started singing, harmonizing with Charlie. My voice is not the croaking rasp I've produced over the last five years. It's my voice, Nona May Taylor's voice, slowly growing louder than the sizzle of the eggs as they turn white around golden yokes.

"You have a beautiful voice," Charlie says, still playing. "Do you sing?"

"I used to," I push out through a thick, narrowing throat. I was singing. I sang. I want to sing more. I want to grab the guitar from Charlie's hands and play. And sing. And sing and sing and sing until I'm hoarse. I want to sing more than I have ever wanted anything in my entire ever-loving cursed life. But what if I can't do it again? What if it was a fluke?

I wipe away hot tears, slide the eggs onto a plate, and walk to the couch.

"Thank you," he says while we make a trade, his breakfast for my guitar. He cuts into one egg with a sweep of his fork, staring at the golden yoke as it spreads across his plate. "Nona, why did you stop singing?"

When Bridge swishes into the room, saving me from having to answer this question, I could kiss her. She sniffs at the still-smoky air, whips her head toward the kitchen, then plops down dejectedly onto her haunches, whining. She loves coffee cake.

I'm staring at Bridge, then down at my hands, noticing the places where the deep crevasses that once cut through my skin have been replaced by shallow gullies. "Charlie, how would you like pheasant for dinner?" I ask. Fresh panic is spinning up in my belly and I need to get out of the house before it detonates.

I'm already grabbing my shotgun and nodding at Bridge, whose red ears perk, her tail shooting straight up into the air. She's usually not super jazzed about a snowy morning hunt, so her sister senses must be detecting my intense need to unload on her.

"I've never had pheasant."

"Tastes like chicken, but sweeter." I pull on my snowsuit, tug on my hat, and stomp my feet into my boots. "You'll love it."

I'm halfway out the door when I turn back to see Charlie nestle my guitar back into his lap. I bite back my smile when he says, "If you're cooking it, I'm sure I'll love it." Then I close the door as he starts to play again.

"I SANG."

"You what?" Bridge circles around me to halt dead center in my path.

I start laughing, hysterically, and I don't know the exact moment when my laughter turns to tears, but it does. "I sang," I blubber through a truly ugly cry.

The snow is up to my knees and as I fall to the ground with my face in my hands because I just can't stand anymore, it folds in over my thighs, blanketing me in fine white crystals. I feel Bridge duck under my hands, her cold, wet nose brushing against mine.

"Nona. Are you okay? Please, say something."

After a moment, I raise my head and meet her eyes. "I'm okay. I mean, I'm not, not at all, but...I just don't understand what's happening."

Bridge says nothing, just sits with me, letting me cry it out.

"Is this..." I wipe my eyes, then I show her my tear-soaked but still less wrinkled hands. "Is this real?"

"I think it is," she says quietly, sitting in the snow in front of me. She rests a paw on my thigh.

"But none of you are changing. Only me. I feel like it's a

trick. Another one of Rebecca's tricks. And tomorrow I'll wake up even older."

She nods. "It could be a trick, but I don't think so. I think it's the loophole."

"The loophole," I repeat.

"Remember when we studied curses before we moved out here? No curse is unbreakable, they all have a loophole, a weakness, if you can just find it and slip through. Charlie is your loophole. Just like Rebecca said."

"That's ridiculous, Bridge. Rebecca said the curse would break only when I had my own love to lose. But I don't love Charlie. I barely even know him. It must be something else."

"Maybe you just don't love him *yet*." Bridge's brown eyes are round as quarters and they stare into mine, unflinching.

"Did you know right away, with Jack?"

She scoffs. "Hell no. When I first met Jack I thought he was a lost cause. He wore sweatpants and velcro shoes. And do you remember his hair?"

I do indeed. When we were in school, Jack had a mass of frizzy curls sprouting from his head and his sunny face was round as a pumpkin. He's cleaned up since then, but Bridge is right, he was a lost cause. "Yeah, but Charlie is gorgeous," I counter. "He can play, sing, he's nice and funny, and he loves hiking in the woods. Plus he's single. By all accounts, he's the perfect man. But, I'm still not in love with him. I don't fall in love with men I've only known for two days. I don't think I do, anyway. So why is the curse getting weaker?"

She shrugs her narrow shoulders, then she cocks her head to the side as a wicked smile spreads across her vulpine face. "Maybe *he's* falling in love with *you*."

I stare at her, and she stares at me, and then I snort. And then we're both laughing, riotously, from our bellies. I scratch her under the chin. "A little far-fetched, sis. True, I do look maybe ten years younger today, but I'm still plenty old for a looker like Charlie."

"Especially when you say things like 'looker.' You're not actually eighty-three. You do know that right?"

"Young people say 'looker.' Don't they?" I start walking again toward thicker brush.

"No, sis. No, they do not."

~

WHEN WE RETURN to the cabin, I've got three cocks dangling in my grip—typically a thing that inspires a heaping serving of double entendre from my animals—and I'm smiling ear to ear. Not just because of the birds, but because my joints only ache a tiny bit and I don't feel winded at all. There is a spring in my step, I tell you! Even if today is all I get, even if I wake up tomorrow frail and aching, I don't care. This is luxurious.

"You did well," cheers Charlie as Bridge and I bustle through the door. "They're beautiful."

I hold the cocks up proudly in front of him. "We got lucky. Bridge flushed a flock out of the brush, and I got these three easy." I don't bother adding that my eyesight is keener, my reflexes faster, and that those were the easiest three shots I've gotten off since we moved up here.

"What do you do with them?" He reaches out to touch one of the birds. The way his hand smooths the bird's ruffled feathers raises goose bumps along my arms. I imagine those long fingers sliding over my skin, cradling my neck, pulling...

"I don't get fancy with pheasant," I say with a weird, too loud, dare I say goofy laugh. "But right now, I'm going to pluck them. Do you need anything?"

He nods, his smile sheepish.

After taking Charlie to the bathroom again, I head to the shed to pluck out feathers and get my shit together. My hormones are out of control, bonkers, like the mummy woke up, shook off the dust, and tried to kill everything in sight.

I feel everything so intensely, more than I have in so long. The smoothness of the feathers as I pull them free, the wind seeping through the shed door, my clothes brushing against my skin. Everything feels so intimate, so sensual, so exquisite. Closing my eyes, I surrender to the waves of pressure, the pull and release, the soft feathers, the prick of the quill. Plucking these damn birds becomes the most erotic thing I've done, probably ever. Which isn't a stretch since I'm an eighty-three-year-old virgin who's never even owned a dildo. Yep, cursed before I could seal the deal. I take what I said about singing back, that is, hands down, the worst tragedy the curse wrought upon me.

My pleasure session is rudely interrupted when Mom and Wally burst through the door. My eyes fly open as Wally booms, "Pheasants!"

"Wally, shut up!" I hiss, scolding his enthusiasm and pointing to the wall across from which Charlie sits still believing that animals are animals and people are people. "You are not supposed to be a talking pig right now."

Mom runs to my side and flits up onto the table where I'm preparing the birds. She pulls a pheasant feather loose with her beak, then says to the birds, "Oh, cousins. I will think of you fondly while I eat you."

"What's gotten into the two of you?" I ask as Mom hops onto Wally's back, nestling her beak into the space between his thick neck and floppy ear.

"Oh, I don't know. Maybe it's the fact that my daughter looks years younger today. Maybe it's the gorgeous man on our couch who can't stop staring at her. But more than likely, it's the simple notion that my Nona sang this morning."

My head whips toward her. "You heard me?"

She shakes her beak. "No. Bridge told me. What did it feel like?"

"Amazing," I say as I pull a handful of feathers free, trying my hardest not to cry, again. "It felt amazing." Everything feels amazing. Every sight, every sound, every touch.

"I see," she says, and I know she can read my every thought, my every fear. It's something she's always been able to do. I can't hide a single thing from Penny Sheldon. "You deserve something amazing, Nona. I don't know what any of this means either and it scares me too. I don't want you to get hurt. But I do want you to live. And today, you look alive."

These words destroy me, annihilating any chance I might have had to not sob in my shed over these dead birds. I weep into my hands while Wally nudges my legs. A flapping rush of air bursts over me as Mom flies onto the table again. Then her soft, round head is brushing over my hands. I wipe my tears and gather her into my arms, kissing the tip of her beak. "I love you, Mom."

She coos, "I love you too, Sweetheart. Don't be afraid, Nona. Never be afraid to follow your heart. You can't control anything else in this world, but you can control that. And that gives you power. The only power we ever truly have."

"Follow my heart," I repeat. I usually do, to the point of recklessness, but right now I'm not. I'm not following my heart and this simple idea stokes a fire inside me. "Yes," I say. "That's it, Mom. You're right. You're absolutely right!"

"You can say that again!" she squawks.

I grimace, peering toward the cabin door. "But seriously, y'all need to be quiet."

"Oh, please," she says with a flip of her wing. "If you keep getting younger, the jig will be up soon enough. He'll take it well. Don't you think, Wally?"

Wally shakes his head, his ears flopping audibly against his cheeks. "Not yet, Penny."

"All right, fine. But I'm getting tired of having to behave like a chicken in my own home." She flits down from the table then hops up into a nesting box and fluffs her feathers. She settles her beak into her breast. "I'm going to lay an egg then take a nap."

"Me too," rumbles Wally, falling to the ground in a thudding heap of skin and muscle. "Minus the egg part."

I smile at them and feel something tight and kinked unravel within me, like an ancient, rusty spring uncoiling. I hum a little while I finish plucking the birds, the down of their feathers floating through the air like cottonwood puffs. It's peaceful, I'm calmer, until Jack races in from outside, Bridge hot on his tail.

Bridge's eyes are wide as acorns and Jack's breath comes out in rapid, rasping bursts as he asks, "Has anyone seen Fritz?"

CHAPTER EIGHT

"HE NEVER CAME BACK THIS MORNING?" I ask, putting my snowsuit back on and slinging my gun over my shoulder.

"No," says Jack. "And I think I heard him shouting through the trees. Nona, what if something got him?"

Fritz and Jack are kindred in the open woods. Both small, both easy prey for nearly any predator, they've taken to looking out for each other. Jack's trembling from whiskers to tail.

"We'll find him, babe." Bridge wraps her tail around Jack's shoulders.

"Will we? I wish I could come," Jack seethes, hopping out from under the shelter of Bridge's tail and throwing her an aggravated glare at her attempts to soothe him. "I wish I could do anything helpful at all in this small, worthless body."

It's been a while since Jack has talked like this. In the early years of the curse, both Jack and Fritz broke down, a lot. Well, we all broke down, but this particular concern was one they shared more than the rest of us, the useless feeling in being small and weak. Being helpless.

Bridget's irritation with Jack's self-pity is apparent as she snorts sharply through her nose and turns for the door. She's had to pick him up so many times from days, sometimes weeks, where he'd let the curse get the better of him and swan-dived into a bleak, despairing depression. It wears on her. Everything about Rebecca's curse has worn on Bridge and Jack. They deserve so much better than this life they've been forced into. Because of me.

"We'll find him, Jack. I promise," I say as I sweep past him and follow Bridge out into the snow.

~

"CAN YOU HEAR HIM?" I ask. Bridge has keen hearing and she'll pick him up well before I can.

"No, nothing yet. But it's amazing how much faster you're walking."

I haven't really noticed, but she's right. Bridge usually has to walk for me to keep up, but she's trotting now and I'm staying with her. "Where is he? Bridge, what if something—?"

"Don't say it, Nona," she cuts in. "Don't even think it."

She's right. Worst case scenarios won't help us, and they won't help Fritz. Fritz, my manager, my biggest fan, my first crush. The man who fought for me and supported me through every inch of my career.

I thought I loved him once, even though I was sixteen and he was in his early twenties. I still love him, if I'm being honest. He was gorgeous when he was human. Dark black skin, square jaw, brilliant hazel eyes, and he kept his head shaved smooth as marble. I tried to kiss him back then, in an ill-advised and poorly executed seduction attempt. He let me down gently, but I was crushed. I learned soon after that, though he has been with women, his preference is for men, and certainly not for teenagers of either gender. He's still the sweetest, smartest, and sexiest man I've ever known and now he could be some stupid hawk's dinner.

"Fritz!" I shout, panic carrying my voice into the trees. "Fritz! Where are you?"

Bridge stops dead in her tracks, her nose pointing to due west, ears darting forward.

"Do you hear something?"

She answers by way of bolting into the trees. I try to follow her, but the snow isn't packed down yet and I post-hole over and over, 'dammit-ing' my way along as my weight plunges repeatedly through the snow and I have to pull myself back out. Then I see Bridget's tail weaving through the trees.

"Did you find him?" I shout.

She's panting, her fur matted with tiny balls of snow. "Yes. I think he fell or something. He's breathing, but I was too scared to move him."

"Show me."

We find Fritz curled in a ball, half buried in the snow. I'm amazed Bridge saw him at all, then realize she probably smelled him. I kneel at his side, frantically brush away the snow covering him, then pick him up as gently as I can. A sob bursts out of me as I press his narrow chest to my ear and hear the rapid but steady thumping of his heartbeat.

"Why won't he wake up?" Bridge asks, circling around me nervously.

"I don't know." I hoist him up, raising his nose to mine. "Fritz, Fritzy can you hear me?" Nothing. Tears prick my eyes as my heart plummets down through the snow. "Fritz, please wake up."

His eyes crack open and he groans, "Bear," before passing out again, falling limply over my hands like a wet rag.

"Did he just say bear?" Bridge sniffs at him. She licks the wet and ruffled fur of his back until it lies straight again.

"He did."

"That doesn't make any sense. All the bears are hibernating, right?"

I shrug, then stand up so I can shove Fritz under all of my layers, cradling him against my skin. "The berry crop sucked this year, maybe they need more food before they sleep." *Fritz-type food*, my very unhelpful brain supplies.

We haven't had a bear up here in years and the notion turns the blood in my veins to ice. I march out of the trees. "We have to get him home, get him warm."

❧

FLINGING the cabin door open and bursting inside, I fish Fritz out from under my clothes.

"Jesus. What happened?" Charlie asks, sitting up and holding his hands out to take Fritz from me. Without a second thought, I hand a still limp and lifeless Fritz over to him and watch as he cradles the ferret to his chest and wraps him up tightly into his arms.

I kneel by the stove and start throwing in logs. "I don't know. I found him buried in the snow." I can't really tell Charlie that Fritz had mentioned he'd seen a bear, since Fritz is a ferret and shouldn't be able to mention anything.

Charlie has one hand petting long strokes over Fritz's back, the other clenching the ferret tightly against him. He looks as distraught as I feel. "He's trembling."

I twist newspaper so tightly it cuts into my palms, then I shove it under the logs and strike a match to light it. As the fire crackles to life, I turn to face Charlie, see Fritz still limp in his arms, and bite hard into my cheek to keep from completely losing my shit.

Charlie hands Fritz back to me so I can bring him close to the fire, hoping he'll warm up. Fritz's trembling comes in violent waves, like aftershocks. My tears fall into his sable fur as Wally, Mom, Jack, and Bridge surround us by the fire. I can see how much they want to speak, how badly they want to ask how

80

Fritz is doing and tell me everything will be okay. But they can't.

"He'll be okay," I say to them anyway, people talk to their pets all the time. "He'll be okay."

I throw more newspaper onto the fire and slowly, Fritz's trembling calms, his breathing settles, slows. Is he dying? Is this…death? I can no longer restrain the tears pouring down my cheeks as I gather Fritz to me and whisper in his ear, "Wake up, Fritz. Please, don't leave me. Don't ever leave me."

And then, suddenly, I'm not in my cabin anymore. I'm with Fritz. We're both human and dancing together under the stars after a show in Virginia, four o'clocks perfuming the humid summer air. That was when I'd loved him most, when I couldn't stop thinking about him or the way his laughter sounded like thunder and his smile felt like moonlight. That was the night I'd pressed my body as close to his as I could and stood on my tiptoes, my hand sliding up his neck making my intentions clear. He'd laughed, a small, kind laugh, kissed my forehead, and then my cheek, and then he'd squeezed my butt and said, "Find a boy your own age."

I was a little embarrassed and a lot disappointed, but we'd danced for hours anyway, waiting for the sun to rise, listening to the waves of tree frog chatter swell and recede. I remember feeling safe with Fritz, protected, knowing that no matter what he would always stand beside me. Even after my botched come on, he'd be there.

"I'd never leave you, baby," he says, barely a whisper against my ear.

I hold him out in front of me, his body dangling from my hands, swinging side to side. "Fritz, you're all right!"

He opens his mouth as if to speak, but seeing my eyes burst wide in warning, flashing between him and Charlie, he thinks better of it and turns the motion into a yawn.

Wally pokes Fritz with his snout, Bridge and Jack collapse

against each other, and Mom *burks* away, flitting ecstatically from the arm of the couch to the floor and back again. I hug Fritz to me and kiss his head a hundred times, tears streaming down my cheeks.

"He's okay?" Charlie asks.

I sniff and wipe my nose on my sleeve. "I think so," I say, but when I look at Charlie, I have to wonder how it's possible he doesn't find this situation the strangest thing this side of that fungus that zombifies ants. I'm sobbing over my ferret while the rest of my animals watch on with very human expressions and Charlie is acting like this is all as normal as Sunday morning. What is wrong with this man? Is he insane? Is there an insane man on my couch?

I stand up and set Fritz down gently on the rocking chair. He immediately curls into a ball while I pull the chair closer to the stove to help keep him warm. After running my hand over his fur and sliding his tail between my fingers, I take a breath and let it out slowly. The sharp knock on our door nearly gives me a heart attack. And a stroke. And I pee myself a little.

"Is that the door?" asks Charlie. He sits up and swings his legs off the couch like he's going to stand up.

"It is. Stay put." I've got one brow cocked at him with the command, just like Mom used to do back when she had eyebrows. "It's probably Sam."

"Who's Sam?" he asks, his tone harsh and clipped.

"He's one of my neighbors. He's a friend." *And why are you on guard all the sudden, Charlie?*

He settles back onto the couch, but his mouth is a thin line and his brows are creased tighter than a walnut shell.

"It's okay. Sam checks in on me from time to time."

Charlie nods and smiles, but it's fake, like a smile painted on a Ken doll.

"What is it? What's wrong?"

His distress seems to transform into this intense sadness,

almost like regret. Then it's gone, just like before. "Nothing is wrong," he says, fake smile firmly back in place. "Nothing at all."

I don't believe him. But as I watch Sam through the window, poised to bang on the door again, Charlie's regret becomes contagious.

Sam has traveled from his property to mine on his snowmobile. His very capable snowmobile. Sam can take Charlie to Three Rivers. He can take Charlie to get the medical attention he needs. He can take Charlie away. And I have to let him.

My hand trembles over the doorknob. Of course Charlie can't stay. Of course the curse can't be broken. And I can't believe I ever thought it could, that I let myself hope. I'm old enough to know better. I am an idiot.

With my jaw set, I pull open the door, but before I can even say hi to Sam, who's standing with his fist poised to knock again and surprised eyes bulging, Charlie is standing at my side. Standing up. On both legs. His hand is resting on my lower back and as I stare up at him, slack jawed, I find him beaming at me, his wide toothy grin bright and utterly baffling.

PART II

THAT MAN, MY MAN

CHAPTER NINE

"Nona, who's this?" Sam asks, staring Charlie down.

Who the flaming fuck is this indeed? I'm speechless, absolutely speechless as I stare dumbly at Charlie. He's standing next to me. He's walked from the couch. His splint is gone and his jeans, his jeans look brand new. No dried blood, no flap hanging open where I'd sliced into them.

Blood drains from my face to puddle at my feet as understanding crashes into me. This *is* a trick. Charlie is a trick. Just another one of Rebecca's games. The pain in my chest is like a vice squeezing.

"Are you all right?"

I hear Sam's voice, but I can't see him. All I can see is Charlie's face, his smile vanishing. And then I see my hands and clench my jaw to the point of pain to hide my shock and my tears and my fucking fury because I'm old again. As old as ever, with crepe paper skin and blue veins bulging over crooked bones. Charlie mouths the words, "I'm so sorry," at me before my vision tunnels, narrowing into a blinding white nothingness.

~

"HOLY CROW, Son. Has she been sick?"

"Not at all, Sam. I don't think she ate breakfast though."

Soft fingers brush my hair back from my forehead.

"I suppose that could be it. Her color's coming back."

"Hey," says Charlie. "Open your eyes."

I don't want to open my eyes. I don't want to see myself again, or Charlie. I hate to worry Sam like this, but I'm so terrified and furious and woozy. Oh shit, I'm really woozy.

"Out of the way," I blurt, rolling off the couch. Charlie hops to his feet to hold on to my elbow, keeping me from falling as I bolt to the bathroom before I vomit all over my floor.

I slam the bathroom door closed in Charlie's stupid face and then shove mine into the toilet, emptying the contents of my stomach into the bowl. Why is this happening? Why would the witch do this to me? It doesn't make any sense.

"Nona, what can I do?" Charlie's voice is quiet on the other side of the door. "Please don't panic. I'll explain everything, I promise."

I flush the toilet, splash water on my face, and rinse out my mouth, refusing to look in the mirror. Then I throw open the door. "You can fuck right off is what you can do," I hiss, stalking past him back to the living room.

Mom, Wally, Jack, and Bridge look even more furious than I feel as I catch them strafing Charlie with irate, heartsick glares.

"Skies above, Nona. You scared me half to death," says Sam.

I give Sam a hug, then shoo my enraged family begrudgingly out the door before one of them loses their cool completely and blows this whole thing wide open.

"I'm sorry, Sam," I grunt, pushing Wally's massive ass out into the snow. "Don't know what came over me. What brings you this way?" After pressing the door shut, I turn to rest against it, still dizzy. "I'm making pheasant if you want to stay for dinner."

"That's kind of you Nona, but I've got Marge waiting."

I'd forgotten Sam found a woman last summer and somehow convinced her to move in with him. That's a feat in and of itself for someone Sam's age, let alone someone who lives out in the middle of nowhere.

"How is Marge?" I ask, motioning for Sam to take a seat on the couch while I collapse onto the rocking chair, repositioning a still sleeping Fritz onto my lap.

Charlie stands in the hallway, where he can stay until he rots for all I care.

"She's good. She would have come too, but she's got the gout with these storms coming through. She told me to give you these, though." He fishes in his bag and pulls out three jars of blackberry preserves. "She just made a huge batch, so we have plenty."

"That's wonderful. Please thank her for me." The words sound wooden as they come out of me. I'm having a hard time focusing on anything but my racing heart and my white-hot rage. "Do you want a drink?" It's all I can think to ask because it's all I can think to do. I need a drink, immediately.

"I'll get it," Charlie snaps to answer, already walking into the kitchen to pull the whiskey bottle down from the cupboard.

I turn back to Sam and smile the most wretchedly awkward smile my face has ever made. It is a smile of lies.

"The reason I came, Nona, is that we have a bear out here."

Of course, the bear. This would be a thing that would make Sam come for a visit. This makes sense, if nothing else does. "Really? This late?"

Sam nods. "The berry crop was shit. Dangerous thing, a hungry bear this late in the season."

"Have you seen it?"

He leans forward, resting his elbows on his knees and

settling his watery blue eyes on mine. "Yep. It's a big bastard. A grizzly for sure, a boar. It's been roaming through my property the last few days and it ransacked our greenhouse yesterday. When I went out with my shotgun to scare it off it just stared at me, like it was sizing me up. Then it turned around and walked back into the woods without a care in the world. Made all my shorthairs stand on end, Nona."

"It wasn't afraid of you at all?"

"Not one bit. Anyway," Sam sits back again and rubs at his graying chin whiskers, "I know you've got your critters and I'd hate for anything to happen to them."

"Thank you, Sam. Thanks for coming. I appreciate you checking in on us."

"Here you go," says Charlie, handing Sam a glass of whiskey.

I grab the other glass from Charlie's hand before he can stretch it out toward me and as I'm downing an enormous gulp, Charlie says, "Here you go, Nanna."

The whiskey I spit out in a sputtering spray wakes poor Fritz with a jerk and drenches Charlie's jeans. Charlie stands before us, swiping at the front of his jeans and giving me a look that says, *seriously?* and I can feel the words bubbling up in Fritz's little body. I can only imagine what those words will be and for a moment, I think it might be worth all the grief just to hear Fritz lay into duplicitous, two-faced Charlie.

Instead, summoning a mountain of restraint the size of Everest, I clutch the ferret to my chest and say, "Shhhh. There, there Fritz. It's all right," and hope it's enough to keep him quiet.

"You okay, Nona?" asks Sam. "You never told me you had a grandson."

Suspicion brews in Sam's eyes and that is not a good thing. Sam can be a little overprotective. Well, I guess pretending to be Charlie's grandmother is what I'm doing today. *Fanfuckingtastic.*

"I'm fine Sam, just got whisky down the wrong pipe. And I

haven't seen Charlie in years." I smile at the fraud, sweet as molasses.

"Not since I was ten, when you left Boston, right Nanna?"

Charlie winks at me and I want to punch him in the throat. "That's right. I remember you were such a little shit back then." I laugh. "Some things never change, I suppose."

Sucking on a tooth, Charlie rolls exasperated eyes to the ceiling, then takes a seat next to Sam on the couch.

Sam's gaze shifts from me to Charlie, then back to me. "Families," he says with a shrug, the gesture simultaneously explaining and excusing our behavior.

I peer out the window to see my own family sitting in the snow and staring through the window at us, inconspicuous as circus clowns.

"Have you seen carrion?" I ask Sam, changing the subject from the liar back to the bear.

"Strangest shit I've ever seen." Sam shakes his head. "Deer with only their heads removed, a badger missing only its legs. That bear isn't right."

"Just the heads?" I ask, shivering even though the fire's burning hot. "You're sure it was the bear? What kind of bear only eats deer heads?" Rebecca's cold, well-manicured fingers dance along my spine.

Sam tilts his head side to side, considering. "Not sure what else it could be. The heads weren't cut from the bodies, but torn off. Same with the legs."

"And it just left the bodies," I mutter, turning away from Sam so I can squint at Charlie. Is he responsible for this? Is Rebecca distracting me with Charlie while she's sent a bewitched bear demon to kill my family? Wouldn't put it past her, but at the same time it doesn't seem like her style.

"Left them bleeding in the snow." Sam finishes his whiskey with a gulp, then twirls his glass in his hand. "Just keep your eyes open, your guns loaded, and your animals close until it passes through."

"Thank you, Sam." I get to my still wobbly legs, setting Fritz who's already fallen back to sleep, back onto the chair, and walk to the kitchen. "Please, take these." I bring him three bottles of cider I'd brewed earlier this fall. "It's apple and pear with a touch of basil. I wish I had more for you."

Sam opens his bag so I can set the bottles inside. "Marge loved your last batch. Basil? Really?"

"Really. Try it, you won't be sorry."

"I sure will, Nona. Thank you." Sam stands and Charlie follows him to the door.

"Glad to meet you, Sam," says Charlie, hand outstretched. "It's nice to know Nanna has good friends out here looking out for her."

Sam's smile is tight. He doesn't trust Charlie. But trust is earned out here and Charlie shouldn't be trusted. Because he's a no-good lying liar and Sam is just perceptive. He gives Charlie's hand a single firm shake. "Good to meet you too, Charlie. Safe travels back to Boston."

I nearly snort. That was definitely Sam's version of, "Don't let the door hit your ass on the way out." I follow Sam out and shut the door behind us, leaving Charlie alone in the cabin. I stop short as Sam wheels around on me. "He's really your grandson? He doesn't look like you."

Sam isn't necessarily a paranoid person. He's not likely waiting for me to pass him a note that says "help me" or to tell him some banal story while I blink SOS at him in Morse code. But he is wary and if I don't set him straight, he'll be back tomorrow, and the next day, and the next. "He is, but not by blood. I never had my own kids and Charlie's mom lived in the apartment below me. She worked nights and I watched him—"

"Enough said." Sam waves me off, shaking his head. I've convinced him enough and now he's ashamed he's asked.

"He's a good boy, just a little overprotective. Thanks for coming, Sam. Let's hope the bear passes through quickly."

The look Sam gives me turns the cold air positively arctic. "I've got a bad feeling about this one, Nona. I may call the ranger station."

I wrap my sweater more tightly around me as Wally stalks over to stand at my side. "That's probably a good idea."

Sam scratches Wally's snout before setting his gaze on me, his wide brow furrowed into ridges. "We worry about you, Nona, out here all alone."

Sam's concern is related to my age, not my being female. And this concern is a strange thing. I'd wager Sam is close to fifty, over thirty years my senior, but also more than thirty years younger than me, depending on how you look at things. So while I understand his worry, it's also irritating on multiple, bizarre levels. "I'm not alone, Sam. I've got my animals, and now I have Charlie." Charlie who I may shoot dead with my pistol as soon as you leave.

"I suppose you're right." One of Sam's Sorels kicks at the snow, then he turns to his snowmobile, finding Mom perched on the hood taking advantage of the lingering warmth of the engine. He laughs, pats her head, and shoos her gently back into the snow. "Take care of yourself, all right?"

"You bet." I wink at him, waving as he turns the key and drives off back up to his property.

"So, Nona," Wally says once Sam is gone, "Charlie?"

"Yeah, what the hell is up with that?" spits Bridge, baring her teeth as she stares at Charlie through the window.

"Isn't it obvious?" I hiss. "He must be working with Rebecca. He's tricked us all and I'm going to kill them both."

"You don't know that. None of us knows that." Mom, the ever-present voice of reason, waddles to Bridge and pecks at her tail until Bridge moves away from the window. "You need to go talk to him, Nona."

"Oh, I'll talk to him all right." I spin toward the door and I can feel my family falling into line behind me. "Oh no. No no no. You lot are staying out here," I tell them.

"Why?" asks Jack. "I'm sure he knows about us already. I mean, he can see us through the window." Jack stands on his haunches, waving his front paw at Charlie. I kick snow at his face until he drops his paw to scratch feverishly behind a floppy ear with his back foot.

"Because, I'll be the one who has to clean up the mess when Bridge decides to bite Charlie's arm off and Wally accidentally sits on Charlie's legs, breaking them for real. It'll be better if it's just me."

Bridge is raising a furry brow at Mom, and I can hear the thoughts pinging between them. Even after this, even after Charlie lied to all of us, they still think he's going to break the curse.

"That," I say, wagging an accusatory finger between them, "that look, you two, is another reason why you can't come in."

"What's she talking about, Penny?" Wally asks.

Mom answers, "Nothing, dear," as I slam the door behind me.

CHARLIE SITS ON THE COUCH, fingers drumming nervously on wide-spread knees. His cheeks are flushed, and he almost looks embarrassed, in an unacceptably charming way.

"It's a little late for that," I say, waving my hand up and down in the air in front of him.

"Late for what?"

"That thing, that look you've got going there. That 'I didn't mean to pretend to fall in your woods and make you nurse me to health and find extra food for me while I pissed in your favorite vase' look."

He scratches his head, grimacing. "That was your favorite?"

I fist my hands on my hips. "Yes."

"I'm sorry. I'll buy you a new one." And he does look sorry; he looks dreadful.

I sit down next to him on the couch, but stare straight ahead. "Are you working with Rebecca?"

His head whips toward me. "What? No. No, I am not working with Rebecca."

"But you know who she is. You know what she's done to me, to us." I point my chin at the window where my family sits staring at us.

"Yes," he says simply. I know he's staring at me, I can feel his eyes on me. "Christ, Nona. You really don't remember me at all, do you?"

Now I turn to him. Am I supposed to remember him? My heart pounds against my ribs as I look at him, really look at him, long and hard. "Why? Do we know each other?"

His breathy laugh is miserable. "We do."

He reaches out to take my hand and I jerk it away, shooting to my feet. "Who are you? How would I know you?" I consider for a moment, then it clicks. "Charlie Brown, Charlie fucking Brown. That's not even your name, is it?"

"That's my name all right, and you never let me live it down. Nona, I..." he pauses and I don't know how, but I know he's not going to tell me the truth. I know it.

"You promised! You said you would explain everything!" I'm frantic and hyperventilating and my composure is crumbling. "Are you another witch? Did she send you here to finally break me? She hasn't been able to break me yet, you know that, don't you? And if you think you're going to be the one to finally do it, you've got another thing coming." I'm standing tall, pointing a finger at him, but my bluster is ridiculous because I'm also sobbing and trembling, gasping for air in between my words.

This, Charlie, whoever he is, *is* breaking me. Into a million, razor sharp pieces.

He stands up and grabs my hands, hard. I try to yank them free and back away from him, but he grips them even tighter, pinning them to my sides. "Nona, listen to me. Just listen." This last word falls from his mouth, his voice deep and measured, like a foghorn over the sea, miles out from shore. He's doing something to me. His eyes meet mine and I can't turn away, even if I wanted to, which I don't because there's so much beautiful truth in them, so much pain.

"I want to tell you everything, and I will, I promise. But I can't, not yet. The bear isn't strong enough."

"The what?" I try to say but my tongue feels wooden, my words moving thick like sludge.

His brows knit together. "I just need another day, just one more day. This isn't how it was supposed to go. Believe me, this is the last thing I want to do. The amount of shit you're going to give me when this is over…"

I open my mouth to speak, but my muscles have melted into useless blobs of goo and my jaw hangs slack. My eyelids droop, my vision blurs, and the sweetest heaviness envelopes me, like I'm sinking into a bath of warm, molten chocolate. The last thing I see before my eyes fall closed is Charlie, or whoever he is, raising my hand to his lips. He splays my fingers against his cheek, presses a kiss into my palm, and then, with his other hand, he snaps his fingers.

CHAPTER TEN

"Hot damn!"

"Good morning," Charlie says, laughing at me as I glide into the front room. "You're looking chipper."

"I'm feeling chipper," I agree, fist-bumping Wally's raised snout then spinning to scoop Fritz from the kitchen counter. I give him a loud, smacking kiss on the head before setting him on the floor. I'm floating graceful through the room, like Snow fucking White, and I half expect birds to fly in through the windows and start singing to me. "I slept like the dead. Best night's sleep I've had in years. How about you, Charlie? Did you sleep?"

"I did. Must have been the pheasant."

"Mmmhmm," I nod, "or the wine." The pheasant was spectacular, sweet and rich, and the Malbec was smooth and velvety. It was a perfect meal. The cabin smells heavenly this morning, the air thick with the aroma of the broth I've been simmering from the pheasant bones all night. I turn off the burner, remove the lid from the pot, and inhale deeply. "Hello beautiful!" I sing to the inanimate golden-brown liquid.

"That smells amazing," says Charlie. He's removed his splint and he's wincing, slowly bending and straightening his knee.

"How does that feel?"

"Not great," he answers, grunting as he straightens his knee again. "But not terrible."

"That's great, Charlie. Truly." I'm smiling at him like a drunken, crushing idiot and when I see my goofy grin mirrored on his face I have to bite my cheek hard to keep it from getting worse. "Coffee?"

"That is the magic word." He lowers his feet to the ground and sits up, rolling his head from side to side. Wally, who is sitting at the foot of the couch now, catches Charlie's eye. "Good morning, Wally," he says, then after a beat, "Nona, why is Wally staring at me like that?"

When I look at Wally, my smile vanishes. Something is wrong. Wally is staring at Charlie like he's a stranger, a trespasser. I've seen Wally stare people down this way before, both in his human and pig forms. It is the icy peak of intimidation. But why is he doing it now? To Charlie?

"I don't know." I walk over to my stepdad and settle my hand on his back. "What's wrong, Wally?"

It's a barely perceptible signal, but Wally's squinty eyes slide to the door, then back to Charlie. *Message received.*

"I think he just needs to go out. He's probably wondering why you haven't opened the door for him." My laugh is cringy in its high-pitched loudness, but Wally's got me nervous. I step into my boots and follow Wally to the door.

"I'll be right back," I say unnecessarily to Charlie before I trail Wally into the snow.

The tension radiating off Wally's rolling hide is palpable as I follow him back behind the shed. His head whips edgily from side to side. He's scanning the grounds. He's doing recon.

"Wally, what is it?" He doesn't answer me.

Wally is a vet, Viet Nam. He doesn't talk about those days,

ever, but occasionally he acts like this. Withdrawn, hypervigilant, guarded. "Wally, stop. What's wrong?"

Slowing his pace, he finally turns around, sniffing at the air. "Something's off, Nona."

"And you just realized this now?" I jape, trying to lighten his mood because he's right on the edge.

"What happened yesterday?" Wally's skin is twitching like it does in the thick of summer when the biting flies descend upon him.

"What do you mean?"

"I mean, what happened yesterday? Do you remember? Precisely?" he asks, shifty eyes darting everywhere but toward me.

"Of course I remember." I'm frowning at him. "Wally, are you having a stroke? Say your ABCs."

Now he looks at me, glowers, actually, if we're going to get technical about it. "I am not having a stroke, and that's not at all funny."

"Fine, then tell me what's gotten you so upset?"

"We had pheasant last night, right?" he asks, his agitated ears flapping back and forth.

"We did."

"And wine?"

"Yes."

"Nona, what happens to me when we have pheasant and wine?"

My head cocks. "You get heartburn." This is an understatement. Wally has been known to spend the entire day after a dinner of pheasant belching and farting while wallowing in the mud. "What? You're freaking out because you have heartburn?"

His tail flips wildly over his back like a tiny unmanned firehose. "No, Nona. I'm freaking out because I *don't* have heartburn."

"Wally, getting lucky with your gastrointestinal tract is not typically something that freaks people out."

He paces over to me until he's standing directly at my feet. "Maybe not, but something is wrong. I don't know what it is, but I'm sure as hell going to find out."

Before I can respond, Wally's stomping back to the shed. "Wait up!" I shout, ducking into the shed behind him.

Mom swoops down from her box. "What's wrong?"

Fritz, Jack, and Bridge pile into the shed, rowdy and demanding, loudly, to know what's happening. I put my finger to my lips, making the universal "shut the hell up" sign.

"Wally is freaking out because he doesn't have heartburn," I whisper.

Bridge and Jack glance at each other quizzically as Fritz sneezes into the dirt.

"It's not just that," Wally blurts. "Something is wrong. I can feel it."

Mom sashays to Wally's side and starts pecking at his knees until he drops his head to meet her eyes. "Honey, let's take a walk."

"Don't condescend to me, Penny. I know when something isn't right."

"And I know when you need to take a walk." Mom stares Wally down until, eventually, he submits.

"Fine," he snorts, "but I know what I know. And something happened yesterday, to all of us."

As Wally follows Mom out of the shed, fear sits cold in my belly. I don't particularly feel like anything strange happened last night—we saved Fritz from a bear, I roasted pheasant, we ate, we talked, we went to bed. But Wally's apprehension is getting to me. We are all easy prey for paranoia and suspicion— see how well you do after you're cursed.

"What was that all about?" Bridge asks, trotting to stand in front of me.

"I have no idea," I say distantly, scratching her behind the ear then following her back into the house.

"Is Wally all right?" Charlie's sitting up, running his hands through the tangled mess of his hair. My fingers remember what it felt like to run through those soft waves and I promise myself I'll offer to brush it for him again later today.

"I'm not entirely sure." I set the kettle to boil for coffee. "He's a strange pig."

When I bring Charlie his coffee, his fingers brush over mine, gentle and warm like a summer breeze when it sweeps my hair off my shoulders.

He takes a sip, then shakes his head. "Jesus, this is amazing. What is this?"

"I know right?" I say, sitting carefully onto the rocking chair. "I get it at the farmer's market in Three Rivers from this young couple who roast their own beans. Best coffee I've ever had. I didn't think I had any left but found a bag in the pantry this morning. This is the last we'll have of it until the snow melts in May…" I trail off. "Charlie, it could be months before you can leave this cabin. The snow will keep coming; it doesn't let up all winter."

He glances up from his mug and shrugs. "I know."

I can't not ask him this question anymore. "You're so calm about being stuck in a cabin in the woods for months with a stranger. How do you do that?"

His breath is as deep as the sea. "Nona, do you ever feel like you don't have a place in the world? Like maybe you did once, when you were younger, but now there is nowhere you fit?"

I'm frozen in place, my heart stalling mid-beat. Charlie is speaking to my soul, to the deepest parts of me I never show anyone. "I did," I tell him. "Until I moved out here."

"You fit here," he says and it's not a question, it's a truth, a certainty.

He's right. I didn't truly know who I was until I grew my

first tomato, shot my first pheasant, chopped my first haul of firewood. My life, as insane as it is, makes sense up here. It's simple and hard and sweet and right. And I fit. Old and wrinkled and quiet and sure, I fit. But I can't say this out loud. While my family suffers, missing out on the lives they wanted to live, their careers, the families they wanted to have. As they go on not fitting, it's not okay for me to admit that I've finally found my home in this cabin. But now, alone with Charlie, maybe just this once I can.

"I suppose I do. I love it up here."

He smiles at me. "This may sound completely insane to you, but I love it up here too."

"Really?" I ask, setting down my mug on the table with a clunk.

"I do. It's peaceful and beautiful, really beautiful."

When he says "beautiful," his big brown eyes are locked onto mine, like he's not talking about the cabin at all, like he's talking about me. I'm so flustered by the entire exchange that I punt completely by changing the subject. "Tell me about your woman. The one who left you."

He sits back on the couch, grabbing a pillow and holding it in his lap. "What do you want to know?"

"What was she like? What did she do?" Wally catches my eye through the window as he trudges through the snow with Mom on his back, nestled down in her feathers. It seems like he's calmed down, his tail hanging limp between his legs.

"She was a singer."

My head swivels back to Charlie. "A singer?" my voice cracks. "Like as a career?" What are the odds?

He nods.

"Did she sing for your band?"

He tilts his head side to side, then says a non-committal, "Sure."

"Sure?"

"Yes, sometimes she sang in my band." He hugs his pillow just a bit closer, the corded muscles of his forearm flexing and releasing. "She had the most amazing voice. Like water spilling over rocks and wind whispering through pines."

Evidently I'm not the only who makes overworked similes about singing voices. "What happened between you?"

"I'm not sure. I think she wanted something different."

"Like a different person?"

His laugh is a huffed breath. "That's what I thought, at first anyway, that she didn't want me anymore. I thought I'd ruined everything."

"Why?" I can't imagine Charlie ruining anything, aside from my vase.

"Isn't it obvious?" His reluctant, lopsided grin is the saddest thing I've ever seen. "I proposed."

"Oh," I say and the word feels like the period at the end of a truly awful sentence.

"Yeah, I guess being engaged is a big deal. Some people don't take to it."

"I'm sorry, Charlie." I take a sip of my coffee. "What do you think now?"

"What do you mean? About what?"

"You said you thought she left because she wanted someone else, but only at first. You don't think so anymore?"

He shakes his head. "I don't. It just never made any sense."

"Why is that?"

He sits up a bit straighter. "Because I am the perfect boyfriend. And I'd make the perfect husband."

I'm laughing. "Well, of course. Anyone with eyes can see that."

"She loved me. I know she did. And I loved her so much it still hurts. But there are things out there that pull stronger than love."

"Like what?" I take another sip.

"Like finding your place. Like finding who you are. Sometimes that path has to be traveled alone."

"That's, um—" I swallow, trying to hide the way his words are shaking me to my core— "that's very wise." I might understand Charlie's woman. When I was younger, if I'd met someone like Charlie, who in all likelihood is the perfect boyfriend, I'm not sure I would have been ready for him. I found myself up here. I know so much more about who I am and what I want. And he's probably right, I had to do that on my own. "You never know though, Charlie. Once she finds her path, it might end up leading her right back to you."

An electric silence buzzes between us. I watch him raise his coffee cup to his lips and just as they part, his eyes flash past me to the window and he bursts into laughter.

I turn around and see that outside, Bridge and Jack are playing in the snow. When Bridge tackles Jack into a deep drift, then pounces on his belly, Charlie and I are both near hysterics. It's not until Fritz darts from the porch to come to Jack's rescue, heroically latching himself onto Bridge's back, his body flying through the air as she whips around and takes off bounding through the snow, that tears start streaming down my cheeks.

They haven't played like this since we found Charlie in the woods and watching them now is a cloud lifting. They are critters after all and critters play. I'm just usually out there throwing snowballs at them.

I'm wiping away my laughter tears when Charlie says softly, "I think that's why I stopped looking for her, so if she ever did decide to come back, I'd be in one place for her to find me."

I know it's not possible, that I'm seeing something that isn't there, but the pain in his eyes, the desperate way he's staring at me, it feels like he's not talking about some woman in his past at all. It feels like he's talking about me. "How long do you think you'll wait for her?"

"Forever," he answers immediately. "Forever and a day."

Forever and a day. It's just like the second verse of "Lilies".

> The wind keeps our secret
> Over the field where we lay
> In the summer when I loved you
> Forever and a day

I stand, walk to the couch, and bend down to press my lips onto Charlie's forehead. "I hope she finds you again," I tell him. "You probably are the perfect boyfriend."

When he raises his face up to mine, a bolt of lightning shoots straight through me, white heat gathering in my belly, my toes. We're so close that I can see these tiny copper lines radiating through the brown of his irises, like sunflower petals.

He looks like he wants to say something to me, but he doesn't.

"I'm going to bake some bread," I say in lieu of anything more profound.

"All right," he replies evenly.

I straighten up, ignoring the hitch in my back and the ache in my hips. After gathering my flour, sugar, and yeast, I stand at the counter, registering how quiet the cabin is, the only sound an occasional squeal or snort from my family still rowdy in the snow. I consider turning on the radio, but there's something I haven't asked Charlie yet. "What was her name? Your fiancé?"

"Lily."

Record scratch. *Lily? Her name was Lily? Of course it was. He's Charlie and she's Lily and I'm the Queen of England.* "Just like the song, huh?" is all I can manage.

Charlie doesn't say a single word.

I pour the yeast into a bowl with water and sugar and while I watch the mixture bubble, foam rising to its surface, I wonder what it would be like to have someone love me the way Charlie loves Lily.

She probably had no idea how lucky she was. She probably thought love like that came along every other day. People are idiots. Which reminds me, I'd better get my idiots inside before they get eaten by our new neighborhood bear.

JESS K HARDY

CHAPTER ELEVEN

PROCESSING the buck in the shed is, in a word, really fucking hard. I'm sweating and shaking and my hands are cramped claws, but I'm making stew tonight and once that first spoonful meets my lips, the pain will miraculously vanish, or at least be entirely worth it. Still, when I'm finally finished I'm dog tired and would love nothing more than to take a nap, but I have one more rather large task ahead of me. This morning I decided it's time to get Charlie on his feet, or foot anyway. I'm going to make him a set of crutches.

I sit with Bridge, Jack, and Fritz for a while, sketching out what the crutches should look like with a stick in the dirt of the shed. Then Bridge and I search for two hearty branches with 'y' junctions and several smaller sticks for the handles and armrests. I use screws, twine, glue, and finally, the master of all home doohickey creation, duct tape. The finished crutches are too tall for me, but they hold steady as I hop around the shed. They're about as comfortable as barbed wire underwear though and the rough wood gives me a fresh skin tear on my left arm.

After wrapping my arm in gauze, I wrap the armrest and handle of the crutches in rags and ace bandages, securing them in place with more duct tape. I don't try them again, not wanting to make the skin tear worse, but I think they'll work.

"I have a surprise for you," I say, smiling at Charlie, the crutches hidden poorly behind my back.

He moans. "All I care about right now is having some of that bread when it's done. I'm drooling like a dog."

"Really though," I swing the crutches out in front of me, "I think you might like these even better. Want to get up?"

He squints, eyeing the crutches skeptically. "Did you make those? They seem," more squinting, "janky."

I gasp, wounded. "Yes, I did. And they're just fine, thank you very much. I tried them out myself."

Charlie sits up and tries to straighten his Albert Einstein hair which is getting crazier by the minute. "Yeah, but I'm probably seventy-five pounds heavier than you."

"More like a hundred, but I think they'll hold you. I used duct tape." My smile is proud.

"Duct tape," he says, one hand landing on his chest. "They'd probably have worked for Andre the Giant if you used duct tape."

"Ha ha, very funny. I figured you'd be courageous enough to risk them, because then you can take a shower."

His jaw drops open and he blinks rapidly, tears springing into his eyes. "Dear lord, a shower. Yes, yes I want a shower. Gimme."

I'm giggling as he waves me over enthusiastically with both arms. When I lean over him to help him stand, he notices my bandaged arm.

"What happened?"

When his fingers run over my arm, my heart stutters then kicks hard at my chest. The skin under his fingers is tingling and warm, but also sagging and wrinkled and still so old. Worlds older than his. My oldness is sobering. "Oh, just a skin tear," I say, waving him off. "You'll find out when you grow up, but they're easy to get."

I help him stand and settle the crutches under his arms. My vision catches the flap of his cut-away jeans as it falls open to expose his thigh. The stitches of his wound look good, the muscles of his thigh look even better as they flex to raise his foot from the ground.

He takes a hesitant hop, then another. His surprised eyes are gleaming in the sun pouring through the windows. "Nice job, Nona. These are perfect!"

He looks so happy. "Yep, perfect," I agree, not talking at all about the crutches.

I offer to help Charlie get out of his clothes—I know, I'm a lech, don't judge me—but he's able to manage on his own. I have a shower chair for my own benefit after that near fall last month, so I feel safe enough leaving him in there alone to do his thing. I hear the water run and cover my laughing mouth as Charlie looses a barrage of colorful swearwords and professions of undying gratitude for me and for the hot water.

In desperate need of a distraction from the vivid images of Charlie showering my mind is conjuring, I check on the bread, then make my way to the greenhouse to gather veggies for the stew. Fritz follows me.

"How'd the crutches work?" he asks.

"Like a charm. Charlie's taking a shower."

"A shower, huh? A hot, steamy shower? Nona?" says Fritz, drawing my name out until it's practically five syllables.

"Yes, Fritz."

"You're smiling."

"And?" I say, pulling up a carrot.

"You're smiling like you're dreaming of having a hundred of his babies."

I snort. "I am not. I'm just happy he's off my couch."

"Sure you are."

I drop the carrot to grab Fritz. Spinning him around, I hug him against my chest. Then I hug him tighter and kiss his head. "You scared me. You scared the shit out of me, Fritz. I thought I'd lost you."

He nestles between my neck and chin. "Not yet. But thank you for coming to find me."

"Always. I love you. I love you so much."

He licks my neck. "I love you too, baby."

When I set him down, he scampers immediately back into the shed. "Hey, where are you going?" I shout after him, but he doesn't look back.

I gather an onion, some celery, a few more carrots, a head of garlic, and several potatoes for the stew. By the time I walk back into the cabin, I hear Charlie talking to someone in the bathroom. Who the hell is he talking to? Then it dawns on me. Fritz. Fritz is able to squeeze his rubbery ferret body under the bathroom door. That little voyeuristic shit. I'm feeling indignant and offended on Charlie's behalf, but, let's be honest, I'm mostly just jealous. "Charlie, how's it going?" I call outside the door.

"Good. I feel like a new man. Fritz pulled a towel over for me."

"I'm sure he did," I mumble. "I have some of my husband's clothes. They might fit you if you want to try them on."

They're actually Wally's. When we moved up here, I brought a few outfits for each member of my menagerie, just in case. They've been hanging in my closet and folded in my drawers ever since. Wally's clothes will be big, but Jack and Fritz were too short or too trim, respectively.

Charlie's quiet for a moment, then he says, "That would be wonderful."

He looks good in Wally's clothes. Dark green chinos and a soft gray crewneck sweater. They hang from him a bit, but it just gives him this irresistibly boyish vibe. After hopping from the bathroom with his crutches, he passes the couch to sit on the rocking chair and stares into the fire. His hair is still wet and after he rakes a hand through it, his bangs settle back over his eyes in wispy strands.

He smells good, really good. Fresh and clean. I want to sit in his lap and nestle my face into his neck so I can breathe him in for hours. As Fritz bounds smugly from the bathroom, I wonder if Charlie is some sort of sex wizard and he's having his way with all of us, severely deprived patsies that we are. Then I realize that if anyone has been taken advantage of, it's Charlie who just unknowingly had a man-ferret watch him take a shower.

I wander to the kitchen and pull the bread from the oven. It's steaming and golden and perfectly hollow when I tap its bottom. I set it on a wire rack to cool and start cutting veggies. My skin tear aches a bit as I push my knife through stalks of celery and thick carrots. Then I'm sniffling and crying while I dice a stupid onion.

"Are you all right?" Charlie turns in the chair so he can see me over his shoulder.

"Just an onion. I'm fine." I wipe my nose on my sleeve and groan, the noxious onion fumes setting fire to my eyeballs.

"Can I help?"

"Nope. Well," I reconsider, "I wouldn't object to more music."

Charlie plays while I cook. Wally and Mom joined us after their walk, Wally still on edge but much calmer. Calm enough, as a matter of fact, to pass out cold, now sprawled and snoring at Charlie's feet, flicking an ear whenever Charlie plays a certain chord. After nestling in Charlie's lap for a while, luxuriating in his feather petting in between songs, Mom finally retreats to her nesting box for some proper rest, winking at me on her way past the kitchen.

Aside from Charlie's guitar and Wally's nose, the cabin is filled with the sweet and heavy silence of afternoon naps, the blissful calm before the storm of empty bellies and full plates. As I stir the roasted vegetables into the pheasant stock and wait for it to come to a boil, Charlie starts to sing an old Tom Waits song. It's one Mom and Dad listened to all the time when I was a kid, before Dad died. In the song, an older man calls a woman he loved when they were younger and asks her to meet up for coffee, eventually confessing that he still loves her. I always thought it was so sad, and now it feels even sadder. I start to sing along, testing my voice, pushing into my vocal cords, feeling out my range.

"Your voice," says Charlie, not stopping his strumming during the chorus. "It's stunning." His next words are almost a whisper. "You sound just like her."

I swallow involuntarily and burn the shit out of my fingers as my hand drops, trembling to rest against the side of the scalding soup pot. "Like who?" I ask, shaking my hand out.

"Nona May Taylor. You have that same perfect tone she has." Unintended, I'm sure, but his words are an anvil hurled at my chest.

Eventually, I manage to push, "Thank you, that's a very kind thing to say," through the geyser of emotion shooting up my throat. Just then, Wally provides much-needed comic relief by way of a loud and prolonged snort, then an even louder fart, before resuming his customary snoring.

"Oof. That's awful." Charlie's waving his hand in front of his nose.

I laugh, knowing exactly what he's dealing with. Wally's farts are epic; they've forcibly emptied this cabin more times than I can count on both hands.

"Sorry," I say. "He's the absolute worst. Wine?" I pop the cork on a cabernet.

"I'd love some, if I don't die in the next few seconds."

I reduce the heat under the stock to simmer. "You really might. And what a way to go, huh? Can you imagine the obit?"

He laughs while I cover the soup pot, lay a towel over the bread, then pour two glasses of wine.

"What do you think about sleeping in a bed tonight?" I ask while I hand him his glass.

He shakes his head. "I won't take your bed." Then one of his brows does this saucy little hop. "Unless you're suggesting we share it."

I choke on my wine, again. It burns, but at least I manage to swallow it down instead of spitting it out this time. My mind wants to reply, 'Yep, yes sir, that is precisely what I'm suggesting,' but my mouth intervenes. "Not quite. But there is more to this cabin than meets the eye."

His eyes sparkle as he whispers conspiratorially, "Is this a magical cabin? Is it really a mansion with a pool and a bowling alley in the basement?"

I lean toward him with the widest smile and reply, "Yes."

No, the cabin is not a magical mansion, but it does have two adjoining back rooms that I'd closed off shortly after we'd moved up here. Nobody used them and trying to keep the entire cabin warm in the winter seemed stupid.

I push open the door to the first bedroom with my eyes squeezed shut, terrified of how it will appear after four years of neglect. Will there be dog-sized spiders? A million moths? Lung-infesting mildew? Through a crack in one lid, I see the room pretty much just as I'd left it. A little musty, the lightbulbs are all burned out, and there's a Mission Impossible laser maze of cobwebs strewn across the room, so I've got some work to do. But I'm sure Charlie won't mind a little mustiness if it means he gets his own bed.

After this cursory glance, something on the wall snags my attention. I blink, my eyes focusing on an image so foreign to me now that a gasp of stale, dusty air flies into my lungs and my eyes fill with tears. I'd forgotten. How could I have forgotten?

This is where I'd hung our pictures.

I'd debated bringing them with when we moved up here, but we were all so certain we'd break the curse in those first few months that the pictures were nice to have around. Eventually, this evidence of our old lives became painful to see, and then unbearable, so I stowed the pictures in here.

I walk around the four-poster bed, wiping thick layers of dust from the frames, and I see…us. There's a picture of Mom and Wally on their honeymoon in Vegas, sitting at a poker table, Mom held tight in Wally's lap and laughing, her head tilted up to the ceiling. Another one is a family picture of that beach trip in South Carolina when I fell asleep in the sun and got fried red as a beet. I'd ruined the entire trip, laid up in bed, moaning and delirious with pain. That was the summer when, despite my agony, Mom and Wally fell in love with Charleston. On the far wall there's a picture of me and Fritz holding my first gold record, our smiles so big and bright the record pales in comparison.

Then I dust off a picture of Bridge and Jack on their wedding day. They're so happy. Could they ever have been that happy? I step closer to the picture, running a finger over Bridge's smiling mouth, and it cores me out. I bring my trembling fingers to my lips, then press a kiss to both of their beaming, beautiful faces.

On one of the bedside tables I find an old picture of my Mimi and Poppop. They're sitting on the cabin porch, Mimi reading a book about canning and Poppop balancing me and Bridge on one knee each while we pretend his legs are horses. I remember this like it was yesterday. Poppop would sing to us about spurs jingling and jangling while he bounced us around wildly, usually until one of us gave up and hopped, or more likely, fell off.

How could we have kept these pictures back here for so long, hidden? Forgotten? I want to take them out and hang them up all over the cabin. I want to sleep with them clutched in my arms. But then I remember that the decision to put them back here did not come from me. In fact, it had nothing to do with me.

I am still human, they are not. These pictures make me sad and sentimental, but they were absolutely devastating to my family—bleak, painful reminders of a life they might never get back. They aren't ready for the nostalgia of their human lives, and they may never be. They didn't have the luxury of rage-burning their pictures after the curse, like I did. But back here, where they won't see them, where they won't see me, I let myself clean all the dust from the frames and pull back the curtains to let the light in. I want to bask in these memories for as long as I can. I want to stare at my loved ones, my human loved ones, until my eyes turn so dry they burn.

Then I remember this room will be for Charlie. He can't see any of this. He can't see pictures of Nona May Taylor or her family in this room. So I wipe my eyes, pull the pictures carefully from the wall, and open Poppop's chest at the end of the bed. The smell of mothballs assaults me as I move aside one of Poppop's coarse wool horse blankets so I can hide the pictures beneath it. I nestle them next to a cigar box full of old coins and one of Poppop's corn cob pipes. I take the pipe out and puff on it, then shove it in my pocket—I'm keeping it.

After shutting the cigar box, then the chest, sealing our memories away again for who knows how many more years, I make Charlie's bed, dust off the lamp on his bedside table, replace the bulb, and stand back to admire my work. This room is where Bridge and I slept whenever we came to visit. We'd stay up late into the night talking about boys we liked or searching for fireflies out of the window. We were certain they'd show up, even though Mimi told us they never came this far north. She was right, they never came. But we never stopped looking, waiting for that single blink of yellow light in the blackness of the woods.

Finally ready for him, I show Charlie into the room, leading him as he hops along with his crutches.

"There *is* more to this cabin than meets the eye," he says, sitting carefully on the foot of the bed.

I sit next to him while he looks around the room. Eventually we both wind up staring out the window, watching new snow fall in big white flakes. They float aimlessly through the sky, looking a lot like fireflies.

"Nona, are you okay?" He rests a hand over mine and suddenly I'm crying again. I haven't cried in years and now it seems to be all I can do. It's too much. Everything about this room, the pictures, the memories, all of our missing lives. I can't hold it all in.

Charlie's just here, letting me cry it out for as long as I need, gently closing his fingers around my hand and waiting silently beside me.

I take a breath and blow it out, wiping my eyes. "I haven't been in this room for a long time. It used to be mine, when I was a girl. It reminds me of them, of my grandparents. I miss them. I miss so many things." It's not a lie, just not the whole truth.

"Is that a pipe?" He slides a brazen hand into my pocket and pulls out Poppop's pipe. His fingers grazing my thigh yank me straight out of my melancholy. He doesn't wait for me to answer, but pops the pipe into his mouth. "This is a fantastic pipe."

I laugh at him, sitting on my childhood bed with my Poppop's pipe in his mouth. "I know. I found it in the chest." I lean in, conspiratorial. "So I took it."

"I can see why. Do you have any tobacco?"

My dirty little secret. "I do."

His mischievous smile sinks into something more meaningful as he notices my red and wet eyes. He brushes a tear from my cheek. "You've got a sensitive soul, Nona. A sensitive soul and a warm heart. It's a good combination."

It is at this moment that I realize I have absolutely never wanted to kiss someone so badly in my entire life. So I do, but only on the cheek. "Thank you. You're a good man, Charlie—" I snort, then laugh.

"What? What's so funny?" He's laughing at me laughing at him.

"You're a good man, Charlie Brown."

"Ooh," he says sportingly, grinning wide. "You make that one up yourself?"

Still laughing, I help Charlie from the room and we sneak out to the rocking chairs on the porch. It's cold but quiet, the wind so still the only sound is the tinkling of the snow landing on the roof. There's even a ray of setting sunlight peeking below the high clouds, spilling yellow over the gray gloom and glinting off the snowflakes as they fall.

"Montana skies are big enough to hold all four seasons at once," I say, repeating something Mimi used to say.

"Beautiful," says Charlie, his eyes to the sky, and then to me.

I unroll my stash of tobacco, inhale the sweet vanilla and raisin scent, then pack the pipe, light it, and take a puff. Charlie and I sit, silent, passing the pipe back and forth while we watch the snow fall. It's nice. It's really nice. Wonderfully, perfectly, nice to sit with him, not needing to talk, not feeling any need at all to say a single word. Then Mom spoils it by flitting onto the porch, flapping her wings at my feet, and glaring at me in abject disapproval. She hates it when I smoke. I nudge her off the porch with my boot and she explodes into a feathery, squawking, ball of indignation. The only thing louder than her protestations is Charlie's chuckle.

After a while the temperature plummets, the sun vanishing behind the western mountains. Ash floats to the ground as I flip the pipe over, tapping the bottom of the bowl with my finger. I stamp the tiny fire out with my foot and, reluctantly, tell Charlie about that stew I need to finish. I help him up, open the door for him to hop through, then deposit him onto the couch.

~

HOURS LATER, after we'd all eaten and Charlie and I talked in front of the fire until we both grew drowsy, I fall into a fitful sleep, my pillows too hot and my sheets too cold.

I dream of snow and wind and a scared little girl lost in the woods. She's running between the trees, dress torn, knees bloody, bright red shoes covered in mud. Something is following her, chasing her. She trips over a tree root because she's looking frantically behind her. I watch her scrabble in the snow and mud, clawing her way back to her feet. I'm trying to help her, to get to her, but I can't move. I can't even scream.

An unearthly roar shakes the branches above her and rumbles the ground beneath her feet. The little girl screams as white teeth and yellow eyes pierce the night sky behind her. But it's not a little girl, it's me. I'm the one trying to run, trying to scream as the bear roars hot breath into my face, its teeth dripping saliva, its claws lashing out to slash across my chest.

"Nona, wake up. Wake up!"

I come crashing out of my dream, heaving myself upright from my pillow, covered in sweat. I'm panting over my legs, my heart galloping inside my chest.

"You were screaming," Fritz says, trembling in my lap.

Groaning, I fall back to my pillow while Fritz scampers up my body to sit between my boobs, his favorite spot. "Bad dream," I choke out. "Really bad dream."

"What abou—" Fritz jumps from my chest like he's been electrocuted, then races around me to slide under my pillow.

The roar from my nightmare shakes my window, rattling the glass against the frame as the silhouette of an enormous, hunched form prowls outside the window. I can hear its huffed breathing through the glass and the low growl rumbling in its throat. Aside from my raised head, I don't move a muscle.

Fritz's head pokes out beside my right ear. "It's the bear. That's it Nona. That's the bear I saw. I know it is."

My heart is still hammering against my ribs, but it's slower now that I've got my bearings. Fritz and I wait, silent as mice, then I say, "We locked the shed, right?"

I can feel the pillow moving with his nodding. "You did. Right before bed, right after you kissed Charlie goodnight."

"Dammit, Fritz," I hiss because he's teasing me even now, even with death skulking outside my window. Then I press my lips together and hold my breath as snow crunches under the bear's massive feet. My windows are locked, the garbage is secured, and my family is safe in the shed, yet the fear barreling through me is primal. That bear is huge and hungry and far too close to the cabin, to my family.

After what feels like hours, the bear's footsteps move away from the window, away from the cabin, and fade into the howling wind. Fritz doesn't come back out from under my pillow for the rest of the night.

CHAPTER TWELVE

"Jesus Christ! Nona! Nona, what the hell?"

Charlie's bellow jerks me from a fragile, shitty sleep. I haul myself out of bed, groaning as Fritz finally slides out from under my pillow to bound past me in furry rainbow arcs. I throw my robe over my shoulders, step into my slippers, and shuffle down the hall.

When I enter Charlie's room, the scene that unfolds is so peculiar that I wonder for a moment if I'm still dreaming. Charlie huddles in the corner, the bedside lamp in his hands and pointed out like a weapon. Wally sits at his feet and Mom stands on his bed, and they're all just staring at each other.

"What's the matter?" I ask around an enormous yawn.

Charlie tips his lamp at Wally. "The pig just talked! That's what's the matter!"

My mouth snaps shut, my eyes bulging painfully from their sockets. "What? No he didn't. That's ridiculous." My laughter is shrill and twanging.

"No, it's not," says Charlie, his voice shaking as much as his lamp-gun. "Your pig just asked me a question."

I blow loud dismissive air through my lips, at the same time wondering what the holy hell Mom and Wally are thinking. "Maybe you were dreaming? Pigs don't talk."

"That one does." His finger trembles in Wally's direction.

My mouth opens to rebut when, to my utter fucking incredulity, Wally swings his swine head to me and says, "He's right, Nona. I did ask him a question."

Charlie shrieks as Mom bursts into motion, running in circles on the bed and flapping her wings in a frantic spasm.

"Dammit, Wally," I seethe, throwing myself between Charlie and the pig. I turn to Charlie and raise my hands in front of me. "Charlie, I want you to stay calm."

"Calm? You want me to stay calm? Your pig talks, Nona!"

"Not just the pig," say Mom and Fritz in unison.

"Oh, for fuck's sake!" I spin to face my family, imploring, "Seriously guys, all at once? Are you trying to kill him?"

"I figured he could handle it. And he's done something to us; I'm sure of it." Wally's voice holds the same paranoid edge it did yesterday.

"Come off it, Wally," I snap, turning back to face Charlie. "He hasn't done anything to us."

"Nona." The tone of Charlie's voice pulls me up short. It's the hushed, severe tone of someone who's seeing a ghost. He's studying me, and his eyes shift between opened wide and squeezed tight like he's trying to focus on something inherently blurry.

"What?" I blurt out.

"Oh, honey," whispers Mom.

"What? What is it? Why are you all staring at me like that?" I'm starting to panic. Did something happen to me while I was sleeping? Am I sick? Disfigured? Even older?

"Go to the bathroom," Wally orders. "The mirror."

I nearly slip, skidding around the corner and racing down the hall. I'm breathing heavy, my chest heaving, throat burning.

What I see in the mirror, how it makes me feel, it's a difficult thing to explain.

There's the simple changes, my skin and hair, those are obvious enough. This change, this Nona in the mirror goes beyond the tightening of my neck or the fullness of my lips. It's deeper. Bone deep. When we age, we don't just look older, we look…different. Our cheeks hollow, our noses extend, our eyes sink deeply into their sockets. We grow beards. In the mirror now is a woman no older than fifty years. It's me. This is *my* face. It's a face I've only seen in pictures and on magazine covers, or on Rebecca, for so many years. This is my face, Nona May Taylor's face. And it is fucking beautiful.

I feel Charlie's hand land softly on my shoulder. Over the thumping of my heart in my ears, I didn't hear him hopping from his bedroom, but his touch doesn't startle me. His hand is gentle and warm and he steadies me while I hover over the sink, my ribcage cinching so tightly I can barely pull air into my lungs. "What's happening to me?"

His hand runs up and down my back. "I was going to ask you the same thing. While you've been in here I've been," he pauses for a dry swallow, "talking, I guess, to your family. They told me you've all been cursed." His voice swoops up an octave on the word, 'cursed,' like it's a question, like it's a ridiculous, impossible question he can't believe he's asking.

I run cold water into my palms and splash it over my face. My skin is so soft under my fingers, so smooth. I push my fingertips into my cheeks. They're plump like peaches and covered with the same soft fuzz.

"Yes, we've been cursed," I say through the towel I'm using to dry my face. "But something is breaking it." My voice belongs to someone else. No, that's not right, it belongs to me, it's my voice, I just haven't heard it in so long. Staring at myself in the mirror again, I run two fingers over my pink lips. "At least it's breaking for me."

Without another word, Charlie pulls me to him and wraps his arms around me in a crushing embrace. I wince, waiting for the pain, but none comes. My bones, my skin, they're so much stronger now. They can take it. I can take a real hug. So I throw my arms around him and weep into his shirt while he strokes my hair.

"Nona?"

Charlie and I both turn to see Bridge sitting in the doorway.

Bridge's voice wobbles. "Nona. You're so young. You're so beautiful."

It is with these words from my sister that I fall completely and entirely apart in Charlie's arms.

"This is, hands down, the strangest day of my life," he says as he stares at Bridge, his chin resting gently on my head, his arms still wrapped tightly around me.

I wipe my nose on his shirt and then pull away. There is laughter in his eyes. "You're taking all of this well," I tell him.

He wipes a tear from my cheek, then shrugs. "Oh, I think I've probably just gone insane, seems silly to be upset about it."

"Well, then," I say evenly, "welcome to the nuthouse."

THE TIME it takes to tell Charlie about the curse is brief compared to the time it takes him to respond. He just sits there on the couch, chewing on his lip and sort of nodding his head. We all glance at each other, brows furrowed, mouths and beak frowning, and I become seriously concerned that we've broken him.

"Are you all right?" I ask. "I know it's a lot to take in at once."

He clears his throat, takes a sharp inhale, then asks, "So you were cursed by a witch who is now pretending to be you because you kissed a boy at a concert?

I swallow hard. "Uh, yep." It does sound absurd when he puts it like that.

"And you don't remember anything from that night? Nothing at all?"

I shake my head.

"None of you remember?"

We all shake our heads.

"Have you seen the witch since?"

Fritz hisses and I give him a pet where he sits on the armrest of the rocking chair. "Yeah. She visits every once in a while. She was just here a few days ago, as a matter of fact."

Charlie sits bolt upright. "What? She was here? While I was here?"

"Yes," I say at length. "She was in the woods when I shot the buck. It's always the same. She appears from nowhere, reminds me what I used to look like, says some stupid bullshit, then threatens to make our lives even worse before fading into the air like dandelion fluff." I wiggle my fingers in demonstration.

"Have you tried—"

I cut him off. "We have. We've laid traps, tried ambushing her with a hidden Wally, shot at her. We even tried a very unfortunate attempt at a counter-spell one year with a pentagon made of deer bones. There was chanting, torches, it was all very dramatic. She'd just laughed at us then took away Bridget's voice for three months for trying to bite her. We didn't know if Bridge would ever speak again."

Bridge's hackles rise, a low growl rumbling from her throat. "The only way out is to break the curse," she says, calming as Jack leans against her and nestles into her fur.

"How do you do that?" Charlie asks.

Bridge opens her mouth, but I interrupt, "Uh, no clue. But I started getting younger when you showed up, so maybe it has something to do with you."

Bridge side-eyes me, glaring. She wants to tell Charlie everything, I can tell. But I can't. I don't want Charlie to know his part in all of this yet. I'm not sure why, but I don't want him thinking he's nothing more than a pawn in this whole game. Instead of...what? A friend? An ally? A cute boy I have a massive crush on?

Charlie's smile grows wide.

"What?" I ask carefully. "Why are you smiling?"

"It all just makes so much sense now."

Mom flaps her wings and lands on the couch beside him. "What makes sense, Charlie?"

After his initial, reflexive flinching at the bird talking to him, he leans toward her and scratches under her beak. "The change. The drastic change in the music, your music," he says, nodding toward me. "Not that I don't like the pop, but I was, am, a die-hard fan of your older stuff. Or, I guess older isn't the right word, is it? Your original stuff?"

I nod, smiling back at him, blood shooting like a firehose into my cheeks. "Thank you. I like my stuff too. But I don't hate the pop either and that really pisses me off sometimes."

He laughs. "Flashlight Dancing?"

I sigh, staring at him, dreamy-eyed. "Yeah. It's a damn good song."

"You did something to us." Wally's insinuation shatters this little moment Charlie and I are having.

Charlie frowns at the hog hunching in front of him. "I'm sorry?"

"Yeah right, you're sorry."

"Wally, behave." I'm more than a little concerned. Wally is huge and he's aggressively pointing his snout at Charlie.

"Something happened here, Nona," snorts Wally. "I know it. He's not what he seems."

Wally flicks his tail and the room shudders with each stomp of his hoof. There is a lather working at his mouth and Charlie presses into the back of the couch and as far away from Wally as he can get. That's real fear I see in Charlie's eyes. "What makes you think that, Wally?" Charlie asks.

I'm not sure whether to stay put or jump on Wally's back and try to tackle him to the ground before he eats Charlie's face. I've never seen my stepdad so agitated. His withers twitch and his ears dart back and forth like manic antennae.

"I know you're lying. You're hiding something." There is so much emotion in Wally's voice, it's ragged and hoarse and most of all hurting. Mom is desperately glancing from Wally to me, like she doesn't have a clue what to do.

This is not good, not good at all.

"Wally," Mom says, flitting down to sit in front of Wally as Fritz jumps up to sit protectively on Charlie's lap, "what's going on?"

"I want him to tell us the truth. I know he's hiding something." Wally turns toward all of us. "I know you all think I'm crazy, or shell shocked, but I'm not crazy. I'm not—"

"We don't think you're crazy," interrupts Bridge, a little too-sweetly. "But sometimes you get carried away. Like the time you thought there was a sniper in the woods."

"Or the time you were convinced an invisible drone was recording us," adds Jack.

"Or the time—" starts Fritz.

"Stop," Charlie interrupts. "Stop, please. Please, I can't do this anymore." His chin drops to his chest. "Wally's right."

We're all staring at Charlie now, dumb and blinking. You could hear a pin drop until I finally blurt, "What?"

Charlie scratches his head, his hair flopping around under his fingers. "Wally's right. I haven't been completely honest with you."

He's quiet for a moment.

"Go on," I encourage, waving an impatient hand at him.

"I didn't wind up out here because I got lost. I was out here on purpose, searching for something. I still am."

After another pause, "Seriously, Charlie. Spill."

He takes a deep breath. "My family, my great-grandfather, owned land out here. His name was Rufus Brown, you may have heard of him."

A wave of head shakes surrounds Charlie, he laughs. "Knock 'em Down Rufus Brown? No? Nothing?"

Silence, until: "He robbed trains," says Jack. "He was infamous in the 20s for stealing more money than the Newton Gang."

"The Who-ton Gang?" asks Bridge, staring at her husband like he's a rabbit she's just now met.

"You don't even know the Newton Gang?" Charlie asks in pure disbelief.

"Charlie, dear. We are a family of talking animals and you're upset we don't know about a long-dead gang of train robbers? Are you all right?" Mom asks.

Charlie barks a laugh. "That's true. I'm not sure how I've become the one trying to explain myself to all of you."

"Keep talking," grunts Wally, not the least bit amused.

Charlie grimaces, but continues: "The last time I was home, my dad gave me a book he'd found under the floorboards of the house Rufus lived in up here, the house he'd passed down to my great grandmother. It was a collection of poems. Rufus was a poet, a rather good one in fact, and several of the poems alluded to a treasure he'd hidden in the woods, under the 'tallest pine in the deepest valley'."

"What sort of treasure?" asks Jack, whiskers twitching.

"Have you ever heard of the Rose of the Desert?" Charlie's eyes twinkle.

"*The* Rose of the Desert?" says Jack. "You're serious?"

I stare at Jack. "You know what that is?"

Jack hops closer to Charlie. "Your great-grandfather stole the Rose of the Desert?"

Charlie's smile broadens, taking up most of his face. "That's the story. And I think he hid it up here."

"That's…" Jack stops to stand up on his hind legs, his front paws resting on Charlie's left knee. "Where? Where is it?"

"His property was a few miles north of here. It's national forest land now. Papa Rufus had land in three states: Arizona, Colorado, and Montana. And I've already been through his properties in Colorado and Arizona with a fine-toothed comb. Nothing. It's up here. It has to be."

"So that's what you were doing up here, searching for the Rose," states Jack.

"What is the Rose? What are you talking about?" Bridge looks at Jack, then Charlie, and finally to me.

"Don't look at me," I say, hands up. "I have no idea what these two are on about."

"The Rose of the Desert is a huge ruby, like over two hundred carats. It belonged to a wealthy railroad tycoon who'd found it while excavating. He was traveling with the ruby to give to his daughter in Colorado Territory when it was reportedly stolen in a train robbery and never recovered." As Jack speaks, we stare at him, expressions blank as a snow field. He shrugs. "I like to read and there aren't many books up here. One of your Poppop's books is about the fifty biggest train heists in the Wild West. The Rose is chapter sixteen."

"Really?" Wally asks, skeptical. "That's quite the coincidence."

"Maybe not," says Charlie. "My Grandmother lived up here after Rufus died. Probably around the same time as your Grandparents, Nona. Maybe they knew each other. Hell, *you* might have even known her. She died several years ago. Her name was Lulu."

I gasp. *Holy shit.* "Lulu!" I practically shout at Mom and Bridge. "Aunt Lulu!"

"Aunt Lulu," says Mom. "Charlie, Aunt Lulu was your Grandmother?"

Aunt Lulu was not an actual aunt, but she was a close enough friend to my Mimi and Poppop that she felt like family. Every summer when we'd visited the cabin, she'd come riding down the trail at least once on Alistair, her gigantic black Percheron. She'd bring us these muslin dolls she'd made with brown and red yarn hair, dressed up in floral aprons and colorful bonnets that drooped to their chins. She'd weave daisies and lavender from her garden into our braids, then call us her wood sprites and beg us to dance for her. Occasionally, she'd take our hands and trace the lines of our palms, divining which of the boys at school liked us and which would break our hearts. She was never wrong. We thought she was our fairy godmother. Thinking back, knowing what I now know, I wonder if we were right.

"You called her Aunt Lulu? Man, that's fantastic," says Charlie "I'll bet my shirt she gave your grandparents that book about the Rose. She was obsessed with it. I always thought it was because she was trying to find it, but now I wonder if it was because she might have been guarding it."

Bridge's smile practically cracks her face in half. "I loved Aunt Lulu. Nona, do you remember her horse, Alistair?"

I smile back. "How could I forget?"

Alistair had a glossy, entirely black coat aside from a brilliant white star that sat between his eyes. This was almost always covered by a thick forelock that hung past his nostrils. His mane flowed in waves over his neck and his hooves were the size of dinner plates. Aunt Lulu would let me and Bridge ride him bareback through the woods whenever she visited. Riding Alistair was like riding a mountain.

I'm surprised to see tears gathering at the corners of Charlie's eyes. "You all knew her better than I did. She was my dad's mother and they'd had a falling out when I was a kid. I only met her once."

"I'm sorry, Charlie," I tell him. "She was wonderful."

He swallows. "Do you know what happened to her?"

I don't, so I look at Mom and Wally, wondering if they do.

Wally rocks back onto his haunches, finally letting down his guard. "Sam found her in the woods, years ago like you said. He thought it was probably a heart attack. Crazy thing about that, her horse had died right beside her, his neck under her head, cradling her like a pillow."

"You never told us that," I say. Mom shrugs. I knew Aunt Lulu passed away before we moved up here, but I never knew how.

Charlie sits back on the couch and blows out a breath. "Well, this is my secret. I was in your woods searching for an ill-begotten 100-year-old family heirloom. Wally, I'm sorry if me keeping this from you has made you distrust me."

Wally flexes his snout a few times, then says, "It's all right, Charlie." And after a pause: "I'm a vet. The war is always with me, but sometimes it gets a little too close."

I watch them and I'm in awe. We all know Wally's struggle with what happened to him while he served, but he's never actually talked about it. Not once. I've never even heard him say the word 'war.' And yet here he is, disclosing to Charlie of all people.

"You guys need to go out?" I ask my family, feeling like we could all use a break. I pull the door open for them and close it behind Fritz who is last to leave, almost reluctantly diving from Charlie's lap.

I turn around and rest my back against the door, then I meet his stare. "Charlie Brown, Ruby Hunter."

He laughs. "You really do look like her." His eyes are roaming my body, head to toe and back again. I feel them like an electrical x-ray.

"I suppose that's because I am her."

"You're beautiful."

A truly unfortunate snort comes out of me. "All right, Prince

Charming. Let's not get carried away." My face burns hotter than a midday sun in August.

He licks his lips. He actually licks his damn lips. *I* want to lick his lips.

"It's true," he insists.

"I'm old enough to be your mother."

"Yeah, but yesterday you were old enough to be my grand-mother. Who knows what tomorrow will bring?"

Staring at him, at his smiling whiskey eyes and full juicy lips, I wish I had my own magic so I could will the sun to set and rise again immediately.

CHAPTER THIRTEEN

I SPEND the day out of the cabin, away from Charlie, away from my family, who were so elated to speak freely again that they talked non-stop once they came back inside, loud and excitedly over each other. Charlie's flirting, their chatting, it all made me happy, so profoundly happy, which scared the living shit out of me. So I geared up, grabbed my gun, and left to the sound of Charlie's laughter while Wally and Fritz took turns telling him stories about the first time we ate one of Mom's eggs or that one spring when a wild female rabbit took a liking to Jack and how awkward that was.

Maybe I'll find more pheasant, or maybe some grouse. Maybe I'll just walk and let the heavy work of slogging through the snow clear my head. It feels so good to walk today, I'm steady on my feet and my lungs are bottomless. The cold air is fresh against my face, not biting, and I'm smiling, thinking about Charlie, his fingers strumming my guitar, the way he looks at me, and this strange feeling I've been willfully ignoring ever since he woke up on my floor.

I feel like I know Charlie. Really know him, like I've known him my whole life. It's so strange. I know I haven't. I know he's a stranger, but he doesn't feel like a stranger. At all. I'm lost in my thoughts and my steps and the bright sun overhead in a cornflower blue sky and I'm happy, still scared, but happy. So of course that bitch would choose now to visit.

"Nona." Her voice is a hand on my chest, shoving me back into myself.

I turn around slowly and what I see there sticks me in place. "Rebecca, what's happened? Jesus, what have you done to me?"

She's strung out, thin as a waif, and it looks like she's pulled out clumps of her hair, my hair.

"I could ask you the same thing," she spits. "You're looking rather spry."

Shit. Shit, shit, shit. "Yeah, maybe you're not as all-powerful as you thought, hmm?" I'm trying for hubris, but I'm genuinely worried about her, about me. Or is she really not me? Have I been me all along? I've always been terrified about what she was doing to my body, the stress, the late nights, the parties, but maybe that isn't my body at all.

"Don't lie to me, Nona. Something is going on up here. What is it? What have you done?"

"How the hell should I know? You're the witch, you tell me. For the last two days I've woken up at least a decade younger. Is this another trick? Another awful part of this shitty curse?" I can act well enough, and even if I was the worst actress in the world, she's so on edge I doubt she'd notice if I was lying or not.

She shakes her head, her shaggy white-blonde hair landing in sharp points over her eyes. "I don't know." Her laughter is scathing. "While you're up here getting younger, I'm getting sicker. I can't eat, can't sleep, and I—" her voice cracks. It's a sound I know all too well and it sends shivers down my spine— "I can't sing."

I take a step toward her, because I want to help her. What am I doing? Rebecca has ruined so many lives and she deserves every bit of retribution the cold and empty universe sees fit to visit upon her. But when I see her suffering, it's also *me* I see suffering, my cheekbones so hollow, my eyes hovering dimly over deep blue circles. It's emotionally confusing. "What do you mean you can't sing?"

"I mean I can't fucking sing. Your voice, *my* voice, it's gone. But you have it, don't you? You stole it!" She's stalking toward me and I lurch back away from her, then I change my mind and surge forward, taking the last step separating us before she can.

I jab a finger into her chest. "If you are implying that I stole back my own voice, I hope you know how much you can go fuck yourself. Do you realize how much pain you've caused because you were jealous and wanted to be famous and couldn't do it on your own? You deserve this Rebecca, whatever is happening." I push her and she stumbles backwards. "You deserve no sleep, no food, and no voice!" I push her again, harder, and she lands on her back in the snow.

She laughs again, a dark and sinister sound. "I am not powerless, Nona. I can still destroy you all with a—"

"Shut up! Shut your stupid mouth you petty, vapid bitch! You have tried for five years to destroy us, to ruin us, but you haven't. And you won't. Haven't you noticed? Despite your curse, despite your selfish, evil lies, we still laugh, we still love, and we still live. You've taken nothing from us. Nothing that matters."

She struggles to her feet, swiping snow from her pants. Her expression is a horrible mixture of shame and remorse. "I...I haven't, I didn't," she stammers, her voice breaking, and it's like just for a moment she's a human being. She shakes her head, shaking off her humanity along with the snow. "Something is keeping me away from you, Nona. I don't know what it is, but I will figure it out and when I do, then you'll truly know what it means to lose everything."

Her final words shudder through my bones as she slips into

the wind. And in the place where she stood, in a perfect little pile, lay three dead rabbits.

My heart plunges. I'm running to the animals, carefully checking their bodies for Jack's tell-tale brown patch below his left ear. None of the poor things are Jack, but the message is clear.

I stumble numbly back to the cabin, no birds in tow, but I did take the rabbits. We don't waste food, not even malevolent gesture food.

It's late afternoon when I walk through the shed door, dropping the rabbits on the table and nearly jumping out of my skin when Mom says, "What ghosts did you see out there?" from her nesting box.

I clutch at my pounding heart. "Christ, Mother, you scared me half to death."

"Answer the question, Nona."

"No ghosts, Mom. Just some rabbits."

She hops down from her box. "My foot. Tell me."

I huff, defeated. It's impossible to keep anything from Penny Sheldon. "It was Rebecca."

She fluffs her feathers. "Twice in one month, that's unprecedented."

I nod. "It seems whatever is happening to me is also happening to her."

"But not in a good way, I'm guessing."

"No. Not in a good way." I stare down at the table.

"Did she kill those rabbits?" Mom knows I don't kill rabbits. I don't kill any of the animals we are; I can't.

"She did. It was a message. I was terrified one of them was..."

"Nona, sweetie, you remember the deal? You remember our vow?"

The tears hit me hard and fast. The weight of carrying these rabbits back to the cabin, the electric fear that one of them was Jack, and then, finally, the crushing remorse that I'd talked to

Rebecca that way, that I'd provoked her. It all comes crashing down over me like a tidal wave of shit.

"I remember the deal, Mom. But I don't think I can keep it. You don't know what it's like, knowing how vulnerable you all are. And not just to Rebecca, but to so many other things out in these woods. I'm not strong enough to protect you. I can't lose you, any of you. I can't."

She hops up onto the table and settles down right next to the rabbits. "You can, Nona. You have to. We all agreed, we vowed that we wouldn't let her take our happiness from us too, that we wouldn't live the rest of our days in fear. That we would live and love and that if we died up here, we'd die happy. You can't let her take that from us too. *That's* what you can't do."

I'm crying hard now because she's right. I know she's right.

"I'm sorry, sweetheart. I know your burden is the hardest. But you can't let her take your spirit too. We will deal with this just as we've dealt with every other hateful thing she's done to us, with drink and food and love and laughter. And maybe, if you're lucky, you might even get laid."

"Mother," I reproach through my tears, but she's already burk-laughing so loudly she can't even hear me.

"One of us ought to," she says breathlessly, leading me out of the shed.

And as I walk behind her, watching her tail feathers swish side to side, her words sink in. We *chose* to live, all of us. We chose to live without fear, without regret, and without shame. And, *shit,* maybe she's right, about all of it. Even the part where I get laid.

"What are you laughing about?" snorts Wally as we wander back into the front room, Mom still chuckling.

"I got some rabbits," I answer.

Jack straightens from his spot next to Bridge on the couch, who's lying next to Fritz, who's snuggled next to Charlie. "What?" he asks, fear riding high in his voice.

"Rebecca came to visit," says Mom. The mood in the room darkens like a shadow is passing overhead.

"She's here?" Charlie asks, sitting upright and grabbing his crutches.

I smile at his manly hubris. "She was here, she's gone now. But she killed some rabbits for us." It comes out of my mouth far too thoughtlessly.

"This is a threat, isn't it?" asks Bridge.

I nod. "She's not doing well. She knows something's happening to me, because something is happening to her. She said she's lost her voice."

"You're serious?" Fritz says. "That's not good, Nona."

All of this happened to us at least in part because Rebecca wanted my voice. If she no longer has it, she'll become something worse than an intimidating pain in the ass full of idle threats, she'll become desperate.

"What exactly *is* happening to you?" asks Jack, anxiously wagging his puff-ball tail.

Slowly, one by one, we all turn toward Charlie. Everything started changing when he showed up.

"Don't look at me," he says, innocent as a choir boy. "I don't know anything about anything."

Wally's growl is a low rumble vibrating the floorboards.

"Wally, come walk with me," says Mom, gently pecking at his toes.

As Mom takes Wally out for yet another walk, Bridge turns to me and whispers, "You need to tell him, Nona. You need to tell Charlie."

I shake my head.

"Tell me what?" asks Charlie.

"Oh, nothing. I'll be right back," I call over my shoulder, walking to the shed, Bridge, Jack, and Fritz following in a tight line behind me.

"Nona, why won't you tell him?" whispers Bridge.

I kneel in the dirt, lowering myself to her level. "Because I've been hard-core flirting with him and it's stupidly embarrassing. And I don't want him to think I've only been nice to him because I'm trying to break the curse."

Jack rocks back on his haunches. "No offense, Nona, but isn't that precisely what you've been doing?"

The question hangs between us like a beehive, best left undisturbed. No, it is definitely not what I've been doing because I am an idiot who's decided that I like Charlie a whole lot. I don't want him thinking that my attention has all been to break the curse. But I am not saying that out loud.

Fritz knows I'm not going to answer, so he says, "Nona, time is running out. If every day that you get younger, Rebecca gets sicker, it's only a matter of time before she's on our doorstep."

Then I remember something she said. "Wait, she can't. She can't show up on our doorstep."

"What do you mean?" asks Jack.

"I don't know. But that's what she said. She said something is keeping her away from the cabin. I think we have something protecting us."

"What?" Bridge asks.

I shrug helplessly. "I have no idea. But maybe it *is* Charlie. Maybe whatever balance of good and evil or right and wrong that exists in the world is finally tipping in our favor. Maybe we're getting our chance. And if that's true," I pull my hair out of its braid, shaking my head until it flows over my shoulders, "then I'm not letting this chance pass us by."

Bridge's smile is sly. "That's my girl."

I smile back. "I need the cabin tonight. Can you all stay in the shed?"

"You bet your ass we can," exclaims Bridge as Jack's ears flop forward and back like clapping hands.

"Go get him, Nona. He's a good one," offers Fritz. I squint at him a little. Even with everything going on, it hasn't escaped my attention that Fritz has been snuggling awfully close to Charlie lately, or that Charlie is totally Fritz's type: cute, outdoorsy, wrapped in flannel.

"Is this absurd? Am I just going to get my heart broken?"

Bridge trots closer to me to weave between my legs, then sit neatly at my feet. "Nona, this is a question everyone asks when they're falling in love. You'll never know until you try, and when you really fall, the answer won't matter anyway." Then she trots back to Jack, rubbing her nose against his.

I smile at them all, pinch my cheeks, fluff up my hair, and say, "All right, then, wish me luck."

They do more than that and by the time I rush from the shed and shut the door behind me, my virgin ears burn at the suggestions they offered regarding exactly what I should try to win Charlie's heart.

CHARLIE IS in the kitchen when I return, filling two glasses to the rim with red wine. He hands one to me. "I thought you might need this."

"Me?" I laugh, taking my glass from him. "I mean, I totally do. But I can't imagine your day was the portrait of normalcy."

"Not entirely," he agrees.

The cabin is quiet as we stand in the kitchen, sipping wine. The sun has finally set, leaving only a dusky light behind, just enough to distinguish the trees from the sky out of the window. I set down my glass and reach behind Charlie so I can plug in the twinkly lights strung above the kitchen cupboards. It's not a subtle move, but he lets me make it, not forfeiting an inch when I lean toward him. His breath hitches in his throat as my hand brushes his arm. This close to him, the warmth of his body seeps into my skin and I breathe him in. He smells like pine and rain and wood smoke. I would bottle his scent if I could, bottle it and wear it every single day for the rest of my life. However long that might be.

His head bows toward me, his eyes following mine while I move away from him again. I'm staring into his eyes. I can't stop, the brown of them swimming in a golden light. It's like magic, the way they always seem lit up.

"I need to make dinner," I try to say, but my throat spasms into a nervy gulp halfway through the sentence.

"What's that?" There is a jittery amusement in Charlie's voice.

I take a big step back and clear my throat. "I said, I need to make dinner." Then I leave him in the kitchen to start a fire and go get the rabbits. When I return, he's still standing against the counter, propped on his arms, staring at me, smiling.

"Can I help?" he asks.

"Are you sure?" I stare at his legs. He's been standing on only one leg for quite a while. I can't imagine it's comfortable.

"Yeah. It actually feels good to be up."

"All right, then, you can peel the potatoes."

While Charlie peels, I braise the rabbit in white wine and whole grain mustard. I'll serve it simply with herb-roasted pota-toes, and I'll make a grilled cheese special for Jack.

AFTER DINNER, I put everyone to bed in the shed, suffering through the lewdest suggestions of how Charlie and I should spend the rest of the evening. One from Wally involving a fly swatter, Saran Wrap, and candle wax shocks me so thoroughly that I scream. Bridge joins me when Mom mutters, "Don't knock it until you've tried it."

I shut the door to the shed with a soft thud and wait in the hallway for my face to fade from the fire-engine red I'm quite certain it is. Charlie is singing to the radio while he's doing the dishes and the dumb-ass grin that takes possession of my face when I hear him is considerable. *Be cool, girl. Be cool.* But I am just not cool, never have been.

"Your leg," I shout too loudly. "You're standing on your leg."

Charlie drops a dish in the sink and whirls around, wide-eyed. "Christ, Nona. You scared me."

"Sorry. But your leg?" I point at the leg in question.

He shifts his weight gingerly from his right to left leg, grimacing. "I can't put all my weight on it yet, but a little seems all right." He reaches behind his back to turn off the faucet, then slides the dish towel through the drawer handle next to him and dries off his hands.

I'm mesmerized by him, by his hands and the way they move. His are a musician's fingers, long and graceful. And I want them on me.

"Thank you for doing the dishes." Nobody besides me has done the dishes up here in five years. That he's cleaned them for me tonight without my asking is quite possibly the biggest turn on in the entire history of turn ons.

"Of course." He smiles. "It's the least I can do."

My eyes follow his fingers again while he reaches over to spin the volume dial on the radio. "Do you know this song?" he asks, a corner of his mouth hitching and those eyes, those bottomless brown eyes glimmering the way they do.

I do know this song. I love this song. "'Night Life,'" I say. "It's one of my favorites."

He holds out a hand, and I notice it's trembling a little. I take a breath, feeling strangely relieved that he's nervous too.

"Dance with me, Nona?"

Dance with me, Nona. His voice, these words, why does it all sound so familiar?

I give him my hand and he takes it, pulling, wrapping my arm around his neck as he slides his arms around my waist. It's a good move and I reward it by stepping closer to him. His hands are warm on my back, his touch firm as I rest my cheek against his chest. There's a confidence in this touch, a sureness in the way he sways me side to side while Ray Price's voice floats around the kitchen, swirling through the string lights and falling over us like midnight rain. Dancing with him, being this close to him, the way he smells, the way he moves, it's so unbearably familiar. And then he sings into my ear, his voice soft and low, "Many people, just like me, dreaming of old used-to-be."

His body shudders and I feel something drop softly into my hair. "Charlie, are you crying? Why are you crying?" I pull away from him, and it's my turn now to wipe away the tears streaming down his face.

He stares at me, eyes glassy. "I'm so sorry, Nona."

I don't know why, because he looks completely devastated, but I smile at him. I'm confused and I don't know what else to do. "What do you possibly have to be sorry for?"

He sobs through a laugh. "So much. I have so many regrets." He brushes a stray strand of my hair from my forehead, his soft finger dropping to trace along my chin. "But mostly, I'm so sorry it's taken me so long to find you."

"What do you mean, to find me?" I take a step back from him, but his grip around my waist tightens. Holding me close, with lips wet and soft, he kisses me.

And then I fall.

CHAPTER FOURTEEN

THE ROAR of the crowd is deafening. The force of it, the sheer power of thousands of voices singing my words, cheering for me, constricts my chest until I can barely breathe. But in a good way. In the best possible way.

My fingers finally loosen, releasing the strings of my guitar and I raise my hand over my head. "Y'all have been so wonderful to me tonight. Thank you so much!" I bellow to the sea of screaming fans. "Now I hope you're ready to dance your asses off cuz Rayne Burns is about to get nasty!" This isn't an exaggeration. Last time I saw Rayne in concert he gyrated all over the stage and had women—and men—throwing bras and underwear at him like he was Tom Jones.

I don't want to leave the stage. I want to stay here forever, playing my music to the largest crowd I've ever entertained until the sun sets and the moon rises, but my thirty minutes is up. I am not a headliner. I am just the absurdly lucky folksinger who happened to be available when a spot at this festival opened up after Maria Hobbs got food poisoning.

With hot, grateful tears pooling in my eyes, I fly off stage-left and into Fritz's open arms. He picks me up and I wrap my legs around his waist while I kiss him long and hard on the cheek. He squeezes me, laughing as he twirls me around, then he mumbles something into my ear.

"What?" I shout, pointing to my ear and shaking my head. I can't hear anything but my heartbeat, thrumming like my guitar and clapping like the crowd.

Fritz laughs at me, brushing my sweat-soaked hair back from my forehead. Grabbing my hand, he squirrels me back-stage and into my blissfully air-conditioned dressing room.

"I said, that was beautiful!" Fritz kisses his fingers and flings them into the air. "Absolutely beautiful!"

Jack and Bridge pile in behind us, throwing themselves into a heap on the couch.

"You really were wonderful, Nona," says Jack as he tries to pull Bridge onto his lap. But she struggles away from him and jumps up to hug me.

"No joke!" She slaps my butt. "All those people knew the words to your songs. All of them. It's crazy!" Bridge returns to the couch, spins in a circle, then falls into Jack's open arms. He dips her into a kiss.

"I know, right?" I can barely hear myself, but everyone's laughing at me so I must be shouting. The high of the stage buzzes through me like I'm made of bees. I feel dizzy and my nerves jangle. I can't stand still. Walking around in circles, I shake out my arms and roll my neck. Then I hop in place like a frog on a hot pan.

"Uh oh," croons Fritz with a half-smile. "Somebody's antsy."

This is a colossal understatement. "How can I go from that," I point behind me toward the stage, the crowd still rowdy and electric, "to this?" I stare at Jack and Bridge canoodling on the couch again and then at Fritz who's just taken a phone call, probably from his new boyfriend. Everyone is coupling up, this room is quiet as a tomb, and I'm jacked from my toenails to my hair roots.

"Ouch, Nona. I take offense to that," scoffs Bridge, but she gets it. She whispers something to Jack, and he shakes his head at her with a knowing smile. She kisses him again, stands, and opens one of my bags to pull out my wide-brimmed hat and huge bug-eyed sunglasses that I travel with to hide my appearance. I've literally never had to use them before and honestly probably don't need to now. But it's hot and the sun's blazing, so I'll take them.

Bridge stuffs the hat onto my head and slides the glasses over my nose. "Let's go have some fun," she says with an evil little wink that makes my heart thump.

"That's it," I agree, smiling like the cat who ate the canary. And I haven't even done anything yet.

After changing into a *Rayne Burns* t-shirt and tucking my hair up under the hat, I look like your typical 18-year-old fan here to see the headliner. Which, by the way, I totally am. I may even throw my bra at him later.

I grab Bridget's hand. "Let's go."

"Be safe out there, ladies," says Fritz, waving his fingers at us before returning to his phone call.

The festival is a living, breathing thing. The air is sweet with meadow grass and flowers and smoke. Everywhere around us, as Bridge and I weave through the throng of fans, we see smiling faces, arms entwined, and kissing with such passion my cheeks burn with jealousy. I'm eighteen, single, and Fritz spoke the truth, I'm antsy. I want, no, I need something to happen tonight. I want to be in that guy's arms over there as he slides his hand into the back pocket of his girl's jeans. I want to be either one of those two gorgeous women all over each other under the shade of that cottonwood. I've been touring for six months, writing and recording for twice that long. Tonight I want to live.

"Bridge," I shout, taking her hand and pulling her into a sweaty hug. "I love you so much. Did you know that?"

I feel her laughter through my hands wrapped around her. She pulls out of my arms, smiling like the sun. "You never need to tell me that. I know. I'll always know." Then she winks. "Let's go find some trouble."

She grabs my hand and pulls me through the crowd toward the sprawling hillside covered in tents. She's quick, determined, like she knows exactly where she's headed. This is a three-day festival and the tent city is enormous. The tents themselves dot the hills with bright colors like wildflowers. Blankets hang on lines and drift in the breeze while the smell of grilled meat hovers heavy in the air.

It's another world out here. People sit in circles playing drums and guitars, lovers lie on blankets under the shelter of willow trees, everywhere there is dancing and singing. There is a freedom here and it's intoxicating.

"Hey." A voice shakes me from my reverie. I spin in place, and then I stifle a snort. Now I know why Bridge brought me this way, because there he is.

"Hey yourself," I reply, pulling off my hat and shaking out my hair.

He's so cute, shaggy hair, bourbon-brown eyes, and full, red lips. He's sitting on a camping chair, strumming the strings of his guitar and smiling at me sideways. He's Charlie, my guitarist. "What are you doing out here?" I ask.

"Hey Charlie," says Bridge while crawling into his tent. She reappears with a couple of beers from his cooler and hands one to me. I twist off the cap and take a sharp swig. Charlie laughs at me as the beer overflows white foam onto my novice hands.

"I guess the same thing you are," he says, laughing more as I shake the foam from my fingers. "It's amazing, isn't it?"

We've been on the road for months, playing small clubs and pavilions. None of us has had much time to relax and certainly no time to attend a concert as fans. We have a full day and night at this festival and, apparently, I am not the only one feeling the freedom of this reprieve.

"It really is," I agree. "Are you sleeping out here tonight?"

Charlie flings his fingers over a 'C' chord, then sets his guitar on the blanket beside him. "I am. Either in the tent or on this blanket under the stars. I'm hoping for the latter."

I stare up to the sky. There's a dusky rose light hovering over the horizon, slowly sinking behind the hillside. It's beautiful and, thankfully, finally cooling off.

"That sounds perfect." I walk to Charlie and hand him my beer. Then I pick up his discarded guitar, sit cross-legged beside him, and start playing.

I've been flirting shamelessly with Charlie for months, ever since Fritz found him playing at a bar in Tuscaloosa and signed him to the band. He's older than me by a year or two and he's a fantastic musician. He's also sweet, charming, absurdly fun to flirt with, and I want to kiss him, a lot. He's flirted back, but only a little, smiling that crooked smile and laughing at my stupid jokes, always the perfect gentleman despite my efforts to corrupt him. But up until a few short weeks ago, I'd been jail-bait. This small detail has not escaped my attention and tonight, I intend to find out if it's escaped his.

I can feel Charlie's eyes on me while he drinks my beer and I play his guitar. I'm feeling brazen, so I turn my head and stare back. When his eyes meet mine, I don't look away. I won't, no matter how hard my heart is hurling itself against my ribs, begging me to stop. I ignore it. Thump all you want, you little shit. Tonight, I am fearless.

Charlie doesn't look away either, but smiles at me. "You were fantastic tonight."

I bite my lip, trying not to smile at the compliment. "You too. That part during 'Turning the Tables' when you knelt at my feet during your solo." I'm blushing, my cheeks must be cherry stained. "That was…nice."

"Nice?" He cocks a brow, and I want to suck on it.

"Yep, nice. You should keep doing it." Every single night, forever and ever, amen.

He clears his throat, bringing his bottle up to touch his grinning lips. "Done." He takes another swig.

I'm not sure when Bridge left, but she's gone. *Schemer.* Now it's just me and Charlie in the middle of a suddenly empty city of tents as the sound of Rayne Burns starting his first set puts matching smiles on our faces.

His head tilts toward the stage. "Wanna go?"

I stare down at my hands, at the strings vibrating under my fingers. Yes I wanna go, but not down there. "Not really. You?"

He shakes his head, his hair flopping into his eyes. He swipes it back.

Good.

We sit and talk for a long time, about the tour, our shows, which songs are our favorites to perform and which ones need work. Then we talk about our hometowns, our families. I tell him about my dad passing away three years ago and how it nearly tore my family apart. Then, when my mom found Wally, how his endless kindness and good humor pieced her heart, and my family, back together. I knew nobody would ever replace my dad, but Wally taught all of us that there are so many kinds of love, and ways to be loved.

Charlie tells me about his parents. He lost his mom when he was a kid. I didn't know that and I feel a sudden, devastating kinship with him. He tells me about his overbearing stepmom, his perfectionist stepsister, and his favorite aunt who lives in the woods and can read the future.

I laugh at this. "Really?" I ask, thinking she sounds just like Aunt Lulu.

"Really," he answers. He leans over to whisper into my ear, his breath tickling my neck, "She says she's a witch."

I turn my head to face him, too quickly for him to move

away. Our lips are mere inches away from each other. My eyes flare wide.

He sits back, smooth as silk. "Honestly, I haven't seen her since I was a kid. But she was full of magic. If there are witches, I'm certain she is one."

"I know someone like that," I say, relieved at his composure considering how close I was to falling gracelessly onto his mouth with my face. "She's a friend of my grandparents. She's completely wild and totally awesome."

"Sounds about right." His laughter is so sweet. It's like an ocean breeze. Hearing it reminds me of that night a few months ago when we were driving through North Dakota. We were bored and everyone else was drunk so, naturally, Bridge suggested we play strip poker. When the game ended, Bridge was naked, Jack was in his shirt and shorts, my drummer Danny was fully dressed because wasted or sober, he's insanely good at cards, and Charlie was down to his boxers. I'm pretty good at cards myself, so I was still wearing my jeans, but my black lace bra was on full display. Charlie, as I recall, could not stop staring at me. He'd laughed a lot that night, that sweet, breezy laugh. If I'd been drinking too, I have no doubt I would have tried to crawl into his bunk with him. I should have been drinking.

My ears prick and a smile breaks across my face. "No way! Charlie, this is, like, my favorite song ever." It's a song Dad used to sing, serenading me and Bridge while we sat next to him on the piano bench watching him play.

Charlie turns his head toward the stage, listening. "Is this 'Night Life'?"

"It is. Rayne is covering 'Night Life.'"

Charlie stands up beside me, brushes his hands off on his pants, then extends one out to me. "Dance with me, Nona."

I set his guitar down, slide my hand into his, and let him pull me up to my feet. He takes my hand and snakes it around his neck before stooping a bit to wrap both of his arms around my waist. He tugs me toward him until my hips are pressed against his. It's a good move, a really good move.

He's soft and hard in all the right places and he smells amazing, clean and piney. Then he starts singing in my ear and the vibrations of his voice rumble through his chest where it touches mine. I sing too, harmonizing with him, and we dance.

A firefly blinks over his shoulder, flashing and hovering, floating slowly through the summer air like a fish swimming in a bowl. Soon there is a sea of fireflies swimming around us. That's how it happens with fireflies, none, then one, then they're everywhere.

A fire kindles inside me, burning hotter with each note Charlie sings into my ear, each sway of our hips, each breath that escapes my lungs until it's burning me up.

"Charlie." My voice is quiet as I pull away from him just a little, just enough. His eyes find mine, then he makes the choice for me.

His hand is buried in my hair and his warm, soft mouth is on mine. I've never been kissed before, not really, not like this. This is not an awkward attempt at trying to figure out what a kiss should feel like. This is wanting and needing, giving and taking. It's sweet and hot and my knees tremble as his mouth slides to my neck, my shoulder. As I burst into flames.

"Is this okay?" he asks, breathless against my skin.

"Yes," I whisper. "Yes, this is more than okay."

His laughter brushes over me, making me shudder. Then he grabs my hand and pulls me into his tent.

"Nona."

Someone is shaking my shoulders.

"Nona, can you hear me? Sweetheart, open your eyes."

But I don't want to open my eyes. I'm still lying on the blankets with Charlie in his tent, kissing him all night until our lips swell and our bodies ache, demanding we go further. We don't go further that night, but we do later. In the months we spend falling madly in love with each other, there isn't an inch of our bodies we don't explore together, not a corner of our hearts we don't give to one another. He was my every-thing, my sun, my moon, even my air since whenever he wasn't with me, I felt like I couldn't breathe. Yeah, it was that bad. He wrote me poems, I wrote him songs, and although it made everyone around us groan, I could never stop kissing him. Never.

"Nona, look at me."

I drag myself kicking and screaming away from memories of daffodils left on my bunk in the tour bus, fingertips brushing over my bare belly, brown eyes smiling in the moonlight. The ridge of his collarbone and how my lips would travel the length of it until they met the softness of his neck, settling over the heartbeat pulsing there. His knee in the sand, a ring in his hand. His smile when I'd said yes.

When I finally open my eyes, I say the first thing that comes to mind. "Wait. Wait a second. I'm...I'm not a virgin?"

Then Charlie, the real Charlie, my Charlie, the one standing right here in my kitchen who's been in my cabin for days pretending to be a stranger, laughs and sobs at once as he crushes me against his chest. "No, Nona. You are most definitely not a virgin."

I push him away, but only so I can grab his face between my hands. And then I kiss him. It's a desperate kiss, a hard and messy meeting of lips and teeth and colored by the salty tang of tears. Then I pull away, take a step back, and slap him hard across his face. "What the hell, Charlie?"

He cradles his cheek, staring at me with a baffled mixture of surprise and anger. "Jesus, Nona. That hurt."

"Really? *That* hurt? You want to know what hurts? Being eighty-three, that hurts!"

He flinches like I've slapped him again. But I don't care. I hold up a hand, counting on my fingers. "A. What are you doing here? B. Why have you been pretending not to be you? And C. Where the fuck have you been for the last five years?" This last question breaks from my throat in hoarse sobbing bursts as I launch myself at him, kissing his mouth, his chin, his neck, that perfect sloping collarbone. He kisses me back, his hands knotted in my hair.

I lurch away from him when confusion and sadness and anger well up inside me again, but he covers my face with his hand and pushes me back a step. "No, Nona. No more slapping."

I work his hand free from my face, laughing despite myself. He was always able to make me laugh. No matter how hard I may have tried, I could never fight with him. Every time I got upset, he'd say something ridiculous with his crooked smile and perfect timing and disarm me completely. "I won't slap you again, even though you deserve it, I think. Or maybe you don't." The tears come again. "I don't know. I don't know anything."

He pulls me back into his arms. "Take a breath, babe. A deep, deep breath."

I look at him, really look at him. I reach out, running my fingers over his cheekbone, his jaw, his lips. He's older than the last time I saw him, but he's still the same. How could I have not known it was Charlie? My Charlie?

"The witch. She made me think it was about a cat." I press my cheek into his chest, feeling his heart thumping against my skin, fast like hummingbird wings.

"What's that?" He brushes his hand over my hair.

"'Missing Charlie.' It was about you. Not a cat."

He snorts. "Of course it was about me. You wrote it when I had to take that break from the tour after I fell off the stage."

"Oh shit, that's right." I'm laughing now.

"That was your fault, I might add. You looked so good that night, I couldn't focus. Then you grabbed my ass after 'That Man, My Man' and I lost it. Right off the stage."

His face is blurred by the tears dotting my eyelashes. "Well, Rebecca made me think I'd written 'Missing Charlie' about a damned cat. I could never understand why I'd written such a beautiful song about a stupid cat. I've never even had a cat."

I can tell he's trying not to laugh for my benefit. But I take pity on him and burst into laughter so he can join me.

"What happened? How? And why? Why did she do it?" I'm not laughing anymore, my voice coming out thin and quiet as my strength disappears, like water slipping down a drain.

Charlie takes my hand and leads me to the couch.

"You're walking. Your leg?"

His sigh is almost a grunt. "I felt like shit lying to you, but I needed to be with you. I needed a reason for you to take me in and the injured hiker thing seemed like my best chance to not seem like a weirdo stalker and get shot. You do have a lot of guns, if you haven't noticed."

I squeeze his hand. "You might not be wrong about that," I admit.

"I tried to wait until everything was ready, I really did. But when I saw you out there, chopping wood like Paul fucking Bunyan and looking like the sexiest grandma I'd ever seen, I just, I couldn't wait. I'd been searching for you for a year straight, Nona. And I'd finally found you. When I did, I finally realized what Rebecca truly did to you, to all of you."

Rebecca. He knows Rebecca. Like a rogue wave, the memories assault me, crashing over my head. I knew her.

"Charlie. The witch, she's your sister."

CHAPTER FIFTEEN

"STEP-SISTER," amends Charlie, one finger raised.

"Semantics."

"Important semantics," he counters.

"Why? Why did she do it? We were friends, Rebecca and I. I thought we were at least."

His lips press into a grim line. "I know."

My eyes fly wide open. "Wait? When did you find out? She looked like me. Pretended to *be* me. How long did she convince you she *was* me? Did you…did she…did you two ever…" I can't even finish.

"It was bad, Nona. So bad. You'd changed overnight. You were you, but also not you. I thought I was going crazy but the first, and only, time I kissed her, I knew. I knew it wasn't you."

I remember now, the spell. She'd invited me to lunch right after Charlie had proposed. She'd said she wanted to celebrate. Instead she'd sliced my palm open, and then her own, grabbed my hand and hissed some bullshit incantation that erased my memories, months of my life, all the way back to that night at the festival. That first time Charlie and I kissed. I'd woken the next day an old woman, screaming at the fox in my room until it spoke with Bridge's voice.

"We were going to get married," I whisper these words because they hurt, passing through my throat like broken glass. We were going to get married. What might my life have been like? Our lives? What has his life been like without me?

"Charlie, you said you had a woman. Lily. Did you find someone else? Did you fall in love with another woman? It's okay if you did." It's so not okay if he did, not even close.

"No. No no no," he says, reaching for me, his fingers wrapping around my arm. "No, I made all of that up. I was hoping I could jog your memory with your music, with 'Lilies'. With anything I could think of because it really sucked being with you and not being able to touch you. Each time you looked at me like I was a stranger, it broke my heart. But it's only you, Nona. It's always only been you."

I kiss him again. I kiss him fiercely with the weight of five years of wanting and needing and missing him. He pulls me into his lap and I straddle him. "But you broke the curse," I say between kisses. "You gave me my memories and...wait." I sit up straight, pushing him away. "Did Sam visit? He did. I remember. Christ, Charlie, you told Sam I was your grandmother!"

"I can explain."

My breath catches in my throat. "My family. Are they?" Fresh, hot tears sting my eyes. I move to stand, ready to run to the shed. My family, Fritz. They're human again. I can already feel their arms wrapping around me.

"Wait." His voice is low, hesitant, his arms wrapping tightly around my waist. "Wait, Nona."

My heart sinks like a stone. "It's not broken, is it? Not for them."

"No. Not yet."

"Why not?" There's an angry edge to my voice. How could he only save me? He has to know I'd never be okay with that.

His hand brushes over my back. "The curse isn't broken at all. Not for any of you."

"What? But," I hold my hands up between us as evidence, "I'm younger."

He shakes his head, brow furrowed. "I'm not strong enough to break the curse by myself, but I've weakened it enough, along with some glamouring, to restore your age and memories. I don't have as much magic as Rebecca—"

"A glamor? So, you're a witch too?" I interrupt.

"We menfolk prefer warlock, but pretty much," he says with a shrug.

"Were you ever going to tell me, before? Before all of this happened?"

He sighs, his arms dropping to hang loosely around my hips. "I was hoping I'd never have to. I never embraced this life the way Rebecca did. The way Julianne forced her to."

"Forced? Really? Rebecca was forced to be a massive dick?" I'm calling bullshit.

His smile is tight. "When my dad married Rebecca's mother, Julianne, I could tell right away that she was an overbearing parent, abusive even. Rebecca did everything for Julianne, everything and anything to try to please her."

I put my hand over his mouth. "I'm gonna stop you right there. I am in no way, shape, or form ready to hear about how hard Rebecca's had it."

He kisses my hand, sending tiny electric shocks through my palm that travel straight south. "Fair enough." My eyelids fall heavy over my eyes as he takes my hand and kisses my fingers, one at a time. He pulls me close, his lips brushing over my shoulder while his hands slip under the hem of my shirt.

"I have more questions," I assert weakly. I want him to tell me everything, to explain everything, but his hands feel so good over my skin and when one of them grazes up the side of my body, I can't seem to care about anything else at all.

"On second thought," I gasp when that hand finds my breast, cupping it gently. "Can we talk about all of this later?"

He stands from the couch, bringing me with him. I wrap my legs around him and hang on.

"We can do whatever you want," he breathes.

"Bed," I say, clinging to him. "Now."

He walks me down the hall, kicks open the door to my bedroom, and spins around, pushing my back into the door to shut it again. Pinning me in place, he presses his hips against mine. He kisses me again and I moan as I feel him hard against me. I rely on his strength to hold me up and release his shoulders to undo the buttons of his shirt. I'm feeling possessive now, greedy. These are my shoulders I push his shirt over, my arms I slide his shirt down. These lips I kiss are my lips. She tried to steal them from me, but they are mine.

"I've missed you. I love you. I love you," I tell him. Even though I didn't miss him, not really. Until a few moments ago, I didn't even know he existed. But this doesn't matter, I feel it all now, all the pain, all the longing. I wrap my arms around him and crush him to me, sobbing sudden, fat tears onto his shoulder. Then I feel him shuddering as well and for a long moment, we stand there, holding each other, crying years of stolen tears.

He carries me to the bed, lays me down gently, and I scoot up to the pillows while he crawls over me. His eyes are heavy-lidded, but the intensity in them burns straight through me. "I love you, Nona. And I've missed you more than I can put into words. But we're here now. We're together now."

Slowly, one by one, he unbuttons my shirt, sliding the flannel fabric open. A warm breeze rolls over my exposed skin along with this strange, tightening sensation. I sit up so quickly I nearly head-butt him.

"Charlie. Holy shit!" I'm staring down at firm breasts, soft skin, a smooth, flat belly.

Smiling, he runs one hand from my throat straight down to

my stomach, then he slides that hand around my back to pull me into his lap. "I knew you'd want to be you for this. Your age, your actual age."

My actual age. I'm young again. I feel it in the gliding of my joints, the way my muscles sit tightly under my skin.

My fingers are thick and clumsy as I undo the buttons of his jeans. But when I reach in, I'm not clumsy anymore. He hisses as I take him in my hand. I'd forgotten how perfect he was, how well we fit together. He took my virginity, so I'm not sure what other men feel like, but I can't believe they'd be more perfect than Charlie. That first night together, he'd waited for me, holding still as my body adjusted to him. He was so slow for me, so sweet. I remember feeling safe. Loved. Worshipped.

He backs away from me, despite my protestations, and undoes the tie on my pants. He slides them off, sitting on his heels at my feet, staring at me.

I prop up onto my elbows so I can see him. His torso is long and lean, his shoulders broad, muscles tensing. With his jeans unbuttoned, they hang open, loose around his hips. I lean forward to touch him again, but he slips away from me, backing up to the edge of the bed to kiss my toes, the arch of my foot. He slides the tip of his tongue around my ankle, up my leg, then he bites the fleshy mound of my calf and I fall back to the pillow, lost.

I'm lost in his lips moving up my inner thigh, higher. My fingers fist in his hair as he settles between my legs, emptying my brain of every single thought except for him, his hair, his breath, his mouth. His tongue. My back arches off the bed while he teases me, tasting me, working me over until my body surrenders, shuddering in rolling electric waves.

I emerge from the sea of sensation with his mouth on my breast, his tongue drawing a perfect circle around my nipple. I pull him up to me and I'm kissing him again, digging my toes into the waistband of his jeans to push them away so that nothing stands between our bodies but a few inches of air, inches that vanish as I take him in my hand again and guide him into me.

I gasp. It's been a long time and it hurts.

"Are you okay?" he whispers, his eyes finding mine.

I wrap my legs around him and hook my heels together, squeezing him close, pulling him as deeply into me as I can, no matter the sharp sting of pain. "Yes. I've never been so okay." I brush his bangs back from his forehead then run a finger over his lips. "I love you," I say. Then I angle my hips up to his, taking him even deeper.

This is a joining five years in the making. We move slowly, carefully, feeling every inch of each other. My body made a home for him years ago, a spot where only he could fit. And even though I didn't know it, that part of me has been empty, waiting. And now with Charlie kissing me, his hair brushing over my forehead and his hips pressing against mine, I feel complete again, full.

I want this to last forever. I want to be sore and breathless and raw so that every movement I make will remind me of him, of his body living in mine, that he's mine again and I am his. I know it's not going to be that simple. But right now, I don't care. I only care about this man and as he trembles under my fingertips, as I squeeze him even tighter to me through his spasms of release, I can only cry and laugh and cry, and kiss him. And kiss him again. And again.

But I don't let him go, I can't. He's heavy on top of me and I hold him close, my legs still wrapped around his hips. I trace my fingertips down his spine and over his shoulders, kissing his neck, nibbling on his ear. I tell him how much I love him and how much I've missed him. How my body has ached for his. How my fingers have tried to make me feel the way he does, but never could, no matter how many times I'd tried. How he is beautiful and warm and mine. Forever, mine.

He's ready again quickly, so I roll him over and sit astride him, pulling him up so we sit together. We don't speak, we don't kiss, we only cling to each other, moving together. Eventually he leans forward and pushes me onto my back. It's not long before his name comes out of me in a harsh whisper as he tenses above me again, straining through a stifled groan. He falls, his body completely covering mine, substantial and centering and everything. Everything I've ever wanted.

We're sweaty despite the cold and I'm not sure I've ever felt so good. I'm young. I'm strong. And I'm completely worked.

"Thank you," I finally manage.

He pulls me back up into his arms, my limbs limp as a doll's, and he holds me tight. "Anytime."

I laugh. It's an exhausted laugh, but also the happiest laugh I've had in years.

Our lips meet, a slow kiss, then he turns around to lay me on my pillow. I roll to my side and he curls up behind me, wraps his arm around my waist, and nestles his face into my hair. Like we've done this every night for the last 1,800 days. Like our time was never taken from us.

With the heat of his body behind me, the soft kisses trailing over my neck and shoulder, sleep claims me quickly, pulling me into strange dreams of withered hands, black horses, and a bright red ruby buried six feet underground.

CHAPTER SIXTEEN

CHARLIE DOESN'T GIVE me a second to worry if he's still here, if all of this is real. He's inside me again before the sun rises, before I'm even fully awake, his chest pressed against my back, his arm snaked over my side. But this time it's sweet and slow. And it's quiet, so quiet, like we're holding sleep close, keeping it draped over us like a blanket. The finger he's slipped between my legs plays me as skillfully as he plays my guitar. I grip him tightly as he strums me over the edge, pulling him down right behind me.

"Charlie, can I get pregnant?" It seems like a strange question given how old I was just a couple of days ago, but we haven't used any form of birth control, and I'm young now.

"I certainly hope so," he mumbles against my neck.

Rolling onto my back, I wrap an arm around his shoulder as he slides down the bed a little so he can rest his head on my chest. I'm smiling. "Me too." I bury my nose into his hair and breathe deep. "Where have you been?" *Why did it take you so long to find me*, I think, but don't ask.

His sigh brushes over my bare skin. "She," he pauses, swallows, "Rebecca, or it could have been Julianne, stole my memories too."

Of course. Of course she did. Charlie loved me, and I loved him. He would have searched for me. If he'd remembered me at all, he would have searched for me just as long as I would have searched for him. And I can't imagine I would have ever stopped searching for him if the tables were turned.

"They'd concocted a story that Rebecca had been invited to train with a coven in Iceland, so when Rebecca left, Dad and I had no idea that it was to become you. Once Rebecca realized I'd figured it out, that I knew she wasn't you, she fired me from the band and wiped my memory clean of you, the real you, and of her becoming you. I went from being madly in love with you and willing to kill Rebecca to get her to tell me what she'd done to you, to royally pissed that some young hot-shot folk singer fired me from her band for no good reason. All with a snap of her fingers."

"When did you find out she was pretending to be me?"

"The first time she tried to kiss me. Felt like I was kissing my sister, and I just knew."

I roll over and sit up to straddle him. "Well, it *was* like you were kissing your sister. Technically."

He huffs a laugh.

"I'm sorry she fired you from the band. I would never have done that." I lean down to trace my lips over his collarbone.

"I know you wouldn't." His hands slide up my thighs. "I'm far too good."

"You really are," I tease, kissing the soft spot just behind his ear. "When did your dad and Julianne get married?"

He's gripping my ass now, his voice diving low. "They met after Mom died. They married quickly and it just broke my family apart. My relatives on both my mom and dad's side had magic, but a light magic, earth-based and limited in power. They could make flowers grow, summon animals, whip up a breeze, that sort of thing. But Julianne and Rebecca, they come from a family of immensely powerful witches. They practice darker magic, spells and hexes...*curses*. My dad wanted those powers, he wanted their strength. My mom's death nearly destroyed him. More than anything, he wanted their immortality, for me. So he wouldn't lose me too."

"Jesus tapdancing Christ!" I bark, bolting upright. "Rebecca is immortal?"

His face scrunches up into an apologetic wince. "Um...yes."

"Are you immortal?" I've got my hands braced on his stomach and I'm staring him down. "Because I have zero interest in being in a long-term thing with someone who's going to stay young and beautiful and live on forever while I get old and die. I love you, but not that much."

He laughs. "No, I'm not immortal. I'll get old and die right alongside you, sweetheart."

"Good," I say, relieved to have dodged that preposterous relationship bullet.

"My real parents' sides of the family were completely against the marriage and we lost all contact with them when Dad decided to marry Julianne anyway. They just stopped calling, writing, and I never saw any of them again."

Stories are beginning to align. "Aunt Lulu?" I ask.

"Yeah." His brows pull tight. "At the time, I did not understand. I mean, I knew Julianne was a difficult woman, but she seemed to make Dad happy, so I never understood how the rest of my family decided she was so bad that they had to stop talking to us, to me."

"They were probably all afraid of being cursed and waking up turned into skunks," I mutter.

He snorts, the tips of his fingers grazing up and down my back and making goose pimples prickle over my sensitive young skin. "I was devastated but, yes, now I know that they were probably afraid of getting cursed."

"But why did Rebecca curse me, us? What did we ever do to her?" I've spent so many sleepless nights asking this question. I've even asked her, repeatedly. There have never been any answers. She could have taken anyone's career. Why mine?

He blows out through his cheeks. "I don't know anything for certain, and Julianne had a lot to do with it, but it might have been simple jealousy. I was around fifteen when I began to suspect Rebecca wanted more than a brother-sister relationship with me."

"No," I gasp. "No, seriously?" I'm flabbergasted. "She did all of this to us because she wanted a *Flowers in the Attic* moment with her brother and I was standing in the way?"

"Stepbrother," he reminds me.

"Semantics!" I repeat, throwing my hands up.

"Important semantics," he insists. "Very important. I really don't think I can stress how important this particular semantic is."

"If that's what you need to tell yourself." I wink at him while I pinch his side, hard enough to make him swat my hand away. "So when did you figure out I was up here? When did you get your memories back?"

"Last year someone left a wooden box on my porch. There was a picture inside of an old woman shooting cans off a stump while a pig with a hen sitting on its back stood behind her, watching."

I remember this scene he's describing. I'd just gotten a new pistol and I was practicing in the yard. "Who gave you that gift? Who took that picture?" *Is someone else watching us? Someone besides Rebecca?* My hackles rise.

One of his hands roams up my side, his thumb brushing the underside of my breast. I can't help but notice him stirring beneath me. "I don't know, but it was charmed. The second my fingers touched the picture, I remembered everything. I knew it was you, the old woman, and you were the most beautiful thing I'd ever seen."

He sits up, both hands grasping my hips. "I didn't know where you were. There was no note, no markings, nothing. I went out of my mind."

My fingers slip into his hair so I can cradle his head against my chest. "How did you find me?"

"Later?" he asks, leaning down to take my nipple into his mouth.

Yes, later.

He starts to lift me up so I can guide him into me when there's a scratching at the door.

"Shit. Shit, Charlie. Under the covers!" I climb off of him. "Now!"

"What? Why?" he asks, but it's too late.

I jump under the blankets, then throw as much cover over his hips as I can before Fritz slides in under the door. He scurries across the floor and climbs up onto the bed.

"You two done?" He tilts his head at us. "We're hungry." Then his eyes slide to Charlie. "Hi, Charlie."

This is not the "Hi, Charlie," of a ferret addressing a relative stranger. This is knowing, remembering. This "Hi, Charlie" is slathered in thick insinuation.

Charlie laughs. "Hi, Fritz. Damn, I've missed you."

CHAPTER SEVENTEEN

I'M SMILING, feeling as satisfied as a well-nursed baby while I make breakfast for everyone. It's simple, bacon, eggs, toast, but it feels like the height of decadence. My body thrums and aches and every step I take reminds me of Charlie. Just the way I wanted it to.

Even though I only have a few left in the pantry, I pop one of my remaining bottles of champagne and make orange juice for mimosas. The OJ is the concentrated shit, but it'll do.

After Fritz woke us up, I'd snuck into the shed to bring everyone up to speed. Everyone except for Bridge who was still snoring like a lumberjack. Nobody had been overly surprised since Charlie's magic had restored their memories as well. Not their bodies, not yet anyway, but at least they had their memories.

Charlie left with Wally a while ago to "talk things over". Wally was pissed at Charlie for sure, but also relieved that he wasn't losing his mind, that his suspicions surrounding Charlie were sound instead of some trauma-induced paranoid delusion. Charlie apologized profusely, nearly getting onto his knees before Wally to beg his forgiveness. But while Wally is quick to anger, he's even quicker to forgive. It didn't take much self-flogging before Wally's squirrelly tail was wagging happily while he pushed Charlie out into the snow with a step-fatherly shove of his snout.

"Morning, Nona." My name is drawn out like the punchline to a very dirty joke as Bridge slinks into the kitchen, finally awake. Jack, who apparently spared no detail when he caught her up, bounds in sheepishly behind her.

"Morning," I chirp like the happiest bird. Balls to the lot of them.

"How was your night?" Bridge croons. She's goading me.

Careful what you ask for, Bridge. "My night? Oh, my night was phenomenal. Charlie fucked me twice, then a third time this morning. I'm spent."

"Nona!" Mom reprimands, warming her feathers by the fire. "Language! But good for you."

Bridge is in hysterics now, cackling and rolling around on the floor until she gets distracted by her own tail and winds up stuck in a frenzied loop chasing it.

"Some of us were trying to sleep, you know." Fritz scampers into the kitchen to join in the roasting. It's fine. I knew I'd take a mountain of shit from them this morning.

"Well, Fritz," I reply calmly, "perhaps you shouldn't have insisted on sleeping right outside our door with your ear to the floor."

Fritz starts nipping at my heel cord until I'm forced to fend him off with little kicks aimed at his face.

"Touché," he says, finally ceasing his assault on my feet. "But honestly, Nona. What do you expect? Nobody in this cabin has had sex in years. We're starved for it." Fritz's sentiment is accompanied by vigorous, agreeable nodding from Bridge.

"Nona had sex?" Wally snorts sardonically as he lumbers

back through the door, Charlie stumbling over the door jamb behind him, eyes wide and cheeks bright red. Whether it's from the brisk morning air, his talk with Wally, or the fact that we're all sitting around chatting about what he did to me last night, who could say? If I was a betting lady, I'd say all three.

"Ha ha," I say, "Very funny, Wally."

"Seriously though, when do we get to have sex?" This comes from Jack and it makes me inhale my swallow. Jack never talks about sex, or anything personal at all in front of anyone but Bridge. But while I'm coughing, trying not to laugh, Jack is obviously completely serious.

I pull myself together. "I'm sorry, Jack. You're right. You're absolutely right. Charlie," I say after clearing my throat, "when does my family get to have sex?"

Charlie's red cheeks flare positively crimson. "Uh, soon?"

"What's the hold up?" This time it's Mom who makes me choke, so much that I'm forced to spit my gulp of mimosa into the sink, missing a direct hit on the bacon by a hair. Evidently the prospect of getting their human bodies back has everyone thinking of only one thing, and they're making no bones about it.

"What's gotten into all of you? If this isn't the biggest group of animals I've ever met. Where are your manners?" Wally's disapproving tone wipes the smiles from our faces. But then he saunters over to Mom, rubs his snout against her waiting beak, and murmurs, low and seductive, "But really, Charlie, what is the hold up?"

Even Charlie's laughing now, doubled over, hands on his knees.

I turn the stove down to simmer to keep the bacon warm, pour him a mimosa, and walk across the living room to give it to him. I'm grinning like an idiot and when his eyes find mine. They pull me toward him, like the tide toward the shore, like magnets, like gravity. He takes the glass, then wraps his arms around me and kisses me, a chaste little peck.

"Was that nice? That kiss?" asks Bridge, nettled. "It looked nice. It looked super nice. It looked, in fact, like something I'd really love to be able to do with my husband as soon as possible."

"Help me," I mouth to Charlie, imploring him to fill us in on whatever his grand plan is.

He takes a swig of his drink, then says, "All right, everyone. Gather 'round."

I fill bowls with mimosas and plates with breakfast for everyone as we surround Charlie near the fire. He's sitting on the couch and, out of respect for my family, I sit beside him instead of on top of him like I want to.

He tells them about the curse, Rebecca, his magic, Julianne. Everyone is silent as he speaks, intent eyes wide, mouths slowly chewing or pecking at their breakfasts.

"That's," Mom massively understates, "interesting."

Charlie presses his lips together and nods evenly. "Yep."

"If you knew we could speak, if you knew who we were, why were you so scared when Wally started talking to you? Why didn't you just tell us who you were? Or give us our memories back sooner?" Mom's questions are met with silence while Charlie seems to be deciding how to answer.

At length, he says, "Well, it's one thing to know that an animal is a person, it's something else entirely to have a 500-pound hog threaten you. It was terrifying. No offense, Wally."

"None taken," Wally replies, oddly proud.

"I should have said something sooner," Charlie admits. "But I couldn't. Not until Nona had her memories back. Rebecca is watching, she's probing this cabin all the time with her powers. She'd know if I used too much magic at once up here."

"How did you free Nona from the curse?" asks Jack.

"Well, I didn't. Not really. I can't actually break the curse, yet," he adds quickly, heading off the growing din of animal grumblings. "I can weaken the curse, a little. Any more would be too dangerous. What I'm doing to Nona is more like a glamor. And I might be able to glamor the rest of you, too. But I can't do it yet."

"Why not?" Mom asks. Her tone is that skeptical mom tone, the one she uses when she knows we're trying to hide something from her.

He bites his cheek, his fingers gripping at his jeans like he's nervous about how we're going to respond. "Do you remember the bear who almost ate Fritz?"

Fritz pops upright to balance on his hind legs. "I certainly do. Why? Did you bring that thing here?"

Charlie stiffens beside me. He's right to be nervous. Whatever he's about to say, I don't think it'll go over well.

"I did."

"What the hell, Charlie? You brought a bear to our woods? Are you nuts?" Bridget's hackles are spiking and the tip of her tail flicks aggressively at the air. Rightly so, Jack has barely left the yard since we learned about the bear. Fritz barely leaves the porch.

Charlie's got his hands up in surrender. "Please, let me explain."

"Go on, then. We're waiting," snaps Bridge.

"Bridget, please," I implore her, even though a part of me agrees with her. "Just listen."

"The bear is a totem. My family doesn't have a ton of magic, but this is magic we can do."

"What's a totem?" Mom says. She's hopped up to perch on Wally's back in an attempt to meet Charlie eye to eye.

"A totem is like a protective spirit, a guardian."

"Is a protective guardian supposed to do things like eat Fritz?" asks Jack matter-of-factly.

Charlie shakes his head. "It wouldn't have eaten Fritz. I promise. It won't harm any of you, ever."

"It's eating the heads off deer," I remind him.

"Well, it is a bear." Charlie shrugs. "It gets hungry. It eats. But it won't eat you. You have nothing to fear from the bear."

"So you, like, conjured this bear? To protect us?" Jack asks.

Charlie nods. "Against Rebecca, specifically. She won't be able to come within the bear's territory. If she does, he will find her, and he will do whatever it takes to protect his family," he glances around the room, "you all. She won't know this, but she'll sense a barrier around the cabin keeping her away."

This pulls me up short. "Charlie, she knows something's up. Last time I saw her she looked like hell. Whatever you're doing to me, it's having an effect on her. She'll want it to stop. She'll want revenge."

He shrugs again. "That's Rebecca for you, so intent on what she wants, she'll never be satisfied with what she has. She's not entirely a bad person. Her mother, Julianne, she's really done a number on her."

It sounds like a tuberculosis ward in here with how many animals choke on their drinks or eggs.

"Yes, she is, Charlie," growls Bridge. "She is a very bad person, the worst in fact." Everyone nods their agreement. "What? Underneath that bitchy 'I'm going to destroy everything you know and love' exterior lurks a sad and wounded heart? Well, screw that!"

"Fair enough," he concedes, scratching the side of his head. "Not the right crowd for Rebecca sympathy. Duly noted."

"If the bear is protecting us, why can't you break the curse. Or at least glamor the rest of us?" asks Fritz, licking bits of egg from his whiskers.

"The bear isn't strong enough yet. A totem is formed by magic, but grows stronger on its own as it learns the hearts, dreams, wants and needs of those it was formed to protect. I instructed it to home in on Nona first. Sorry," he offers, "but I hope you can all understand that. When I first found the cabin, I was planning to wait in the woods until the bear was strong enough to protect all of you. So I could restore all of your memories and bodies right away. But," he turns toward me, "I just couldn't wait." He turns back to the room. "I'm sorry. I'm sorry I lied to you."

"That's actually kind of sweet," Bridge admits, swinging her tail so it curls around Jack.

"What happens when the bear is strong enough?" asks Wally.

"I can, well, I hope I can weaken the curse enough to make you all human again. But, my magic will probably only be strong enough to keep you human when you're all close to me, or to the bear."

"So we're still stuck here, then. Even if you're able to turn us into humans again, we're still stuck."

This statement from Fritz knocks the breath out of me. His hunched shoulders and shiny black nose pointing miserably at the floor make me wonder if I'll ever breathe again. I know it's been hard for him up here, harder than the rest of us. He doesn't have family here, or a partner. All he has...is me. How could I ever have thought for one second that my friendship would have been enough for him? Even though it's been the one thing above all others that has kept me going over the last five years. I feel like the most selfish, inconsiderate, unbearable ass that I've never truly realized how stuck he's probably felt. Stuck with us. With my crazy family. With me.

If Charlie is privy to the Fritz-life-crises I'm having beside him, he doesn't say so. Instead he shocks us all by saying, "No. None of us are stuck. The curse will be broken. It's just that Rebecca has to do it. And I have to make her do it."

I scoff so loudly Fritz's head whips back up and his tail poofs. "Fat chance of that."

Charlie's staring at me, plaintive and exasperated, like I'm not being at all as helpful as he'd prefer.

I try a little harder. "Look, Rebecca told me that she can't break the curse. She said the only way the curse would break was if I had my own love to lose. That's why we thought I was getting younger, because I was falling in love with you. But that's not even true, is it? I've already had you, and already lost you."

"Hmm," he murmurs, "sounds more like Disney than Rebecca. If I had to guess, I'd say she was messing with you. Sending you on a wild goose chase. She can break the curse. I'm sure of it. Which brings us to the rest of my plan."

"The rest?" Bridge asks.

"Remember me telling you about the Rose of the Desert? My great grandpa's ruby?"

"That wasn't bullshit?" Wally asks, voicing what we're all thinking.

"No, that wasn't bullshit," Charlie says, settling back on the couch. "Rufus Brown wasn't just a train robber. He was one of the most powerful earth-magic warlocks in recent history."

"There are different kinds of warlocks?" Jack is perking, his ears pulled forward so they point directly at Charlie.

"Sure, lots of them. Witches too. Some can do fire magic, or water magic, some can read minds. Some can even slip through reality, transporting themselves from one place to the next."

"What sort of magic does Rebecca practice?" Jack asks, curiosity sparked.

"Rebecca and her mother, Julianne, work in a darker kind of magic, hexes, curses, transfiguration. Their magic is ancient and, especially with Julianne, formidable."

"That's not all," I add, mulish. "Those assholes are immortal, too!"

"Thanks for that clarification, Nona," Charlie says tightly under the chorus of "What!"s blurted from Mom, Wally, and

Fritz, which is only slightly louder than Bridge's barked, "Are you shitting me?" Jack remains silent, far too busy gawping, his blue-gray bunny eyes bulging, his little bunny mouth hanging wide open.

"How on earth are we supposed to stand a snowball's chance in hell against immortal witches!" asks Wally, snorting indignantly on every third word.

Sitting here, listening to my family freak out, watching Charlie trying hard not to wince while they do, I'm feeling no small amount of remorse for letting the whole immortal thing out of the bag so carelessly. I take Charlie's hand in mine, lace my fingers through his, and squeeze apologetically. "Why don't we let Charlie speak?" I suggest.

"Nona's right," says Mom, one wing petting Wally's head in soothing strokes. "Charlie, what do we do? How do we beat them?"

Charlie clears his throat, runs a soft thumb across my wrist, then says, "Well, that's where the Rose comes in. While it's true that the ruby is an extremely valuable gem, its real worth goes much deeper than that. The Rose of the Desert is a powerful magical relic. Whoever holds it can shield themselves from any magic."

"Amazing," whispers Jack reverently.

Wally has calmed down enough to admit, "That'd come in mighty handy," without a single snort.

"It sure would," Charlie agrees with a frustrated head scratch. "If I could only find the stupid thing."

"But you think it's up here," I say.

"I'm positive. I can feel it. The Rose is my inheritance and I know it's up here."

"Well, then," I pluck Fritz from my lap and spring to my feet, "that settles it."

"That settles what?" asks Charlie. He's hesitant, squinting at me. Wary.

"There's an enchanted gem in these woods that will free my family, a magical totem bear out there to protect us, and a blizzard expected later tonight. As far as I can see it, there's only one thing left to do." I pull on my snowsuit, walk to my rack to strap my shotgun over my back, and belt on my pistol. "Come on, Charlie. We're going hunting."

CHAPTER EIGHTEEN

THE TEMPERATURE PLUMMETS while Charlie and I hike out north of my property, the sharpness of the coming storm biting at my cheeks. Charlie's following his warlock nose magic, I suppose, because he keeps whipping his head around, sniffing the air like the best-looking bloodhound. I'm watching him as he trudges along ahead of me, admiring his broad shoulders and long back, the little curls of hair peeking out from under the hat I'd pulled out of the snow that first day we'd found him.

"You getting any…smells?" I'm not sure how best to word the question.

"Maybe. I don't know. I know it's up here, I know it. But," he glances around, waving his hands, "up here is a pretty big area."

He turns a sharp left, catching a scent on the wind, and starts climbing up a steep embankment.

"That leads to Sam's place, about two miles up," I tell him. "And a mile or so further north is where Aunt Lulu used to live."

He turns his head north, sniffs. "It has to be up there. It has to be." Shoving his hands into his pockets, he lowers his head and picks up his pace. He's a man on a mission, a mission to make things right, to fix what his family has done to us. Finding the Rose, I realize, is just as important to him as it is to us.

"Charlie, wait." I run to catch up to him. As he's turning around to face me, I throw my arms around him and try to kiss him, but my lips are cold, numb. His are too. It's a disaster, this kiss, but we don't care. We laugh and mash our useless, frozen lips together. I pull away, holding his face between my gloved hands. "I love you. No matter what. No matter what happens, if we find the Rose or not, if Rebecca wins or not, I love you. And I always will."

He leans forward, his forehead coming to rest against mine. "I love you too. But I won't fail you again."

"Charlie, you never failed me. I've never thought that for one single minute."

"Of course you haven't." His head lifts, lips tilting into a somber smile. "You didn't even know I existed."

"It doesn't feel that way. It feels like I've always known you and I've always missed you and wondered when you'd find me. But I've never blamed you. Not once."

He pulls me to him, hugging me hard through my snowsuit. I breathe him in, memorizing his piney Charlie smell, holding it deep in my lungs, just in case. Just in case this time together is all we get.

"We'd better keep going if we want to make it back before the storm," I say, reluctant to release him. But after I feel him nod against my cheek, I do.

We pass by Sam's place around noon, trying for a wide berth since I don't want to give Sam and Marge heart attacks when they see a younger Nona hiking with her "grandson".

In another hour or so, we reach the edge of Aunt Lulu's clearing.

"I can't believe it," I gasp as we crest the small hill over-looking her homestead. "I can't believe it's still here."

I'd only visited this place a handful of times, but Aunt Lulu's little cabin is impossible to forget. Its doors are blocked by two feet of snow, but it's still here and in surprisingly good shape, all jagged shingles and odd angles considered. "Charlie, this is where your great aunt lived."

He's silent beside me, a storm of emotions passing over his face.

"Are you okay?" I take his hand in mine.

"I don't know." His voice is so quiet, barely a whisper, like he's hiding from ghosts.

"Do you want to get inside?"

He turns to me, his eyes glistening with the beginning and ending of tears as he pulls himself upright. "I do."

We clear a path to the door, which isn't even locked, and Charlie pushes it open. My boots are stuck to the ground as I peer inside. Everything is exactly like I remember. Exactly. Lulu's couches, covered in this bright canary-yellow fabric, seem untouched in her living room. Her walls are still crowded with pictures she'd taken of Paris, New York, of live oaks in Louisiana, their roping branches forked and spreading out across the frame like lightning. And pictures of these woods, the towering pines, the jagged cliffs, the mountainside lit up in the purple and white of lupine and beargrass in full bloom. "Does someone else live here?" It seems impossible this cabin would be so clean, feel so warm, if it was still empty. "Hello," I call out, but there's no answer.

"Some sort of magic must protect this place," Charlie says while he runs his fingertips over the back of a couch.

"Is it the Rose?"

He shakes his head. "No, this is something else. I don't know what, but it's not the ruby."

I laugh out loud, running toward one of Lulu's shelves. "Holy shit, I loved this guy! I used to play with him whenever we came up here." I pluck the Charlie Weaver bartender toy from the shelf and flick its switch. "Unbelievable. It still works."

Charlie and I stand together, watching the tiny mustached man sway side to side, shaking up a martini. He pours the martini into his mouth and his round face turns red as a turnip as smoke streams out of his ears.

"That is amazing," says Charlie. His eyes, lit-up and smiling, remind me exactly of how I'd felt the first time Aunt Lulu sat cross-legged on the floor with me to show me this toy when I was just a kid. I thought for sure he was real, that he was just another part of Lulu's magic.

"He's the best, right?" I brush my fingers over his bushy mustache.

"I wonder if this is where I got my name."

"What do you mean?" I ask him, flicking the switch to turn off the toy.

"Dad always said it was Aunt Lulu who came up with my name." He turns to face me, grinning. "Maybe I was supposed to be a bartender."

"I bet that's it. Charlie the bartender. It's never too late to fulfill your destiny," I tell him.

"As soon as I recover a priceless magical artifact, use more magic than I've ever used before to glamor a bunch of animals, then somehow convince a couple of super-powerful witches to relinquish their control over my fiancé, I'll totally become a bartender."

A painful lump takes up residence in my throat. "Is that what I am? What we are?" I swallow. "Am I still your fiancé?"

He grabs my hand, eyes wide and panicked as if he only now realized the words that just dropped from his mouth, what they meant. "Yes. I mean, if you, if yes is what you...You want yes right?" he stutters hopelessly.

I'm laughing at him now through fat, blurry tears. "Yes. Yes, I want yes. Do you want yes?"

Wrapping his hand around the back of my neck, he pulls me to him. "Yes," is all he says before I crush my lips to his.

After a long while kissing my fiancé, I place one Charlie back on the shelf, and follow the other down the hall and into the back bedroom. It feels a little like an invasion of privacy to enter Lulu's room. She lived alone, never married from what I remember, and her room is just as eccentric as she was. Elegant floor lamps with intricate beadwork dripping from their shades sit on either side of her four-poster bed, silk scarves draped like a canopy between the posts. The walls are burgundy with black detailing painted along the upper border that looks exactly like lace.

"She was definitely unique," Charlie says, taking a seat on her bed.

"Decadent, even." I take a seat beside him. We're both staring straight ahead at Lulu's wall, at a photograph hanging in a distressed wood frame. It's an old black and white of a young boy and girl holding hands in front of a pond. They're facing the water, turned away from us so we can only see their backs.

"Do you know who those kids are?" I ask, squinting at the picture.

"I don't think so. Could be my mom and my uncle. I've never seen this picture before, though." He scans the room. "I wish I knew them all better. I feel like I missed out on so much."

My hand runs up and down his back. "I'm sorry."

We sit there for a moment, living in Lulu's house, looking at Lulu's pictures. Then a brisk wind rattles a window. The storm is still coming.

"We should start searching," I say, knowing we only have an hour or two before we need to head back.

He turns to face me, slides a hand over my cheek, and leans in for a kiss. This isn't a sad kiss, or a needy kiss. There are no tears now, no blinding passion, only a deep and true tenderness. For a little while anyway, because eventually I reach my hands into his hair and he grabs the back of my coat. He yanks me closer and I am sorry Aunt Lulu, but I will absolutely defile your bed today if Charlie wants to. Turns out, thankfully, he has more self-control than I do.

"You're right, we should go." He says against my lips and the hoarseness in his voice settles directly between my legs.

I groan my protest, then get a grip on myself and take Charlie's hand to follow him out of the bedroom.

We search the cabin from top to bottom. It's not hard, it's a very small cabin. We find spell books, dried flowers, jars of herbs, bones, feathers. But not a single ruby.

"This isn't the best time of year for digging up buried treasure," I say, staring miserably out the front window where the snow has started to fall.

"I honestly wouldn't know where to dig anyway. I was hoping," Charlie laughs, pinching the bridge of his nose between his thumb and finger. "I don't know what I was hoping."

"That it would call to you?" I offer.

"Something like that. I know. I'm an idiot."

"Charlie, you are a warlock who can summon magical bears and trick people into thinking they'd stitched up your wounded leg. It's not at all idiotic to think you'd be able to sense your family heirloom. Not trying to find the ruby, that would be idiotic."

"Either way," he says, running a hand through his hair, "it's not here. Or if it is, I can't feel it. And you really did stitch up my leg, by the way. It hurt like hell. For some reason, I didn't think you'd actually go through with it."

"I did?" I grimace, brows crinkling. "Charlie, I'm sorry. I guess next time, don't glamour a gaping wound on your thigh."

"Sound advice," he says with a half-smile. Then he puts his coat back on and wheels on me. "Well, the Rose is a lost cause, for now. So on to Plan B."

I cock my head like a dog who's heard a whistle. "There's a Plan B?"

"There is."

"What is it?"

He takes a deep breath and blows it out. "It's a lot harder."

THE SUN SETS as we hike back from Aunt Lulu's, but the snow now falling in earnest lends the sky a wooly gray light. I'm huddled in my coat, walking with my head down and my hands crammed into my pockets. It's that wet type of cold, the kind that seeps deep into bones and can easily convince a person they'll never be warm again.

Charlie doesn't elaborate on his "Plan B" during our trek, only telling me that it involves getting Julianne, Rebecca, and his father James up to the cabin, which sounds completely bananas to me. But my teeth are clacking together so hard with my chattering I'm worried I'll chip a tooth, so I decide pressing him on this plan can wait until we're curled up by the fire.

When we reach the cabin, Charlie pulls the door open and we hustle inside. Everyone's cuddled together on the couch, except for Wally who lies next to the dead fire like he's trying to soak up whatever warmth might be left in the coals.

"Shit, guys," I manage through my shivering. "The fire died. I'm sorry." I'd put enough wood in it to last most of the day, but we've been gone longer than I thought we'd be. I jerk out of my snowsuit, pull off my gloves, and blow into my cupped hands as I turn toward the stove. Charlie's long fingers wrap gently around my arm. "I got this, Nona. Why don't you go take a shower? You're frozen."

I kiss him, not bothering to argue, but then I remember something. "Sorry, Charlie, but we need more firewood. The stack is just outside the door."

He nods at me, smiling, and my knees buckle. Not just because his smile is as cute as a basket full of kittens, but because, just like the dishes, he's offering to help with chores that have been mine alone for years. On my way to the bathroom, I watch him pull his cap down tight and walk out into the storm, for me. It's the single sexiest thing I've ever seen.

I make the shower hot, almost scalding, and dump my clothes on the floor. I'm standing still as a post, moaning gratuitously as water pours over my head and down my body in sheets. I don't know how long I stand there, but some part of my thawing brain registers the curtain sliding back as Charlie steps into the shower with me. He gave me long enough to warm up, otherwise I wouldn't have left this stream of water for Elvis himself. But I step out of the way a little, just enough for him to squeeze in beside me.

"I'm freezing," he chatters, his freezing cold fingers running over my breasts.

"I see that," I squeal, swatting his icy appendages away from my finally warmed up boobs.

He's turned so that he's facing me, his head tipped back and eyes closed as the shower spray beats down on his face, dripping off the rounded tip of his nose. I'm thinking, while I survey the narrow rivulets of water pouring over his chest and slipping down the hollow plane of his hip, that I'm being inexcusably uncharitable. He deserves nothing less than a proper, enthusiastic thank you for taking care of the fire for me. After licking my lips, I drop to my knees so I can warm him up the old-fashioned way.

"CHARLIE," I say, drying my hair with a towel, "does it ever make you feel bad?"

"Does what make me feel bad?" He's standing before me, towel slung low around his hips.

"You know, that here we are able to love each other, touch

each other, do," I tilt my head toward the shower, "*that*, and nobody else can?"

He considers this for a moment. "I guess it does. Do you want to stop? We can cool our jets until they're all able to be human again too."

"Woah there, killer. Let's not go overboard." I'm grinning as I rip the towel from his waist.

"Oh, thank fuck," he replies, grabbing my wrist and yanking me into a kiss.

CHAPTER NINETEEN

THANKFULLY, nobody says a single word to us as we leave the bathroom and wander back to my room to get dressed. I decide, screw it, I'm wearing jammies. I pull on my thickest fleece pants, knee-high socks, wool slippers, and zip up a hoodie sweatshirt over a tank top. This is the type of outfit I want to be buried in.

I toss Charlie a pair of Wally's sweatpants, which are way too big, and a sweater that is also too big but hangs on him in a way that makes him look soft and delicious. He brushes his hand through his hair and eyes me head to toe. "You look comfy." His eyes narrow. "Wait, I remember those jammy pants." He's prowling toward me now. "I remember taking those jammy pants off with my teeth."

I slip out of his reach, proclaiming, "I don't recall that at all. You'll have to remind me later." Then I exit the bedroom before he convinces me to stay in there all night. I do indeed remember the night he depantsed me with his teeth, and I'd very much like him to do it again, but we've got to at least eat dinner first.

"You didn't find the Rose, I take it," says Mom. She's sitting on the kitchen counter, pulling the feathers of her right wing through her beak.

"We did not," I confirm. "Found Aunt Lulu's cabin though."

"Really?" She starts in on her left wing.

"It's in perfect condition too, like she never left. Strange, don't you think?"

"Strange," Mom agrees. "But no ruby."

"Not even a cubic zirconia." I pet her head, then turn to open the fridge and try to figure out what to make for dinner. There's a block of cheese, some sausage, tomato sauce. "Pizza?" I yell back over my shoulder. The rambunctious hoots from the front room confirm that this is an acceptable choice. I'll just have to make dough.

I flip on the radio, hoping for music, but it's a weather report. Another foot is possible tonight with winds gusting up to 40 mph. My rattling windows agree with the forecast, but it's toasty in the cabin now and I pop open a bottle of wine, pouring bowls for everyone and glasses for me and Charlie.

Mom hops over to me. "Will you go back out to search for the ruby tomorrow?"

My own selfishness takes me out at the knees. What is wrong with me that I didn't even consider how much everyone has probably been waiting to hear about the Rose? Wondering if we'd found it, if we were all one step closer to freedom? No, I've been too busy making out with my boyfriend. My shame must be written all over my face because Mom says, "Oh, sweetheart, it's okay. Don't feel bad. Don't ever feel bad about this."

"How could I not feel bad? This sucks. I'm happier than I've been in years, but it's totally unfair to all of you."

"Now you listen to me, Nona May Sheldon, we are thrilled you have Charlie again. Thrilled. You know "Missing Charlie" was always my favorite song. I might have loved him as much as you did. It's all right for you to be happy."

Tears fill my eyes. "But why do I keep forgetting? Why do I keep forgetting how hard this is for you guys?" I wipe away my tears, angry at myself for even crying them. "I'm like a child."

She looks at my outfit. "A little."

I laugh through a sob.

"Sweetie." Now her voice is breaking, reminding me that there is not a single thing in the world that rivals the impossibility of trying to hold myself together while my mother is falling apart. "For the last five years, I've had to watch my own daughter grow older than me. Much older. You've been breaking your back to take care of us, to keep us fed and warm and as happy as any mismatched group of animals could ever hope to be. My heart is bursting seeing you now, young and vibrant and happy. Aside from the same for Bridge, there is nothing else I want in this world. Nothing." She takes a few steps closer to me, her eyes wet, voice soft. "When you have children, everything changes. So much of your happiness hinges upon theirs. And now, not only do I get to see you happy, but maybe I'll get to watch you learn this lesson for yourself when you give me grandchildren."

I grab Mom and crush her against me. We're both sobbing now, as much as a hen can sob, but there's another person in the kitchen with us and his sniffling pulls our red-eyed attention to him. It's Charlie.

"Charlie, are you all right?" I blubber, sniffling.

His breath hitches. "No. I'm not. Not even a little. I'm sorry I'm so emotional, but that was just so…beautiful," he blurts, dabbing at his eyes with a too-long sleeve of his sweater.

I kiss Mom on her head before setting her back down on the counter. Taking Charlie's glass of wine, I lead him to the couch. "There, there," I say, rubbing his shoulders and shooting Mom a baffled expression as Charlie sits with his head buried in his hands. She only shrugs at me.

After a moment, Charlie pulls himself together, raising his head to find all of us staring at him, or at each other with worried expressions. "I'm sorry, everyone. I'm okay, I promise.

I've just made a decision. A decision I should have made days ago, no matter the stupid consequences."

"What's that, son?" asks Wally, still sprawled on his side near the fire.

Charlie doesn't answer him, instead he sears me with the most intense expression, heated and daring. "I think the storm will keep her away. But this is just for tonight." He turns to the room. "Only tonight, okay?"

"Sweetie," I say, pulling his face back around and brushing his hair from his brow, "nobody has a clue what you're talking about."

His eyes meeting my eyes spark like flint against steel. "Kiss me, Nona."

"Right here? Now?" I catch Bridge rolling her eyes so hard they disappear into her skull.

"Trust me."

Yes sir, I think, staring at his lips, slanted into a mischievous smirk. I lean in and just as my lips meet his, I hear his fingers snap beside my ear.

For a sharp moment, the world flips on its axis. I gasp, grabbing onto the couch to steady myself. Then the whirling stops, gravity reasserting itself.

"It's okay, Nona. Open your eyes," Charlie whispers.

Slowly, I let my lids float open.

My family and my Fritzy are standing before me. Naked as the day they were born, but human. All of them, human.

My eyes slam shut again and I scream hard into my fists. Relief and pain, regret and ecstasy, they swell inside me all at once until there is no room left for air. There's this feeling that's haunted me, a fear I've never once voiced to anyone, not even to myself, that no matter how much we loved each other, no matter how hard we tried to make a life up here, that none of it was real. I wasn't real, they weren't, and all of this was only a dream. This might sound crazy, but when you live in another woman's body with talking animals in the middle of nowhere, reality becomes a slippery thing.

Now, in my real body, surrounded by my real family, that feeling vanishes, years of uncertainty vanishing with it. But I still can't look. I can't see them. It hurts too much. It feels too good.

"Nona, sweetie. It's all right." It's Mom. It's her voice, her real voice, not the approximation made through the vocal cords of a chicken.

"Nona, open your eyes. We're okay. We're all okay." This time it's Bridge and her voice wrenches a trembling sob from me.

Their hands are on mine, the warmth of them soaking into my skin. Charlie must have left my side because Mom now sits to my left and Bridge to my right. They wrap their arms around me. Then I feel Fritz come to sit at my feet, his hands squeezing my knees.

"We love you, Nona. Take a breath, baby. Open your eyes."

It's Fritz that finally pulls me down from my panic attack, his deep voice setting my feet back on firm ground. Fritz always centers me like no one else.

When I finally open my eyes, I'm gazing into the most spectacular shade of hazel. "Breathe," he tells me. "Just breathe. We've got you."

Fritz is still unbearably gorgeous, a little older, but it just makes him seem more distinguished. Then my gaze shifts south and I realize he's still naked. Holy Hannah. My eyes snap back up again.

"Hi Mom. Hi Bridge. Hi Fritz." My voice is hoarse, thick with tears. "Looks like you all need some clothes, and I..." My fingernails dig deep into my palms. "I didn't bring enough clothes. Why didn't I pack more clothes, just in case?"

"I got it," Charlie says from the kitchen, wiping his eyes with his sleeve. He slips down the hall, Fritz joining him. Charlie returns alone a minute later with a handful of blankets. He hands one out to every naked person in the room.

Jack doesn't bother with his, he simply stands, grabs Bridge by the hand, and pulls her squealing down the hall into the guest bedroom Charlie's no longer using.

I help Mom drape a blanket around her shoulders, taking as much care as I can to cover every naked inch of her body. And then I hug her, hard. The feel of her arms around me, the softness of her cheek as it presses against mine, her sweet, floral scent. I haven't allowed myself to fully realize how much I've missed this. How much I've missed her. The relief is overwhelming and it makes me a kid again, waking up from a nightmare and she's here, holding me in her arms, rocking me side to side and singing softly in my ear. Growing up, I never knew how she always sensed when I was having a bad dream, but she did. They may not all be witches, but mothers have magic too.

"I've missed you," I say, squeezing her even more tightly when she tries to pull away. I'm not ready yet.

She settles against me, letting me hold her as long as I need. Eventually, I let her go but only enough to look at her. She's achingly beautiful, high cheekbones, narrow nose over a smile that says, 'stop taking everything so seriously all the time.' She's barely aged a day since I last saw her. I cup her cheek and she grabs my hand, turning her head to kiss my palm.

A shadow passes over us. It's Wally. He's got his blanket wrapped around his waist like a beach towel, his hand stretched out toward Mom, and tears standing in his eyes.

"Penny."

It's all he needs to say.

Mom stands from the couch and wraps him in her blanket. I watch them hold each other, Mom with her face buried in his chest, Wally with his lips pressed into her hair. They stay that way for a while. There's something about Mom that makes it hard to let her go.

I say to no one in particular, "I'll have to open up the other bedroom in the back, once Bridge and Jack are finished." However long that takes. I'll sleep on the floor and give Wally and Mom my room if it comes to that, but I won't interrupt them, not for anything in the world.

Fritz strolls in from my room like my teenage dream. He's found a pair of my pajamas, black velvet with a drawstring, that somehow fit him perfectly and he's got one of my robes wrapped around him; it's a bright red satin number with a wide sash. To top the whole black Hugh Hefner thing he's rocking, he's got Poppop's corncob pipe between his lips. Fritz is pure fucking class, always has been.

He stops next to Charlie, extending his hand for a shake. Charlie takes his hand in his, shakes it once, then pulls Fritz into an embrace. The men hold onto each other tightly, like brothers who haven't seen each other in years. Which, in a way, they are. Fritz and Charlie had a bond, similar senses of humor, same taste in music. And I know Fritz had a thing for Charlie at one time. A strange little love triangle, we three. I loved Fritz, then Fritz loved Charlie, then Charlie loved me, and I loved him. I love them both, really. A person can do that, love two people at once.

Bridge screams from the back room and I throw a hand over my mouth, covering my smile. Charlie and Fritz turn to stare down the hall, laughing quietly.

Mom clicks her tongue. "At least you and Charlie were quiet."

As discreetly as I can, I offer my bedroom to Mom and Wally. But they wave me off. "We can wait. They can't go at it all night. At some point they're going to want pizza."

I disagree with the first point, but concede to the second. Standing from the couch because I've got pizza to make, a woozy dizziness rushes through me.

Wally catches me before I stumble, his big burly arms wrapping around me. I stand inside of them, letting him crush me tight. Then I rise onto my tiptoes so I can kiss him on the cheek. "It's good to see you Wally. I've missed your face."

"What, this ugly mug?" He makes a face at me, his bulb of a nose turning red as a beet while his cheeks blow out like a puffer fish.

"That's the one," I say, laughing at him, then I leave him to cuddle with Mom on the couch.

I pass between Charlie and Fritz, turning to kiss Charlie on the lips before wheeling around and throwing myself into Fritz's arms.

"Hi, Nona," says Fritz.

"Hey, baby," I manage, fighting tears, my face buried in the space between his neck and shoulder. Fritz, my lap buddy, my first crush, my closest friend, my lifeline for the last five years.

When I finally let him go he says, "Mind if we smoke?" holding up the pipe.

"Fritz, tonight you can do whatever you want."

His smile is brilliant, but with a wry twist. "It's good to see you, eye to eye."

Charlie's arms wrap around my waist, his chin coming to rest on my shoulder. They're staring at each other, Charlie and Fritz, and I'm settled firmly between them. The air around us is suddenly sparking and electric and... complicated.

"All right, boys," my voice wobbles while I slide out of the Charlie/Fritz sandwich, "I've got to make dinner. Smoke in the shed, though. I'll be in once I pop the pizza in the oven."

Fritz turns on his heel, stopping in my room, presumably to grab my tobacco, then heads to the shed. Charlie spins me to face him and kisses me deeply, grabbing my hips. He moans against my mouth as he lifts me up so I can wrap my legs around his waist. Bridge and Jack, Fritz in his robe, Mom and Wally on the couch, and Charlie's tongue caressing mine, I'd better feed everyone STAT before this cabin bursts into flames in the middle of this blizzard.

"I need…to make…dinner," I say between kisses.

He grudgingly sets me down. "All right, fine. But hurry up."

I laugh at his impatience, then watch after him as he saunters down the hallway toward the shed, stopping once to adjust himself in his sweatpants since things got a little stirred up when we were kissing. I laugh even harder and he flips me the bird over his shoulder.

This pizza is going to be dogshit. I make a half-assed dough, roll it out without any particular care, slather it with sauce and throw the toppings on like I'm throwing clothes into the dryer. Whatever, it's pizza. It'll still taste good.

After putting the pie in the oven, I set the timer and head back to the shed, averting my eyes from Mom and Wally's full on make out session on the couch. I'm so happy for them I could cry, again, but there are things a child just never wants to see their parents doing.

"I guess when a curse breaks, all people want to do is bone," I say, squeezing in through the shed door.

"The curse isn't broken," Charlie reminds us. "Only suspended for the night."

"How does that work?" asks Fritz before taking a big drag on the pipe and blowing the smoke out in tiny, perfect rings.

Charlie shrugs. "It's magic, hard to describe. The curse is still here, it's still on all of you. I can only dim it, like throwing a blanket over a lamp. The rest is a simple glamor. If that makes sense."

"As much as any of this does," offers Fritz while passing the pipe to Charlie. "But why only for tonight?"

Charlie's shoulders slump a little. "Because this much magic is exhausting. Also, Rebecca is sensing my tampering. It's affecting her in ways I hadn't anticipated. If I use too much magic on her curse up here, she'll know, and she'll come. And, like I said before, the totem isn't strong enough yet to protect everyone here. But tonight, with the storm, I think, I hope, the weather will shield us."

I look at Charlie, dubious. "Really? Have you felt the vibe in this cabin? It's practically buzzing. We'd need a category five hurricane to shield this place tonight."

"How much is it wearing on you, using magic like this?" Fritz asks. He's always so thoughtful about things like this, always checking in on the people he loves.

Charlie exhales a streaming cloud of smoke. "A little, with Nona. With all of you? It's hard. I'll be a wreck tomorrow. But it's worth it." He turns to me. "I'm just sorry I didn't do it sooner."

I take the pipe from him. "Don't ever be sorry, not about this. You've given us the most amazing gift, even this one night. Even if I wake up a crone and everyone else turns back into critters in the morning, this night means everything."

"Speak for yourself," says Fritz with a low, humorless laugh. "I'll be madder than a hornet when I'm a ferret again tomorrow. Y'all have any idea what it's like living with a ferret's brain?"

We stare at him, biting back our smiles and shaking our heads.

"It's like living inside a psychotic toddler who's constantly wanting to have the best time of their lives every second of the day, while at the same time always trying to find somewhere to take a nap. Oh, and 'what can I bite?' all day, every day, 'what can I bite and attack?' It's all I can do to make sure I eat and drink in between the madness and the sleeping."

"Fritz," I say, trying not to laugh and doing a miserable job of it, "that sounds terrible."

"It really does," says Charlie, not bothering to hold back his laughter.

"I think Jack has it worse though. All he thinks about is food and sex."

I cough on my smoke. "Jack thinks about sex?" Jack is a private man, in every way. And even when the rest of us have a night where we feel raunchy, Jack never joins in telling dirty jokes. He barely even laughs when the rest of us are rolling.

Fritz nods. "He told me once, a few years ago. Said it was driving him crazy."

"Damn," Charlie mutters, taking the pipe back from me. "What do you think Wally thinks about as a pig?"

"Food," Fritz and I answer in unison.

"Not too different from real-life Wally," I mutter.

"And Penny?" asks Charlie, blowing out smoke as he hands the pipe back to Fritz.

"Mom is unaffected by the chicken brain, I assure you. She is just Penny, always has been, always will be. And Penny Sheldon is impervious to the hang-ups of mere mortals, and mere animals." I take the pipe from Fritz.

"True words," says Fritz, one corner of his mouth kicked up into a grin.

I stamp my feet in the dirt, trying to bring feeling back to the frozen stumps I'm standing on. "I'm going back in guys. I'm freezing. And the pizza's almost done."

"We'll be in in a second," says Charlie. He's got this look on his face, like he's trying so hard to appear innocent that he slips straight into mischief. Like he's got secrets.

"All right," I say slowly, suspiciously. I give him the pipe, and a kiss, then I leave Charlie and Fritz alone in the shed.

After listening in the hallway for a while and only hearing their soft whispers, I rap softly on Bridge and Jack's door. "Hey guys, dinner's almost ready. If you want, I can just leave some pizza by your door."

Footsteps thump over the hardwood, then the door swings wide and Bridge stands before me. She's glowing, curly red hair long enough to barely cover her naked boobs. Nothing at all covering the rest of her.

I smile at her. "Feeling better?"

"Starting to," she says, smirking at me.

I peek into the room and see Jack lying on the bed with his blanket down to his waist and his arms crossed behind his head. He's staring up at the ceiling, wearing the most satisfied smile I've ever seen on him.

"Coming out, or staying in?" I ask.

Bridge spins around. "Get up, Jack. There's pizza."

Jack's head rolls indolently toward us. "What's pizza?"

"Lord, Bridge. What did you do to him?"

She throws her hair back from her shoulders in a wild fling, exposing everything. "What do you think?"

When Charlie and Fritz walk through the shed door, she stops them dead in their tracks.

"Gentlemen," says Bridge, nodding in their direction.

"Close the door, Bridge," mutters Jack, his discretion returning. "You're naked."

She grabs a robe from the door and throws it over her shoulders. "Close it yourself, honey. If you can walk, that is."

Charlie, Fritz, and I watch silently as Bridge swings her hips down the hallway and into the kitchen. Then we turn back to Jack. His eyes are back on the ceiling, the smile planted firmly back on his lips.

"I really don't think he *can* walk," jokes Fritz.

"Bridge," I shout over my shoulder. "Take the pizza out to cool, will ya?"

She shouts her affirmation and I slink around Jack, apologizing as I go, to set up the back bedroom. He doesn't seem to care.

THE PIZZA'S PASSABLE, the wine flowing, the wind howling, and the laughter booming. We celebrate like soldiers before a battle, all of us knowing, even though nobody says a single word about it, that this reprieve is brief. That tomorrow the realities of our situation will weigh us down as heavily as the snow building up against the windows. We know, but tonight, we don't care.

"Do you remember Bridge and Jack's wedding day?" Mom asks with just the tiniest slur thanks to three glasses of cabernet. We're all crowded in the front room, the fire blazing. "Remember Wally caught the garter and tried to put it on me with his teeth."

"I remember," I say. "He had his whole head under your dress, but he couldn't breathe. So he flung your dress up nearly over your head."

Wally is roaring. "I was so embarrassed. And also very, very drunk. And half-mad with desire for your momma."

"Ew," Bridge and I exclaim simultaneously.

"Wait, that was the night Fritz met Danny, wasn't it?" Bridge asks, then takes a great big swig from her glass.

"Oh yes," Fritz replies. "Danny was tending bar that night. Hooking up with a bartender at a wedding…I am a walking, talking cliché." He rubs a hand over his bald head.

"No, Fritz. You and Danny were everything. It's a real shame how that one ended," I say. Evidently Danny was everything to a few other people as well.

"No harm, no foul. We had fun." Fritz smiles like he has the devil in his mouth. "A lot of fun."

"Remember when Nona hit on Fritz." Jack chimes in, eyes still heavy-lidded, cheeks flushed.

My eyes slide to where Fritz is sitting on the couch.

"What? You did? When was this? Where was I?" asks Charlie, one palm pressed against his chest like he's shocked.

"It was before you joined the band. Oh man, I was so in love with you, Fritzy," I admit, drunkenly. "What can I say? I have a thing for beautiful, older men. Not to worry, Charlie. He shot me down. Hard."

"I should hope so," Charlie says.

"I was then, and remain to this day, a perfect gentleman." Fritz makes a tiny bow, all chivalry and charm.

"You broke my young little heart that night, Fritz. But I forgive you."

"Sorry, sugar. But gotta keep it professional. Isn't that right, Charlie?" Fritz winks, the implication that Charlie taking me to his bed was not at all "professional" as clear as day.

Charlie reels back like he's been punched. "Ouch. Sick burn, Fritz."

We notice when Wally stands and pulls Mom up from the couch, but none of us comments anything other than a simple goodnight as he leads her toward the back room.

"Will you sing something for us, Nona?" Jack has pulled Bridge into his lap on the rocking chair, peppering her neck with little kisses.

"I'd love to. But it's been, well, you know how long it's been. So no heckling, okay?"

"Can I accompany?" Charlie asks.

"Please." I'm smiling at him like he's the sun and I'm the moon and we're spending one of those few, lucky hours in the afternoon in which we both get to share the sky.

"Any requests?" I ask. "And if anyone says "Flashlight Dancing", you're going to bed tonight with a black eye."

"'Fireflies'." Fritz's voice rumbles low and soft.

"Fireflies", of course. If that's not the perfect song for this night...I nod, clear my throat, and wait for Charlie to strum the opening chords.

> The sun hangs low, orange fading west on a warm
> summer night
> And the crickets call through the swaying grass in
> the dying light

The rocking chair my Granddaddy left me stirs in
    the breeze
As if he still sits waiting for me, tapping on his
    knees

But I'm waiting and wishing as I watch the skies
    and the sun pulls down the moon
In the corner of my eye there's a light flashing
    bright and it's hovering, over you

Fireflies
Burning through the night
Only have one chance of ever getting this right
Fireflies
Baby take my hand
When the morning comes, don't think we'll ever
    be the same again

I wrote "Fireflies" the night I met Charlie. I laid eyes on him and the song came to me, fully written. I imagined bringing him up here, to this cabin, even then. Sometimes you get what you want. The road may take crooked, messy, and painful turns you never in your wildest dreams expected, but if you just keep driving, sometimes you get lucky.

My voice comes out stronger as I reach the last chorus

Fireflies
Burning through the night
Only had one chance and Baby, did we get it right
Fireflies
Your ring on my hand
When the morning comes, I know we'll never be
    the same again

Everyone hoots and hollers, clapping like we're at a bar. I stand up and take a bow.

Next I sing "My Heart is a Drum" then "Rain Over the Missions" before closing the night out on "Lilies". We're on our feet, and Charlie's forehead is beaded with sweat by the time we're finished from playing hard and singing backup for me, just like when we were on tour. It feels so good, so amazingly good. But it's getting late and there are other things I'd like to do that feel good too.

"When does this magical amnesty end?" Fritz asks, glancing nervously at the clock on the wall.

"Sunrise." Charlie sets down his guitar and flops onto the couch. "I wish it could be longer, but I, we, can't risk it."

"Well, I'm not wasting another minute," says Bridge. She stands up, kisses my cheek, then pulls Jack by the collar of his shirt back to their room. Not that he needed any convincing.

I look at Charlie and raise a brow, feeling like we've spent enough time with our clothes on. He winks at me, catching my drift.

"I'm going to go freshen up." I walk to Fritz who's sitting next to Charlie, lean over, and say, "Night, Fritz," before I plant a fat, wet, sloppy kiss on his cheek.

He grabs my butt just like he did that night he told me to find a boy my own age, only this time he squeezes with both hands, making me squeal. "Night, Nona."

I lean back again and I'm suddenly, deeply distraught. I don't want to leave him out here, alone. Fritz and I have essentially coupled up these last five years, nearly inseparable and intimate in all possible definitions of the word. Except for one.

He must sense my hesitation. "I'm good, Nona. You and Charlie go have some fun." His lips tilt into a crooked, sneaky smile. "Shame I can't sneak under the door this time, though."

My brows knit together while he removes his hands, which have slid down to rest gently behind my knees. I'm having feelings about Fritz sleeping alone on this couch tonight that are really fucking hard to process.

Charlie's hand rests on my shoulder. "Why don't you go freshen up, sweetheart. I'll be right there."

I stumble into the bathroom, drunk, lightheaded. My world spinning. I brush my teeth, my hair, pinch my cheeks, then slap them a couple times to try and center my swirling head. When I leave the bathroom, Charlie's waiting for me in the hall, grinning.

"I have a present for you."

"Fantastic," I respond enthusiastically, sidling up to him so my chest presses against his.

"Close your eyes."

I do, laughing as he takes my hand and yanks me into the bedroom.

I'm still holding my eyes shut as the door snicks closed behind me. Charlie's breath is warm on my neck. "You can open them now."

I used to know a respectable amount of words, but every single one of them leaves me at what I see. At what it means. I turn back to face Charlie, a question swimming in the fresh tears in my eyes. He nods, small but meaningful. I face forward again.

Before me on the bed, in all his red-robbed splendor, sits Fritz.

"Fritz," I say, the word a rush of air.

I expect his wry smile, his low laughter. But something's wrong. He keeps his eyes down. "I can go," his smooth voice trembles a little. "Or just watch, or join. Whatever you want, Nona."

Like an anchor yanking me back and holding me in place, I'm halted mid-breath by the sheer magnitude of this moment. It's been so long for all of us up here. So many years without human touch, without passion, without sex. And we have just this one night, maybe more, who knows. But this could be it for Fritz, for my family, for me even. There are no guarantees Charlie will be able to break the curse. There's no guarantee the witch won't kill us all tomorrow. This could be our last chance, our only chance to be human, to use these bodies. Well, I sure as hell won't squander it.

"I can leave and come back, too." Fritz still hasn't raised his eyes from the floor. "I just don't want to be alone. I don't want to wake up alone, no longer human."

He needs to stop talking. I walk over to him, raise his chin with my fingers, and stoop to meet his eyes. Then I kiss him. His lips might even be softer than Charlie's. "Fritz, please join us," I say against his mouth. Slowly, I feel him smile against my lips.

I won't say much about this night, about what takes place between me and Charlie and Fritz. Only that it is the single most erotic and at the same time achingly sweet night of my life. Having two men I love, the only two men I've ever loved, worship me for hours, covering every inch of my body with their hands and lips and tongues. And then being able to worship them…At one point I think we break the bed, but it's just a slat shifting under the weight of our writhing, thrusting, pulsating bodies as we grasp and cling to this life that we all know is so fleeting. So fragile.

But even the most perfect nights are eventually devoured by the sun. And in the cold, gray morning, I wake up with a ferret between my boobs, and Charlie nowhere to be found.

PART III

FIREFLIES

CHAPTER TWENTY

Everything is different today. The cabin is hollow, sounds muted, even the air feels flat and stale like I'm eight hours into an airplane ride. The rowdy, unbridled joy of last night has collapsed like a flimsy house of cards into a scattered mess of headaches, despair, and complete and total fucking confusion.

He's gone. I knew it the second I woke up. Fritz was despondent on my chest, probably knowing it too. More likely, though, he was just sad he was a ferret again, or simply suffering through the decision to keep napping or start attacking one of my nipples. He seems all right now. As all right as any of us are. I'm flip about Charlie's disappearance because if I actually put into words how broken my heart is, it might stop beating altogether. And I don't have time for that.

Breakfast is a joke, dry cereal in bowls and I chuck a raw potato into Wally's open mouth. I refuse to get dressed today. There is too much snow to go anywhere or do anything anyway like, oh, I don't know, find my stupid boyfriend. I should know, since I already tried.

After I woke up, I ran outside in my slippers and jammies but there was nothing out there but white. No footprints, no sled tracks, no sign that anyone had come or gone since the snow started falling. So either he flew, teleported, or he's still in the cabin somewhere hiding or wearing an invisibility cloak, you know, as a goof.

Or she got him.

"I'm sure it wasn't her," says Mom, 100% hen again and trying futilely to console her near comatose daughter who's too overtaken by hopelessness to do anything other than sit in her rocking chair and mouth breathe.

"You don't know that," I say, petting Fritz in absent strokes in my lap. "Maybe he just left. Maybe this was all another one of Rebecca's tricks. The worst trick yet."

"You know that's not true," Bridge says, sitting on her haunches at my feet. "He loves you, Nona. He loves you more than anything. He is not working with Rebecca."

I know she's right, but I'm in a spiral of pain, a whirlwind of agony, a tornado of melodrama. And I'm not alone.

"You don't think it was because of me, do you?" asks Fritz. He looks ashamed. "Did I ruin everything?"

I pick him up, holding his drooping body in front of my face. "No, Fritz. No. Not a chance. Last night was beautiful. It was magic," I wince and clarify, "The good kind. Don't even think for one second that we didn't all love every moment of it, okay. I don't know why Charlie left, but it wasn't you. It couldn't be."

It couldn't be, be...B.

My own words jog my memory and I shoot to my feet, still holding Fritz in my hand. "That's it! Plan B!" I cry, hoisting Fritz onto my shoulder.

It only takes me ten minutes of searching the cabin to find Charlie's note, taped to the bathroom mirror. I hadn't bothered doing anything besides pee-cry in the bathroom this morning, so I'd missed it. I open the note carefully with shaking fingers. Fritz, still dangling over my shoulder, and I both read.

. . .

NONA,

I hate to leave you, but I can't stay and watch everyone become animals again. I have to do more, try harder. So I'm going back home, back to Rebecca, to Julianne, and to my dad. I have no idea if my plan will work or not, but I have to try to get them up to the cabin. I left enough magic with the bear to keep you young as long as he's nearby. Keep your eyes open because I'll be sending you a gift. You'll know it when you see it, and I'm trusting you to decide what to do with it. I love you, sweetheart. I love you all so much. And I will see you all again soon, human, young, and free.

Love, Charlie

"WHAT IS IT?" asks Jack as Fritz and I return from the bathroom, Charlie's note trembling in my hand, tears streaming down my cheeks. Jack is sitting in the windowsill where, up until this moment, he's been staring distantly out the window, ignoring all of us. Or so I thought.

"It's Plan B," I say.

"The morning-after pill?" Bridge asks and I snort through my tears.

"No, Bridget, not the morning-after pill. Charlie said he had a Plan B when we didn't find the ruby."

"Let me get this straight, Charlie's Plan B involved sneaking out of the cabin in the middle of the night and leaving my step-daughter terrified and heartbroken?" Wally stomps a hoof hard enough to crack the hardwood. "If that's true, then I think Plan B sucks!"

"Yes. That's exactly it! Plan B does suck!" I say, setting Fritz on the floor. "Charlie said so himself."

"Charlie said his plan would suck?" Mom asks, dubious.

"Well, not in so many words, but he said it would be hard. And it was in his tone. It was the tonal equivalent of 'Plan B will suck.'"

Mom shakes her beak. "But why didn't he say goodbye?"

"It's okay, Mom. Here." I set Charlie's note down on the floor so everyone can read it.

"He's going back home?" Wally asks, his snout flexing. "That doesn't sound like a good idea."

"This is nuts!" interjects Bridge, finished reading. "Why the hell would he bring his parents up here? Isn't Julianne, like, the worst?"

I hold up my hands. "Preaching to the choir, Bridge. But Rebecca knows something's going on up here. Maybe he's just trying to control the narrative because he has an idea of how to get her to break the curse. I don't know." I rub my temples where a headache is starting to press in.

"So what are we supposed to do?" Bridge asks, her tail swishing irritably behind her. "Sit around and wait? For what? For Charlie, for whatever 'gift' he'll be sending us?"

Her tone rankles. "No, screw that!" I say. "Charlie's out there, Plan B-ing, and we're going to help him."

"And how would we do that?" asks Jack.

I flop onto the couch, groaning. "I have absolutely no clue." I bolt upright. "But maybe someone else does, or did." I whip my head toward Mom. "What if we weren't looking for the right things last time we visited?"

"No, Nona. The snow is way too deep now. You can't go." Mom knows. She knows what I have in mind.

"The snow is always deep, Mom. It's always deep out here. Deep and cold and hard. And it will stay deep and cold and hard for the rest of our lives if we don't *do* something. We've stopped fighting Rebecca, stopped fighting this curse. And it makes sense; I get it. We accepted this life and tried to live it as best we could. But if last night showed us anything, it's that we are not satisfied with this life. We deserve more. We *need* more. So it's time to put our big girl, and pig, and hen, and rabbit, fox, and ferret, pants on and start fighting for our lives again. And there's one place where I might find some answers, something we can use to help Charlie, or to hurt Rebecca. And that place is only a few short miles from here. So yes, I can go. I absolutely can."

There is silence, a long and uncomfortable silence, and then a thump, and another, and another, resounding through the floorboards. It's Wally. He must be trying to do a slow clap sort of thing. He's thumping a foot on the ground and smiling at me with this proud, teary-eyed, pig grin. Then Bridge joins in, jumping up in place and pounding her feet into the ground. Nobody else can really produce much noise but Mom's flapping her wings in time and Fritz and Jack are up on their hind legs, clapping their little paws together. It's ridiculous. And touching.

Mom flies across the room, landing in my open arms. "All right, Nona. But if you're going out, then we're all coming with you."

"We are?" Jack doesn't sound enthused. I don't blame him. They could all easily die out there. It's freezing, the snow is indeed very deep, and the journey will probably take all day, possibly even longer with how slow the going's gonna be.

"Now, that really is a bad idea," I say, setting Mom down and turning to head back to my room.

Mom relents easily. Turns out, nobody really wants to trudge through feet of snow and possibly die for a trip I can fairly easily make on my own. Not even Wally.

"Walk fast, but don't try to make it back tonight if you're not going to make it in the daylight. We'll be fine here for one night." Mom clucks diligently around me as I layer my snowsuit over long johns.

"The fire will die," I say, pulling on my boots. "I'll make it back tonight, I promise."

"The fire will die, but we'll be fine. We'll cuddle up. We'll survive."

I pick her up again and hug her, then I kiss her beak. "I'll be back in time."

"Stubborn girl," she says, following me out of my room.

I grab my gun, then my snowshoes, and then I address the group. "I've got enough food and water set out for you to get you through tomorrow night. As long as you don't pig out." I'm staring directly at Wally. He drops a guilty snout to the ground. "But I'll be back tonight."

"Be safe out there, Nona," Fritz says, and I can see it in the deep set of his eyes, how much he wants to be human right now so he could help.

I swoop down to scratch him under his chin. "Just a walk in the woods, nothing to it." But somehow it doesn't feel like just a walk in the woods. It feels final, irrevocable. Like leaping off a cliff overlooking a world covered in fog. Could be a better world, could be a fall that breaks us all. Either way, there's no going back.

THE SUN REFLECTING off the snow is squint inducing without being even a little bit warm. But it's a beautiful day. Blinding white mountains bank both sides of the valley and the sky between them is impossibly blue, scoured clean by the storm. The snow is up to my knees, but at least it's dry. This type of snow is easier to walk through, it parts for you, clinging to your clothes like tiny, sparkling diamonds that never melt. I'm hauling the sled up behind me in case I find anything I need to cart back home, so even with the powdery snow, I'm not making great time.

When I reach Sam and Marge's place, the scent of whatever meat they're roasting is so phenomenal that I nearly hike up to their door, figuring I'll just tell them I'm another one of Nona's long-lost grandkids. Then I remember my face is a touch conspicuous. Not that I think either Sam or Marge would have a clue who Nona May Taylor is, but you never know. I've learned not to judge any fan by their cover.

I reluctantly round their property and charge onwards with frozen toes but a stiffness in my spine. When Charlie and I came up here, we were searching for the Rose, only the Rose. But there were other things in Lulu's house, spell books, grimoires, herbs, odd little animal bones in tiny jars. Charlie didn't want to take any of those things back with us. He didn't think they'd help, and he didn't want to pilfer Aunt Lulu's stuff. Because he is a good boy. Well, I am not a good boy.

A twig snap echoes somewhere in the woods to my right. I swivel, raising my shotgun to my shoulder and squinting to see through the sun-bright trees. There's movement, something huge prowling toward me through the snow. Breath freezes in my lungs. I know Charlie said not to be scared, that the bear wouldn't harm us, but he's massive. The urge to run is primal.

Charlie's bear settles himself lazily onto his hind end in the snow about ten yards from me. My gun is still trained on him and he stares down the barrel, then shakes his head side to side at me, grunting irritably.

I lower the gun, my hands shaking. The bear just sits there for a while, staring at me. He's a big bastard. I bet he'd be ten feet tall if he stood at his full height. And his fur seems thicker and shinier than a normal bear's, looks softer too. His nose is long and wet and his eyes are big, brown, and—strange thing to see on a bear—amused. Like I'm funny to him.

He gets to all fours and my hands instinctively jerk my gun up again, but then he crawls to a nearby tree, sniffs at it, spins around, and starts rubbing his butt up against it. He stands up against the tree and scratches his back, unabashedly squirming and groaning in what sounds like ecstasy. I snort and he stops, cracking his eyes open to side-eye me under his lids.

I grimace. "Sorry, didn't mean to interrupt you."

The ground shudders a little as he falls back to all fours. Then we resume our staring match. We could do this all day, I suppose. But there's no time.

I clear my throat. "All right, so I'm just gonna keep walking because my feet are starting to go numb. So, um, nice to meet you...bear." I frown at how stupid I sound but what the hell does one say to their magical totem bear?

He grunts again as I start walking away, but he follows me, staying in the trees and a fair distance behind. At first it's unnerving, being followed by a bear, but after a while it's almost nice to have his footfalls accompany mine, crunching steadily in the snow.

The bear and I reach the hill above Lulu's cabin around mid-day. The cabin seems painted upon the snow, frozen in time. Its chunky shingles poke out from under the snow drifts blanketing its roof. There's even a tiny glow coming from the windows, like there's a fire burning inside somewhere. Aunt Lulu died years ago but this place still looks lived in. Magic. It has to be.

I'm giving myself one hour before I have to head back to my cabin, and even then, it'll probably be dark when I get home. No help for it now. I park the sled alongside the cabin before I shovel fresh snow away from the door and push my way in.

What I see this time yanks a gasp from me. There is a fire burning, the room glowing a bright orange. Lamps are lit, and it smells like cookies are baking in the kitchen. I tiptoe into the kitchen and even though it smells amazing, the oven is off and empty, the stovetop bare, the fridge unplugged. Magic for sure.

"All right, Aunt Lulu," I say, even though I don't believe in ghosts, but I used to not believe in witches or magical bears either so... "I'm back. Charlie went home and I need your help.

We all need your help." It's a strange feeling, talking to an empty cabin, silly but somehow also rude in a way. It's a very one-sided conversation. "If there's something, anything here you think might help my family or Charlie, maybe you can let me know by, I don't know, turning a light on and off or," I sniff, grinning, "making a cookie appear out of thin air." I'm hungry. It's worth a shot.

As expected, I receive no response from the beneficent ghost of Aunt Lulu.

"Fair enough. I'm going to go through your things now. I hope that's okay." No response again. I shrug. All right, time to get to work. I start in the kitchen since this is where her jars of weird stuff reside. I rifle through the drawers and cupboards, searching for…what? I wish I knew. I brush my fingers over the dozens of glass jars lined up along the kitchen counter. Some are full of what look like floating fish eyeballs, others of delicate, wing-shaped bones. I'm hoping one of the jars will speak to me or something. None do.

Next, I move to the living room. The fire in the stove is blissfully warm, but it only glows in my peripheral vision. When I look at it head on, it's simply an old, empty stove. "Neat trick, Lulu."

Lulu's living room is pure delight. Bright lime-green walls, blue shag carpet, and those canary yellow couches. It's like a spring flower bursting up through the snow. A spring flower that bloomed in the 1960s. I pull up the couch cushions, lift lamps to search for any tiny treasure hiding beneath them, and slide books in and out of bookshelves, leafing through each one as I go. Several of the books seem witchy and promising, so I take a few and pile them beside the door.

Lulu's bedroom is still indescribably charming, but it's even warmer today, brighter, the red of the walls more vibrant. I shuffle through her drawers and find several bundles of aromatic herbs tucked next to her unmentionables. They smell new, fresh, so I take them and slide them gingerly into my pocket.

I push the clothes aside in her closet, tapping on the back wall, listening for a hollow thump that might hint at a secret door. Nothing. I do take a few of her robes because they're lovely, silky and ornate, and I snatch a fantastic pair of silver velvet slippers with intricate scrollwork embroidered over the toes.

I search under the bed, in her nightstand drawers, under her covers. Then I stand and turn around in circles, looking for something, anything. There's just nothing, and my time is running out. I collapse onto Lulu's bed and stare despondently at her ceiling. She's painted the same black lace detailing that borders her walls around the small chandelier over her bed. It's beautiful and as I trace the delicate lines with a finger pointed to the ceiling, it seems to dance and swirl as I will it. Another neat trick.

Tricks. What if that's all Aunt Lulu's magic was? Harmless, delightful tricks that won't stand a chance against the dark witchcraft wielded by Rebecca and Julianne. What if coming up here was a ridiculous idea? Maybe there's nothing at all I can do to help Charlie.

I roll onto my side to curl up like a sad little snail, but in this position I notice the picture hanging from Lulu's wall, the black and white one of those kids standing in front of a pond. I sit up slowly, squinting at the picture, and it's like the scene comes to life while I watch. Breeze rustles furred tips of grass gone to seed, clouds float slowly across the sky, and the children's arms begin to swing, their pinkies entwined.

"Is this important? The picture?" I whisper to the empty room, then scream as a chocolate chip cookie appears out of nowhere in my hand. "Holy shit, Lulu! Best trick yet." I stare numb and disbelieving at the still warm and super gooey cookie I'm holding. "I'm eating this."

What is it about the picture, I wonder as I eat my cookie from the great beyond. I walk to the frame and examine the picture, trying to make out any small detail, any secret meaning hidden in the grass, the water. The little girl has long, wavy hair that's lighter than the boy's wild, curly mop. She's wearing a faded pair of denim overalls and he's in jeans and a checkered shirt, sleeves rolled up to his elbows. It's a sweet picture, but I don't see anything out of the ordinary about it, aside from the magical movements. No faces hidden in the trees. No messages concealed in the shifting blades of grass. Perhaps it's not the picture at all, but the space it takes up on the wall.

Bingo! Another cookie appears in my other hand. This is hands down the best magical communication system ever. "Thank you," I say with a wink up to the ceiling.

I put this cookie in my other pocket to save for the hike home. Then I take the picture from the wall and lay it on the bed. Behind the picture, there's a hidey-hole cut into the wall. It's filled with letters, dozens of letters, all tied together with brown kitchen twine. I pull them out and sit cross-legged on Lulu's bed, untying the knot and spreading the letters out before me. An envelope trembles in my hands as I read who it's from. I pick up another, and another. They're all from the same person, James Brown, Charlie's father.

"James Brown and Charlie Brown," I scoff. "Seriously?"

These letters go back years, each one written carefully in James' slanted cursive. They're letters about Charlie, telling Lulu about Charlie's life. One tells about Charlie coming in third place at the city spelling bee, another about Charlie taking up guitar, another still about Charlie graduating from high school. And Lulu kept them all, hiding them in her wall. Why? Who was she hiding them from?

I read and read until my fingers are so dry I have to lick them to open the next letter. Charlie excelling at math, Charlie performing for his school's talent show, Charlie moving into the city, joining a band, meeting a girl. Me. Some of these letters are about me. I read one of them out loud.

HEY THERE LULU,

Sorry it's been so long since my last letter. She's got me on a short leash these days, but I was able to sneak a moment out to the garage to fix a toaster that won't pop. We're doing okay without Charlie, even though Rebecca's fit to be tied. He seems really happy out on the road with Nona. I think he might even love that girl.

I'm drinking your tea every day and it's working so far, I think. Thanks for keeping me supplied. But honestly, I don't know which is worse, blindly loving a woman I didn't know a thing about because she had me under a spell, or having to live every single day pretending to love the woman who killed our Janey because your tea keeps my mind clear. I don't regret it though, not even a little. Not if it means we can avenge her, avenge Janey.

Charlie doesn't suspect a thing, and that breaks my heart too. But what can I do? He's safe from Julianne as long as I play along.

Charlie misses you. He talks about you all the time. I miss you too, Lulu. I know you're still looking for a way to get us out of this mess. I just wish there was more I could do from here. Stay strong for us, Lulu.

~JM

JAMES' words run through my veins like ice water. I can't believe what I'm reading. Julianne was working a spell on Charlie's dad.

Julianne killed Charlie's mom, Janey. And Charlie's dad knows. Or at least he did while Lulu was supplying him with whatever tea she'd been making for him. But Lulu has been dead for years. Who knows what Charlie's dad thinks now?

Oh, Charlie. Your family didn't disown you, they didn't hate you, they just didn't have the magic to free you. But they were trying. Lulu was trying. Your dad was trying. I wonder if Lulu got too close. I wonder if that vibrant, spirited woman and her amazing horse didn't die of natural causes after all.

Shit. My heart plummets as another cookie pops into my hand. It also goes into my pocket.

"All right Lulu. If you can hear me, if you can hear me at all, you gotta tell me what to do. Those witches have messed with this family, both our families, long enough. What were you working on and how do I finish it?"

I sit, I wait, and then I notice certain words in the few letters still spread out before me growing darker.

"Julianne only wants one thing." It's Lulu. She's talking to me through the letters.

"What is it?" I ask. "Tell me, please."

Slowly, one word at a time, Lulu uses the letters written in Charlie's father's hand to tell me everything. Julianne's family has been searching for one thing for hundreds of years. The one thing Julianne's father was supposed to bring to her, traveling with it west on train tracks forged from her family's magic. The one thing that Charlie's great-grandfather stole from her. The Rose.

Somehow, my family, Fritz, and I have landed smack dab in the middle of a centuries-old, vindictive, witchy family feud. After Lulu fills me in on the plan she'd started hatching while she lived, and continues working on even now from the grave, I blink, shake my head, and finally find the presence of mind to mutter, "Fuck me."

CHAPTER TWENTY-ONE

When I step out of Lulu's cabin, much, much later than I had wanted to be leaving, I shut the door behind me, then turn around and get a face full of bear fur. Screaming like a child finding a tick on their belly, I run back into the cabin and slam the door. It's one thing to have a bear following me at some distance, it's quite another to feel its breath hot on my face. Standing on my tiptoes, I peer out the small window in Lulu's door. The bear is just standing there, staring back at me, and then it yawns. Be brave, Nona.

Slowly, hesitantly, I pull the door open again and stand stock still, waiting for the bear to make the first move. My breath retreats into my lungs as the bear reaches a paw out toward me. Just as it's about to make contact with my shoulder, I squeal, my eyes slamming shut. I wait for it, tense as a fencepost, but the bear never touches me. When my eyes crack open again, I see the bear shuddering, its shoulders hunched. It's laughing at me, thick roping drool slinking from its teeth. I can never keep a straight face when someone, or something, else is laughing, so I giggle, nervous and hysterical.

Stretching out a shaky hand, I take a wobbly step toward the bear. It sniffs my palm, loud and wet, then it leans forward, letting me scratch under its chin, then behind an ear. I squeal again as it nose-dives into my pocket, emerging with one of Lulu's cookies clutched between its teeth.

"You like those, huh?" I ask, scratching the top of the bear's head. He's so soft, like a warm, giant teddy. "Well, bear, you coming back with me or what?"

He grunts and nods, licking cookie crumbs from his mouth.

"All right, mind pulling the sled?"

He takes the sled rope between his teeth and we walk in a pleasant silence, the bear a solid, comforting, and irresistibly pettable hiking companion. But just as we approach Sam and Marge's place, the bear drops the rope and darts off in a surprisingly graceful gallop into the trees.

"Hey? Where are you going?"

He keeps running, ignoring me completely, but maybe he has business to attend to. I mean, what do I know of magical totem bears? They probably need to do all the same types of things every other bear does in the woods.

I grab the sled rope and keep walking, figuring he'll catch up and knowing I'm already way too late, it's way too dark, and my family is probably way too cold.

Dragging the weighed-down sled behind me slows me down even more and with every step my feet turn numb and my fingers ache. Especially when about a mile from the cabin, the weather takes a sudden, terrible turn. It's not snow, not ice, but wind. Howling, frozen, complete asshole, bullshit wind. It turns the few feet of snow I've been mired in all day into massive drifts that become impossible to navigate in the darkness. I'd waited for the forecast before I'd left and there'd been no mention of wind—certainly not this gale force disaster. My steps are slowing, my breath harsh and burning my throat. It's grown so cold that my nostrils freeze shut and I have to narrow my eyes and stare out of tiny slits because keeping them open is excruciating.

I can't feel my feet, my hands are useless blocks, and my lungs feel like I'm inhaling shards of ice. But I only become truly terrified when I start to feel warm, then so hot I become possessed by an overwhelming urge to take off my coat. I know this symptom. I know it well. This is hypothermia. This is how people die, alone in the snow. It happens every year up here. Some dumb schmuck thinks they're above the weather, stronger than the cold, and they're found, naked and blue. And now that dumb schmuck is me. But none of this makes any sense. There wasn't supposed to be a storm tonight. This isn't fair, I think uselessly.

I stumble and fall to my knees, the snow folding in over me until I'm buried up to my waist. That's when I see her. I was right; it's not fair at all. It's witchcraft.

"I should have known." I'm laughing now, the maniacal, jerky cackling of a crazy frozen person.

"I'd tell you to get a grip, but what would be the point?" Rebecca states coolly, floating down from her perch on a tree branch to hover six feet above the snow. She's in four-inch stiletto boots, black leather pants, and a fur coat that looks a lot like rabbit. *Subtle.*

"Hello, Rebecca," I manage through chattering teeth. "What brings you and your ridiculously inappropriate shoes to my neck of the woods?"

I'm assaulted by an icy blast.

"Don't test me, Nona. You know why I'm here." She's healthier, not as thin, her hair is glossy again. And she's vibrating with rage, and something else, smugness. She's smug.

"Charlie?" I offer, innocent as apple pie, hiding a growing concern that I might be dying. Like right now, right this instant.

"I thought it was strange that no matter how much wheatgrass I drank, I still felt terrible. And then when I saw you, looking," she swallows, a hateful little gulp, "younger, I knew something was up."

"Can't pull one over on you, Becks." I've never felt so frozen yet so blazing hot at the same time and the only thing keeping me from curling into a ball in the snow and surrendering to the blissful promise of escape from this agony is a desire to wipe that smug, self-satisfied expression off Rebecca's face.

She floats toward me until she's only a few inches away. While her windstorm turns my hair to icy shards and piles snow up to my shoulders, it doesn't touch Rebecca. "Do you know where Charlie is now?" she asks, voice like silk snagging over thorns.

I shake my head, too brutalized by her storm to answer, or really even care.

"He's warming my bed," she sneers.

"That sounds really nice, if you're into incest. Aren't you two siblings? Last I checked that was super gross."

Something moves through the snow behind Rebecca, and I have to pin my frozen lips between my teeth not to smile when the realization hits me like a lightning strike. *This* is Charlie's gift. Rebecca, she's the gift.

A fresh blast of cold strikes me sideways and I'm pushed face down into the snow. Groaning, I muster all the strength I've got left to push myself back up and ask, "If Charlie's in your bed, what are you doing here?"

She doesn't look angry, or sinister, or even bored. She looks, surprisingly...sad. "Tying up loose ends." Then she twirls her fingers and the snow starts spiraling around me like a tornado turned on its head.

But I won't go down so easily. "Rebecca," I shout through the snow and wind, sitting up onto my knees and shoving my hands into my pockets, "do you like cookies?"

The expression she sets on me is equal parts pity and confusion. She clicks her tongue. "It's not uncommon for people to lose their minds before they die of hypothermia—"

"Do you like cookies?" I ask again, cutting her off as I hold Aunt Lulu's cookie up like it's a shield against her powers. It's not a shield, it's just a cookie.

She stares at me, perplexed, like I've gone completely mental. But then I shout, "You know who does like cookies? Bears!"

A roar tears through the storm, followed by a prowling growl that shakes the trees. Rebecca's death-storm falters as her eyes fly open, round as the moon and black as night. Above her head, as the clouds part, as her magic peters out, stars shimmer in a clear night sky.

"What is that?" she hisses, squinting into the trees and backing away from me, clutching at her throat like she's having trouble breathing.

"That," I spit, struggling to my feet, "is 800 pounds of justice!"

She retreats from the step I take toward her, stumbling back into the waiting, open arms of Charlie's furious, snarling bear.

CHAPTER TWENTY-TWO

I HALF EXPECT Rebecca to vanish before the bear can grab her, but the second his paws touch her arms, she goes limp.

I stand on numb feet and walk to the bear. "Good boy," I say, running my fingers over the soft fur between his eyes. "Thank you."

The bear munches on its cookie while I tie a comatose Rebecca to my sled. I'm not sure what the bear did to her, but she's out like a light and snoring like a Wally after too much wine.

"What should we do with her?"

The bear offers no suggestions as it sits in the snow, licking crumbs from its dinner-plate sized paws.

"Can you make her sleep whenever you want to? Can you keep us safe from her?"

The bear licks each side of its snout, then stares at me for a moment before nodding its huge, fuzzy head up and down.

"Thank you, Charlie," I whisper skyward, then I say to the bear, "Would you mind?" I angle my head toward the sled.

The bear grumbles, picks up the rope in its mouth again, and begins towing the sled back toward the cabin. I hobble behind, still frozen but also warmed by a glorious, fiery satisfaction now pumping through my veins.

Everyone is still awake when I lead the bear into the shed.

"What the shit!" squeals Jack, leaping into the air before bolting into a corner and shuddering, shedding fluff balls of fur into the air.

"Which one?" I ask, gasping for air. "Rebecca, or the bear?"

"What the holy hell happened out there?" Wally stands between Rebecca, the bear, and everyone else like a wall made of pork.

"Well, Aunt Lulu was totally a witch and makes a mean chocolate chip cookie—Charlie's bear is a big fan. This one is Charlie's gift," I say, kicking the sled hard enough to rock Rebecca's head side to side. "She tried to kill me with a windstorm. This bear saved my life and can evidently render Rebecca as harmless as a field mouse. All-in-all it's been an eventful day." I glance around the room and my stomach suddenly feels hollow, my head spinning. I think I overdid it.

"Christ on a cracker, Nona!" Mom's voice is the last thing I hear before the room spins and I hit the dirt.

⁓

"Nona, wake up sweetie."

Someone nudges my shoulder while someone else pecks at my cheek.

"Whut, whur am I?" My head is the size of a planet and just as heavy as I try to lift it up from the cushion. "How'd I get on the couch?"

Mom is standing on my chest. "That is a very helpful bear. It carried you to the couch and started the fire. Can we keep it?"

"Sure," I slur, cracking my eyes open a slit. "It's made of magic and eats cookies."

"Can you sit up?" Wally's nudging my shoulder, sliding his snout under my arm and pushing me up.

"Yep. Yep, I'm good." I lean against Wally's head as he helps me up, but I'm not good. I'm dizzy and exhausted. I'm also starving.

The bear, as if reading my mind, thuds into the kitchen, makes an ungodly raucous opening and closing the cupboards, then the fridge, before finally bringing me back some bread.

"Thank you, bear." I sink my teeth into the bread, moaning at its crusty goodness.

"Does it have a name?" asks Bridge, sniffing at the bear from a healthy distance, tail puffed up.

I mumble through a full mouth, "Don't know, hasn't told me if it does. But I haven't asked either. That was rude of me."

The bear, who takes up an absurd amount of space in this tiny cabin, sits on its rump in the middle of the front room, licks breadcrumbs from its paws, then says in a burly growl, "Larry."

Silence envelopes us as we all stare at each other, eyes flinging wildly across the room, then Bridge snorts.

"Larry?" I ask with a laugh, finding it an odd name for such an intimidating bear.

The bear shrugs its massive shoulders and returns to licking its paws.

"I don't think there's enough room in this cabin for both Wally and the bea...Larry," corrects Fritz from the safety of the kitchen counter.

I furrow my brow at Fritz. "He's a bear, Fritz. He's not going to want to stay inside. Right, Larry?"

Larry nods and murmurs his agreement, which also sounds like a growl, because he's a bear.

"Larry," Mom asks, addressing the apex predator as if he were an old friend stopping by for tea, "would you like something to eat?"

Larry shakes his head and rumbles, "No. Larry will go now. But witch won't hurt you. Larry won't be far."

"Wait," I blurt, sitting up straighter. "What do we do with her?" I angle my head toward the shed.

Larry stands on all fours and shakes out his withers. "Don't kill her. Charlie will come." He opens his mouth wide enough to swallow a bowling ball, and everyone in the room, including me, flinches back away from him. But then he coughs, like a cat clearing a hairball, a giant cat and the world's biggest hairball. When he's done, he licks his lips and says, "Plan B."

"Oh, balls to Plan B," I mutter, trying to get to my feet and deciding against it as my head nearly topples from my shoulders.

The bear laughs, its shoulders hunched and shaking.

"What's so funny?" I ask, incredulous.

"You're funny, Nona. Charlie said you would not like Plan B."

"When should we expect Charlie to arrive," snipes Bridge, obviously annoyed at being left in the dark.

"Soon," says Larry as he heads for the door. "Too hot in here, Larry goes outside. You need Larry, you call."

And then, to six pairs of wide, disbelieving, bugged-out eyes, Larry walks to the door, turns the knob, and lumbers off into the snow.

"So, that's our totem." I say, slow and monotone.

"I don't know about you, but I feel pretty good knowing Larry's got our backs. And he's so fuzzy!" Mom's words are met with slow nods of stunned agreement.

"Well, we've got a bear in our yard, a witch in our shed, and a boyfriend who's concocted some ill-advised plan that evidently included him sharing Rebecca's bed."

"What?" barks Bridge, staring at me like I've sneezed out a kitten.

"That's what she said. She said Charlie was warming her bed."

Fritz scuttles across the floor and climbs into my lap. "She was lying, Nona. There is no way—"

"I know. I know he wouldn't." And it's true. I know Charlie would move mountains to break this curse, but there are things he'd never do. Sleeping with another woman behind my back, stepsister or not, is one of those things.

Then I'm on my feet, Fritz in my hands, as a scream rocks the cabin. It's coming from the shed. I race down the hall and burst through the partially open shed door, huffing and still swaying a little.

"Stop it! Ow, that hurts! Stop!"

My alarm falls dead in the face of my laughter. Rebecca sits on the floor, apparently unable to move her arms or legs, while Mom pecks at her toes and Bridge, growling like a fiend, bites at her ankles. I didn't even notice they'd left the front room.

I watch for a while, arms crossed while I lean against the door frame, grinning.

"Penny, Bridge, that's enough." Wally's deep baritone cuts through Rebecca's yowling. "We don't torture our prisoners." There's a chastising flare in his eye as he stares me down and it fills me with shame.

Mom and Bridge, unaffected by Wally's scolding, smack paw and feather together in an interspecies high-five. I roll my eyes. "Everyone, would you mind giving me and Rebecca the room?"

"You're kidding, right?" asks Jack, huddled in the doorway, still a little twitchy from Larry's visit.

"I'm not. I'd like to talk to her alone. She can't move and Larry's doing something to keep her from using her magic. I'll be fine, I think."

Rebecca eyes me, squinty and cold, but there's something else there too. It's like exhaustion, bone-crushing, soul-weary exhaustion.

"Fine," grunts Wally, "but I'm staying right outside this door."

I smile at him. "I wouldn't expect anything less."

Everyone leaves the shed, except for Mom who walks to my feet, waiting expectantly for me to pick her up. Once I do and we're eye-to-eye, she says, "You have a kind soul, Nona, you always have. You care more about everyone around you than you do about yourself. It's one of the things I love most about you. But don't forget who that is." She points her beak at Rebecca. "Don't forget what she's taken from us. From all of us. And don't forget that she literally just tried to kill you, like just an hour ago."

I laugh a little. "I won't. I love you, Mom." I kiss her head.

"I love you too. Don't stay too long."

Mom is wary. She should be. She knows me too well. And even though I have never said these words out loud, I feel bad for Rebecca. Anyone who has had to steal someone else's life because they've never found one of their own that's worth living has failed spectacularly at being a human. You can't live someone else's life. You just can't. Staring at Rebecca, thin as a reed, pale, shadows under her eyes that look painted on, that's all I see. A failure. Perhaps with a mother like Julianne, there were few other options for her.

"Hello, Rebecca," I say, sitting cross-legged in the dirt in front of her.

Her face is expressionless. "Go fuck yourself."

"Charming." I gather my hair to one side and braid it over my shoulder. "Charlie told me everything, you know. Your mom, his family disowning him when James and Julianne were married, your obsession with him."

"I am not obsessed with Charlie," she grinds out.

"Really? That's not what Charlie said."

"Well, Charlie is an idiot."

"So he's not 'warming your bed'?"

A lifeless smile twists her lips. "No, he's not. Pissed you off that I said he was, though, didn't it?"

I smile right back at her. "Not as much as you trying to murder me with the weather, but sure. So, enlighten me. If you didn't steal my youth, my career, my life because you wanted Charlie, why then? The fame?"

She scoffs.

"I'm guessing you're realizing how fickle that can be," I say.

"You have no idea what I'm realizing. You know nothing about me."

She's pissed for sure, but I'm surprised she's talking to me. Strange, but it feels like she wants to talk, like she needs to.

"You're right. I only know what you've shown me—a vain, vapid, child who tortures others to get what she wants. If I'm wrong about you, then why don't you set me straight."

"Tortures? Please. You love it up here. You can't lie to me, Nona. I know you. I am you."

"No, Rebecca," I retort, "you are just pretending to be me. There's a big difference."

She studies her hands, her bangs falling into her eyes. "Whatever."

"And sure, I've made a home up here. What other choice have you left me? I'm not the lie down and die type, none of us are."

She's silent for a moment, and then, "But how? How are you all still happy? You have nothing up here. Nothing but the snow and the cold. But every time I come to visit, every time I watch you through your windows, you're smiling, laughing. No matter what I do to you, you're all still so happy."

"Do you want us to be miserable? Did you want to break us? Is that what gets you off?"

She raises her eyes to me, and I'm shocked to see tears standing in them. "No, that isn't what gets me off. I just don't understand it. I have everything and you have nothing. Yet you're happy and I'm," she pauses, takes a ragged breath, then shakes her head. "Never mind, you'd never understand."

I wait until she looks up at me again. "Try me."

I LEAVE the shed some time later after listening to Rebecca's story. To be honest, I'm not sure how to feel about it. It seems Julianne was an "'After School Special'" about emotional abuse" sort of mom. According to Rebecca, Julianne masterminded everything, Janey's death, marrying James, severing ties with the rest of James and Janey's families, Rebecca trying to get with Charlie, Aunt Lulu. And it was Julianne who cursed me and my family, not Rebecca. Julianne who forced Rebecca to come up here and try to kill me. And Julianne did it all to keep Charlie from finding the Rose and to punish me and my family for hiding it from her, which, evidently, my family has been unknowingly doing for centuries. Rebecca paints herself as an innocent in this story, a victim of an overwhelming desire to please her impossible to please mother.

It all falls a little flat for me. Not because I don't believe it might be true—I did just speak with a ghost via baked goods so there's not much I wouldn't believe at this point—but because I don't think Rebecca really ever cared all that much about her actions and how they might affect anyone else. But who knows, I'm a little close to the whole situation, I could be wrong.

"She's playing you," says Bridge from the couch while I make dinner. With Charlie gone, Rebecca powerless in the shed, and Larry watching over us, there's not much else to do but think about Lulu's plan and spin out. So I spend most of the afternoon cooking. I bake bread, make lasagna, enough even for Rebecca to have some. What can I say? I'm a softie.

"I know she is," I say, "but what does it matter?"

"What do you mean 'what does it matter?' She's playing you. She'll get you to trust her and then she'll screw you over."

"You sure about that?" I wipe my hands on a dish towel hanging from a drawer.

"One-hundred percent."

I sigh loudly through my nose. "I guess my point is, what does it *really* matter? I don't trust her, whether she's telling the truth or not. I won't let her go, whether she's telling the truth or not. I don't like her, whether she's telling the truth or not. So what does it matter if I consider that her story may be true?"

Bridge tilts her head and flicks her ears. "That's a fair point. But I still don't like it."

Truth is, I don't like hating people. I don't even like being mad at people. So, at the moment, it does me more harm than good to hate Rebecca. She's just not worth it.

"Noted." I pull the lasagna from the oven to let it cool. As I do, I notice that Jack, then Mom, then Fritz, and a surprisingly last-place Wally, have joined Bridge in the kitchen with me. They surround me on the floor, a ravenous, glass-eyed cadre of stomachs with faces. I laugh at them, loving these people so much it hurts. I assemble plates, overflowing with bread and lasagna, set them on the counter and the ground, and as I eat with them, I wonder if Rebecca has anyone who loves her as much as we all love each other. I don't think she does and for that reason, if for no other, I feel for her.

I knock on the shed door, plastering an indifferent expression onto my face.

"What?" she barks.

"Dinner?" I ask sweetly, ignoring her tone.

There is a moment of silence, and then, "Fine."

I open the door. She is still on the floor, still in the exact same position I left her in.

"Larry," I call out. "I'm feeding her now, and in a bit, I'm going to get her a blanket and some pillows. You'll need to release her enough so she can eat and then lie down."

Rebecca and I both stare toward the outer door, waiting. Then I hear the crunching thud of gigantic feet. Rebecca cowers.

"Okay, Nona," grumbles Larry through the door.

"I made you dinner too, Larry. I'll bring it out in a second."

A loud and raspy rumbling crashes through the wall. It sounds like a giant nail file is mating with a cyclone.

"What's happening out there?" Rebecca asks me, eyes wide.

"Larry, is that you?"

Abruptly, the sound stops. "Sorry, Nona. Had an itch. I'll go find a tree."

If I didn't know better, I'd swear a corner of Rebecca's mouth ticks up for a second.

"Anyone going to miss you out there?" I ask. "You have a boyfriend, right? Adam or something?"

She raises a perfectly shaped brow at me. "Following my personal life?"

"Well, until recently I thought you were using my body so, yeah, I had a tiny bit of interest in what you were doing with it. But," I say, staring down at myself, "I guess I was wrong."

"Adam and I broke up. Julianne will be furious with me that I failed up here. Nobody will miss me. Can you leave now so I can eat in peace?"

I get to my feet and wipe off my butt. "Sure. And I'm sorry about Adam. I'll be back in a bit with blankets. It gets pretty cold in here, but, you know, not the murderous-ice-storm kind of cold. I imagine you'll survive."

She doesn't respond, so I leave her with her dinner and return to my family.

～

REBECCA BEING Charlie's gift to me is a bit of a puzzler, but I have a growing suspicion it has something to do with the discussion she and I had earlier. I think Charlie wants me to know her better, to understand her part in all of this. Because if I'm a softie, he's practically goose down.

Wally and Mom and Jack and Bridge decide they'll stay in their rooms tonight. I imagine it's hard to let go of the human comfort of a bed, but now that they're animals again, I don't expect this to last long. Mom's always more comfortable in her coop with Wally on the floor of the shed beneath her. Jack and Bridge might enjoy the bed, but Jack has to go out several times throughout the night, so the shed just works better for them. Fritz, I figure, will continue to sleep where he's slept for the last five years, either on the couch or curled up between my boobs.

Before everyone shuffles off to bed, I clean up the kitchen and serve plates of the apple pie I also made today. Then I gather everyone around the fire to tell them about my trip to Aunt Lulu's cabin and what she told me.

"That's," starts Jack, his tail pressed tightly between his legs. "That seems…"

"Dangerous," finishes Mom.

I nod. "I know. And it won't work if we don't have the ruby and I still have no idea where it is."

"But it's on our property?" asks Fritz, walking around in circles in front of the couch.

"That's what she said. Didn't tell me where though."

Wally nods, snorts. "It could work, Lulu's plan."

We all turn to Wally. He's the only one of us who has ever had to make a life or death decision, the only one with any tactical experience. That he thinks this could work is promising.

"How?" asks Fritz. "We aren't prepared. We aren't smart, devious types. We're just…us."

I stand from the rocking chair, fisted hands on my hips. "Hey! That's…well, that's true."

Everyone groans.

"But," I say, holding up a finger, "the most important thing for this plan to work is that we trust each other and work together. And I don't know any other group of human and animals that does that better than we do. This is the best shot we have, and in anyone else's hands I'd be terrified. But I'm not terrified."

"Well, I am," mutters Jack.

"I am not terrified," I go on, undeterred, "because I know that no matter what happens, no matter who wins or who loses, we will be fine."

"We will be dead," counters Bridge.

"And if we end up dead," I say, completely losing the thread of my speech and just riding on momentum, "we will die happy, knowing we did everything we could to save each other and mete out justice to those who have wronged us!" I shout these last words, waiting for another slow clap or a regular riot of unbridled cheering. I get neither.

"Look, I love you guys," says Fritz, voice exasperatingly reasonable. "And I'm sorry about this, but I have no intention of dying for you people."

I stare at Fritz, mouth open, utterly shocked. "What? You wouldn't die for me? Why not?" I'm almost mad, then I realize how ridiculous this whole thing is and erupt into laughter. It doesn't take long for everyone to join me. We end the night with sore cheeks and bellies from laughing, telling each other all the reasons we will absolutely not die for each other. Like not for Wally because his farts stink. Or not for Jack because, apparently, all he thinks about is giving it to Bridge. Or Fritz because he doesn't appreciate brie and is just too infuriatingly gorgeous. It's cathartic and liberating, even though we all know it's bullshit. Each and every one of us would lay down our lives for any of the other. My job is to make sure it doesn't come to that. And I don't intend to fail.

IT's after midnight when I finally leave my bed. I can't sleep. Bleary-eyed, I walk down the hallway to the bathroom and crunch something crumbly under my foot. "What the hell?" I kneel to examine the smushed item. It's a cookie. Looking up, I see more cookies leading all the way to the door.

"Seriously, Lulu? Now? It's dark and freezing." The only response I get is my shovel falling across the front door to land on the back of the rocking chair. "Oh, hell."

Larry is waiting for me after I gear up and sneak out of the cabin. "Figured you'd be out here." I give him the handful of cookies I picked up from the floor.

"Thanks, Nona. There's more." He points a paw west, and my flashlight illuminates a trail of cookies leading into the woods.

"You coming with?"

He nods, and I feel better just knowing I'm not doing this alone. We have a lot of property up here—something like fifty acres—and I haven't explored even half of it. The path the cookies take us on leads deep into the trees west of the cabin to an area I've never been through before. We hike over peaks and valleys, across open fields and through dense trees. Once we're out of the trees, the moon is so full and bright that it stretches our shadows out before us.

We leave the cookies where they lay so we can find our way home, but I tell Larry he can eat them on our way back. Each cookie leads to another in what feels like an endless parade of flour and sugar. I'm so tired by this point I can barely keep my eyes open, but as we crest one final hill, a valley opens up below us, deep and wide. And there, standing in the middle of the valley like a lighthouse showing us home, is the tallest pine I've ever seen.

"The tallest pine in the deepest valley," I whisper, remembering Rufus' poem.

"It's here," says Larry, like he's certain of it.

I hoist my shovel over my shoulder. "Will you help me dig? I'm not sure I can do it all by myself."

Larry ambles down the hill, swiping a paw at the final cookie in our path and popping it into his mouth. "I can dig. Nona can rest."

IT'S STILL DARK when we reach the cabin, but a pink dawn is contemplating its rise over the eastern mountains. I kiss Larry goodnight on his nose before stumbling inside and back to my room to try to get some sleep. On my way down the hall, I pause, my gaze catching on the shed door.

"Ah, shit," I mutter, knowing every bit of what I'm about to do is supremely stupid. Still, I head to my room to grab my comforter and a pillow, then I walk to the shed. She might have left me to die in the snow, but I can't leave her alone and shivering on the shed floor.

Rebecca is asleep, snoring quietly on her side, blanket pulled up over her face. As silently as I can, I settle my blanket and pillow on the dirt and lay down beside her. Slowly, I curl up next to her, nestle close, and wrap an arm around her waist.

"The fuck?" she says, body going stiff as a board.

Through the door, Larry growls loud enough to wake the entire house.

"Oh, shush," I say to both of them. Then I squeeze her tighter.

"What. Are. You. Doing?" she says between gritted teeth.

I roll my eyes. "Lord, the *drama*. I'm sleeping. It's one of my most favorite past times and knowing you were out here alone was making it impossible for me to enjoy it."

"Seriously?" she asks. She's irritated now, annoyed, but she's not angry.

Rebecca doesn't have a sister; she doesn't know the love sisters share. I wonder if she's ever even had a best friend. "Yes, seriously. Look, we're like twins, sisters. This is what sisters do. Now, shut your stupid mouth and go back to bed."

After a few moments, her hand slides down to cover mine, then she pulls both up to nestle under her chin. I smile a little before her soft snoring finally lulls me to sleep.

CHAPTER TWENTY-THREE

"Next time, we should sleep in my bed." My fingers are clumsy, numb sausages fumbling at trying to pick up my blanket and pillow.

"There won't be a next time," says Rebecca, sitting cross-legged in the dirt.

"If I had a nickel for every time I've heard that..."

"What? That doesn't even make sense."

I shrug.

"How long are you planning on keeping me here anyway?" Her white-blonde hair is disheveled. Mascara is smeared down her cheeks. She's a hot mess.

I squint at her. "What made you decide to go blonde?"

Now she shrugs, and it is beyond bizarre to watch her make my expressions. "Wanted something different. Your hair is so..." Her lips purse.

"Boring?" I offer.

"Something like that."

"Well, I like it, the blonde. It suits you. Funny, though, even though we're identical, it wouldn't suit me. Do you ever miss what you used to look like?"

Rebecca was beautiful before she became me. She had dark brown hair, almost black, that she wore in a long bob that swept over her shoulders, and these piercing blue eyes, the kind you can almost see straight through when you're gazing into them. "Sometimes. I forget, though. I have to look at pictures to remember."

"I had to do the same," I say. "Although, ironically, the pictures I looked at were of you."

She frowns. "What was it like, being old?"

I blow over my fingers, jogging in place. "How are you not freezing?"

She ignores me, sitting still as a statue of the Buddha. "What was it like?"

I sigh. "Creaky, slow, but not as bad as you'd think. There's something peaceful about it."

Rebecca chews on her cheek. "She did it, you know, all of it. I tried to get her to just take your memories and leave you alone. Julianne insisted on changing you, all of you."

I'm staring straight at her. "Did she force you to come up here and try to kill me?"

"My mother can be very persuasive," she states unapologetically.

"Sounds like Julianne is an...interesting person." That's it. That's the best I can come up with.

Rebecca scoffs. "That's one way to put it. She's going to come up here, you must know that. She wants that ruby and a hundred bears won't keep you safe from her. She's old as time and stronger than steel. She could turn you, your family, this entire cabin into ashes with a snap of her fingers."

"What is it with witches and snapping? Is it, like, necessary, or just something you do for flair?"

There's a snorting sound and I look behind me for Wally, but there's nobody here but us. Then I realize the sound came from Rebecca.

"Did you just snort?" I ask.

"No," she says. "Maybe, yes."

I laugh.

The tiniest smile turns her lips. Then it's gone. "It's not funny. She'll kill all of you."

"She might. She already killed Charlie's mom and Aunt Lulu."

Rebecca's shoulders rise toward her ears while her head drops between them. "You know about that?"

"I do. She might kill us. Hell, you might kill us. But over the last five years, despair has tried to kill us, so has the weather, lack of food, not to mention the bears, wolves, spiders—you'd be amazed how bad a brown recluse spider bite can mess you up. But none of these things have killed us yet. She might have a harder time than she thinks."

"You are a resilient bunch," Rebecca admits. "But magic is magic. If I were you, I'd do whatever she asks and give her whatever she wants."

"Rebecca, I never do anything other people want me to do. It's sort of my thing."

Shoulders caving inward, she stares at her hands again.

I wonder if this might be something about me she wanted even more than my fame. Either way, I can tell we're finished talking.

I stand up and walk toward the door of the shed, then I turn back. "We were friends once Rebecca. I really liked you. Sucks things turned out the way they did."

Just before I close the door, whisper quiet, Rebecca says, "I really liked you too."

～

"Did you sleep out there?"

Mom's got me cornered in the hallway. I was trying to sneak

my bedding back into my room before anyone else woke up, but no such luck. I hug my pillow and balled-up comforter to my chest. "Yes," I reply, stretching the word out like if I say it slowly enough, she won't notice that I'm telling her I just spent the night with our arch-nemesis.

Mom pecks at the floor five, six, seven times, hard. I wince because it feels like each peck is a swat on my butt. Then she raises her beak and sighs. "I'll bet it was cold." She doesn't say anything else, just struts past me and stops at the shed door. "I need to lay an egg."

"Sorry, Mom. I know I shouldn't have. I just felt bad for her and I couldn't sleep."

Before she walks through, she turns back to me. "I know. I almost came in here myself last night." She peers through the door at Rebecca, still sitting in the dirt. "Go warm up, honey. I'll take this shift."

"Don't go too hard on her, Mom."

"Wouldn't dream of it," she replies and waddles through the door.

MOM STAYS in the shed for over an hour. Poor Rebecca. After that much time spent with Penny Sheldon, even Hannibal Lector would reconsider his life choices.

I shower, dress, and make breakfast, finally saving a red-eyed Rebecca from Mom's uncanny ability to render even witches into blubbering puddles with an offering of coffee cake and sausage. Then I bundle up to go find Larry.

He's propped up against a tree trunk on the western edge of the yard, paws resting on his fuzzy belly, eyes closed.

"Hi Larry. Want breakfast?"

He opens one eye. It glares at me. "You should not sleep with the witch."

"I'm sure you're right. Breakfast?" I hold up the plate.

He takes it. "They're on the way, Nona. Be here soon. You ready?"

"Can we go over the plan one more time?"

The plan is a mixture of Aunt Lulu's, Charlie's, and some fancy footwork Wally concocted late last night when we tried to put this whole thing together. Drawing in the dirt with his paw, Larry plays through the plan again.

I rock back on my heels once he's finished. "We're completely fucked, aren't we?"

Larry scratches at his head and he looks so much like Charlie doing it, I can't help but smile.

"Don't know. Hard to tell with magic. Could go either way."

"And you're sure you're strong enough now?"

He nods, blowing air through his nostrils. "I've got you all."

I throw my arms around him. "Thank you, Larry. You're a wonderful bear."

He grunts, then hooks his chin over my shoulder and pulls me in closer.

WE SPEND the rest of the morning rehashing the plan, going over positions and cues, loading guns, and devising exit strategies for "when things turn into a Charlie Foxtrot" per Wally, which evidently is military slang for "clusterfuck" and is now my new favorite saying.

I'm cleaning my rifle on my bed when Bridge comes to find me.

"How're you feeling?" she asks.

"Terrified. You?"

"Same." She nestles up beside me, wrapping her tail around my hips. "I know you're doing this for us, Nona. I know you've always been happier living up here than we have."

"Yeah, but I've been human. Doesn't even compare."

"Either way, I just wanted to thank you. And in case we don't make it through this, I hope you know how much we all love you."

I lean over and kiss her head. "Never a doubt in my mind." I stand up, rack my rifle, and say, "Now let's go kick some witchy ass."

Larry is sitting on the couch when we reach the front room. Jack and Fritz are at the window, Wally and Mom guarding the door.

"They're here," Larry growls, setting my hair on end.

I spin on my heel and join Jack and Fritz at the window. In the distance, walking out from the trees and looking, ironically, like a gang of train robbers staring down the tracks, come Julianne, Charlie, and James. And all three of them are pissed as hell.

"Well, that settles that debate. Looks like Julianne's got them both brainwashed, or whatever it is she's doing to them," says Bridge at my side.

I push my hand into my belly, splinting my stomach which just tried to empty its contents onto the floor. "Yep," I manage, blinking back a tear or two at the rage twisting Charlie's perfect mouth. "This had better work."

I sling my rifle over my back, step into my boots, and head to the shed.

"Good luck, honey. We'll be right here."

I smile at Mom, then I go get Rebecca.

CHAPTER TWENTY-FOUR

"Howdy. What brings you three to our neck of the woods?" The slight tremble in my voice is at odds with my devil-may-care facade as I stand with my rifle, chewing on a fingernail and squinting at the sun like I'm Annie mother-fucking Oakley.

Julianne is formidable. She's tall with short, raven-black hair and Rebecca's same piercing blue eyes. She's stunningly beautiful in that "I will devour your soul and then shit you out just for fun" sort of way.

"Where is my daughter?" she asks, voice deep and slow but sharp. Like honey dripping off the edge of a knife.

"Hi Charlie," I say, turning my eyes to the love of my life, who glares at me like I'm a bug he wants to squish under his boot.

"Kidnapping? How could you, Nona?"

I huff at him. "No sir, how could you? Plan B, my foot."

He stares at me, brows creased in momentary confusion. "Where is she? What have you done with her?"

"Back there." I nod my head toward the shed. "And nothing at all."

James takes a step toward me and it's completely distracting how much he looks like Charlie. I'd never gotten the chance to meet the man before the curse. "Ah, ah, ah," I warn him. "Didn't Charlie tell you about our totem?"

Larry's growl rips through the trees, vibrating my bones and making James stumble back a step.

Julianne turns to Charlie. "What is that?"

Charlie shakes his head back and forth, clutching at his temples like his brain is attacking him. "I don't know," he groans.

Julianne reaches her hand into his briefly. This calms Charlie so that he can raise his head and glare all hatefully at me again.

"Neat trick, Jules," I say. "I know some neat tricks too. Lulu taught me a few. You remember Lulu, don't you?"

I have both Charlie's and James' attention now.

"I think you do," I say, spitting out a crescent of fingernail. "If memory serves, you killed Aunt Lulu right here in these woods."

"What is she talking about?" asks James. His voice is just like Charlie's, only a bit deeper and with more gravel.

Julianne ignores him, instead she says sweetly, melodically, "Listen here, you self-righteous bitch. Give me back my daughter and I won't kill you and your barn animals with a sn—"

"Snap of your finger. Yeah, I get it. You witches really need a new schtick. What about a nose twitch or a wink?" My snark is nothing more than a stalling tactic, giving everyone a chance to get into position. "Tell you what, why don't we make a trade?"

She scoffs. "You are in no position to negotiate."

I take a step forward, unsling my rifle, and point it at her. In the back of my mind I see Mimi and Poppop on the porch behind me, rocking in the rocking chairs, Mimi offering me pointers while I took aim at cans on stumps. "I disagree."

"You think I'm afraid of a firearm? Child, do you have any idea who I am? What I can do?"

"I have an inkling," I say tersely as a sudden, hot breeze

swirls around my feet, melting the snow beneath me and burning up my calves. "But do you know how strong a pig's jaws are? One shot from this rifle, and Wally's getting his breakfast courtesy of your daughter's face." This is probably the most ridiculous thing that has ever come out of my mouth. But it does what it's supposed to.

Julianne's eyes widen.

"So, I'd stop burning the shit out of my legs if I were you." I angle my rifle to the sky as I dance on my tiptoes, trying to climb away from the flames that are seriously hot as hell and are starting to really hurt and, thankfully, Julianne pulls her magic back.

She looks absolutely disgusted with me. "What sort of trade? Charlie for Rebecca, I suppose?"

"Not just Charlie." I nod my head at James. "I think you've abused both our families long enough, don't you?"

"What's she talking about, Julianne?" asks James, eyes still trained on me. As I look at James and then at Charlie, I see the weakness, the chink in Julianne's armor. James and Charlie are like puppets, but the strings are thin, constantly breaking and reforming. Both men are fighting her. They just need some help to cut the strings for good. It's time to remind them who the bad guy really is, even though I wish I didn't have to. Reluctantly, I shout, "Come out!"

I watch Charlie, his eyes huge, hands clasping over his mouth as a woman walks from the cabin. She's petite, ethereal, lovely.

"Janey?" James' breathless plea is a knife in my heart.

This was Rebecca's idea. She's the only one who knew what Janey looked like, or had the ability to glamour Bridge to look just like her. She knew Charlie and James, once they saw Janey, would strain Julianne's magic to its breaking point. Sure it's a stretch, trusting Rebecca, but we were low on options. She said it was time James and Charlie knew what happened to their mother, and to Lulu. She said it was time Julianne paid for what she'd done to them, and to her. Call me naïve all you want, but I believed her.

"Mom?" It's Charlie's voice that nearly destroys me.

Janey, Bridge actually, opens her arms to Charlie. "Charlie," she says, her voice brittle with the emotion I know Bridge is truly struggling with.

I watch as Charlie takes one stumbling step toward Janey, and then another.

"Don't move," orders Julianne, but Charlie doesn't obey.

As he cuts through the snow, lumbering toward Janey like he's pulling a train car behind him, Julianne raises her arms and something sparkles between them.

"Think about what you're doing," I say, rubbing my finger back and forth on the trigger. "I didn't feed Wally all day yesterday. He's starving." I hate every word that I'm saying. Wally was right, Plan B does suck.

Julianne lowers her hands and releases Charlie, her face twisted with fury. Charlie runs the rest of the way to Janey, sobbing with each step. When he reaches her, falling onto his knees in the snow and grabbing around her waist, my heart breaks into a thousand pieces. Janey places her hands on his head.

"It's all right, Charlie. It's all right. Stand up."

He does. "Mom, how are you here?"

Janey wipes his tears away while smiling sadly over her trembling chin. She takes his hands in hers. "Never mind that." Then she straightens, eyes going wide, and I know Bridge has made the trade. It's barely detectable, and if you weren't looking for it, you'd miss it. But she cocks a brow at him, a "please play along" brow followed by an "I'm really, really sorry for pretending to be your dead mom" grimace.

Charlie hugs her again and whispers something in her ear. I know Bridge like the back of my hand, and that smile she stifles, even on someone else's face, that smile is the sun breaking through the clouds. We've got him.

Charlie turns to Julianne. "What's happening?" he asks, eyes red and voice shuddering again. He's a pretty decent actor too, thank goodness. "Why is Mom here?"

James starts walking toward Bridge now, sorrow lancing through me with every step he takes.

"Trade," I demand, staring Julianne down. "Before they figure this whole thing out and this all turns into a Charlie Foxtrot."

I can't believe it, but she's panicking, turning from me, then to Charlie, then to James. She wasn't expecting this.

"Never," she spits. But I can see her resolve crumbling. Especially when Larry unleashes a mighty magical growl that's so loud the ground shakes. It throws her off balance and gives me the second I need.

As James walks past me on his way to Janey, I drop my rifle, crumple the bundle of herbs I'd taken from Aunt Lulu's in my pocket, raise my hand, and mutter, "I'm sorry." Then with a deep breath, I blow the herbs into his face. It's the same mixture of herbs, Lulu told me, that she had been sending him to make his tea from. Whatever they are, they're imbued with some power of protection over Julianne's mind control.

He stops dead in his tracks, sneezes, shakes his head, then rubs at his eyes like he's waking up from a dream. He stares at me, trying to place my face. "Rebecca?" he asks.

I shake my head and my wink sends a tear down my cheek. "Not quite."

James turns toward Charlie and Janey again. But it's not Janey anymore. It's Bridge, human Bridge, in all her glory. "Charlie?" James asks, confused.

"Take a breath, Dad," instructs Charlie as he comes to my side. He takes my hand, sliding his fingers through mine, and I feel the Rose of the Desert settle between our palms.

"Where the hell did you find it?" he whispers, mouth turned up at the corners.

"Lulu," I whisper.

Julianne's scream of rage rivals Larry's loudest growl as she thrusts her hands out at me and Charlie. Her howling turns banshee-like when nothing happens.

"You'll have to try harder than that," I shout, grasping Charlie's hand so tightly the ruby cuts into my palm.

An icy calm settles over Julianne's expression as she stares at our clasped hands. "You have it, don't you?" She's laughing now, her red lips parting as her head drops back. "You really are a special kind of stupid."

My heart surges into my throat. This might have been a bad idea.

"Do you have any idea how long I've been searching for the Rose? Ever since that prick, Rufus, stole it from me. And you just deliver it to me? I suppose I should thank you, stupid twat that you are. Because that," she says, pointing to our hands, "belongs to me. To *my* family."

Charlie goes still as a stone beside me.

"Bring me the Rose now and I won't kill everyone you love." As she says these words, clouds thicken above her and I taste the metallic tang of lightning in the air.

But then Rebecca, not Nona, Rebecca, with dark hair and blue eyes, opens the front door of my cabin, walks out into the snow, and takes one long look at her mother. "Everyone?" she asks.

Julianne's eyes are still trained on me and Charlie, which really pisses me off because that's her daughter right there and she doesn't seem to care. Maybe Rebecca wasn't exaggerating about Julianne's parenting skills.

Rebecca walks to Charlie's other side and takes his other hand. Charlie squeezes my hand, then releases it as both he and Rebecca raise their arms over their heads and snap their fingers.

And even though I can't see what they've just done, I can feel it surrounding me, soft and warm like a summer breeze.

"You," says Julianne, finally staring at Rebecca "What the hell do you think you're doing?"

Rebecca's voice wavers, but she stands tall. "You are a terrible mother, and you're a terrible person. What you've done," she chokes on the words, "what you've made me do to these people, to this family, it ends today."

"You weak, simpering idiot," Julianne growls. "Don't you see? Nothing ever ends, ever!" She raises her arms to the sky. Above her hands, clouds gather to block the sun and cast us into a cold and silent darkness. I still have the Rose, but everyone else is vulnerable.

Breaking the silence, Larry blasts through the trees, roaring like a hurricane and lumbering toward Julianne in massive galloping strides. But she's ready for him.

I cry out as Julianne turns toward Larry, lightning forking from the sky above her.

Charlie takes off, running full tilt at Larry as the bear zigs and zags, trying to avoid the bolts of lightning striking the ground all around him. Then Larry zigs when he should have zagged and I scream because he should be down. He should be dead. But the lightning stills, hovering above him in crackling strands of blue and yellow.

I hear a groaning beside me and turn to find Rebecca with her arms raised, her fingertips smoking, turning black while she somehow holds Julianne's lightning suspended in the sky. Charlie slides to a halt in the snow, swinging his head back and forth like he's not sure if he should stay with us or go to Larry.

"Stop!" I scream at Julianne. "You're going to kill her!"

Julianne takes one look at Rebecca—whose fingers are now long black cinders, tips falling to the snow like ash—and whips her hands from where Larry gets to his feet to where Rebecca stands. In an act that makes rage bloom hot inside me, Julianne sends a lightning strike straight at her own daughter.

With the ruby in my hand, I don't think, I just jump and throw my arms around Rebecca. It stops the lightning from hitting her, but so much damage is already done. Her arms are singed, black all the way to her elbows and her fingers are just gone.

In front of me, Julianne screams in frustration as Larry stalks toward her. But behind me I hear windows opening, rifles racking, and pistols cocking. Glancing over my shoulder, I see my family, human, and armed to the teeth. Charlie and Rebecca must have shifted them back when they snapped their fingers.

Bridge comes to stand next to me as Fritz, Jack, and Mom aim their firearms out of windows. Then Wally, looking like he's not at all fucking around, moves to stand in the middle of the open door with his shotgun aimed right at Julianne. With one fluid motion, he squeezes the trigger and sends a slug straight at her chest.

"Don't! Please!" screams Rebecca, writhing in my arms. But the slug plummets like a dead bird in the snow in front of Julianne. Just as we'd thought it would.

Julianne readies herself to send another bolt of Lightning toward us and I flinch at the bullets whizzing by my head as everyone in the cabin starts firing. I expect chaos. I expect bedlam. What I don't expect...is horticulture.

In a flash, James is in front of me. His arms are stretched out wide, palms facing skyward as, one-by-one, tiny vines break through the snow and snatch the ammo from the air before they can reach Julianne.

"Enough, Jules," he says as more vines break through the snow and grow up her legs, slithering around her thighs, pinning her in place.

Her blue eyes are red and wild with fury. "You think your weeds can stop me?"

I reach out to touch James' shoulder, hoping the ruby will protect him from Julianne's magic too. But, again, I'm not fast enough.

Time slows as lightning sparks in the gray darkness of the morning, flickering between Julianne's fingers. Charlie shouts while he runs back toward us, a slow-motion yowl. Wally, Mom, Fritz, and Jack run out the front door, but they're so slow.

Rebecca is screaming behind us, begging her mother to stop as Julianne's lightning bursts from her hands, heading straight for James, for all of us. But then it stops. It just stops. Right in front of James. It sparks out, branching and forking over an invisible shield separating us from her as Larry stands up to his full height behind her, his arms spread wide, his roar deafening.

"It's about time, Larry," pants Charlie as he reaches my side again.

"Lay off him," I whisper. "He was almost just a well-done bear-kabob. This will work, right? He won't get hurt will he?"

Julianne, face now a furious shade of red, raises her hands again, the vines growing up her legs withering to dried husks.

"How long can he keep this up?" I ask, because Larry seems paralyzed. He's been on his feet, trying to reach Julianne since he started shielding us but she must be too powerful. He can't move.

Charlie's concerned. "I don't know. She's so strong."

Then, impossibly, terribly, Julianne turns around to face Larry and sends a bolt of lightning directly into his chest.

"No!" Charlie and I and everyone else scream in unison as Larry is blasted backwards, sliding through the snow to rest in a motionless, smoking heap fifty feet away from where just seconds ago he stood like a glorious, fuzzy statue of right-eousness.

Rebecca, with her scorched arms spread wide, turns around, gathering my family and making them stand behind her, offering whatever protection she can.

James faces Julianne, hands up, pleading with her to stop and for a second, for the briefest moment, she looks at him, letting her guard down. And then the sky cracks and Julianne jerks like a puppet yanked by its strings. Her arms fly forward while she flies back, landing hard on her back in the snow.

CHAPTER TWENTY-FIVE

"WHAT JUST HAPPENED?" I ask, staring at an unconscious Julianne.

James grows fresh vines to tie down her arms and legs as Charlie, Rebecca, and I run to her side. Blood streams down her arm from a smoking, gaping shot-gun hole below her right shoulder. I whip around, staring into the trees. Who the hell shot her? None of us fired our weapons.

I'm squinting into the distance when my mouth pops open audibly. I see someone, no, two someones running from the woods, rifles held low in their hands.

"Sam? Marge?" I ask no one and everyone.

Sam slides to his knees at Julianne's side as Marge stands above him, breathing hard.

"What are you two doing here?" I'm staring at Sam in utter disbelief.

"Is she dead?" Rebecca asks, settling to her knees at Julianne's head.

"No, dear," says Sam. "I just clipped her wing is all. Not sure why she's unconscious."

"That would be me," says James, joining my family and Fritz

to come sit at my side as we surround Julianne. "I can keep her down now that she's weaker."

"Yeah, but how, Sam? How did your bullet get to her? And what are you two doing here?" I repeat.

Sam shakes his head. "Strangest thing, Nona. Last night, Marge and I were up late, drinking wine and playing Scrabble, when someone knocked on our door. When I looked through the window, there he was. Your bear, standing on its hind legs, holding a bunch of chocolate chip cookies in his hands. I screamed, turning to grab my shotgun, but then he started talking. Thought I was finally going 'round the bend, but then he told us everything about you and your curse, asked for our help. And I wouldn't have believed a single word of it had the message not come from a freaking talking bear!" His voice rises on this last part.

"But how," I say. "She's brushed everything we've shot at her off like snowflakes."

Sam shrugs. "Oldest trick in the book and no magic required. Distraction. All part of the bear's plan. Told us to wait until shit went sideways, then let her have it. Guess he was right." Charlie stands from my side and walks to where Larry lies in the snow. I can't watch.

"She killed Janey? And Lulu?" James' voice is soft but heavy with pain.

Mom, sitting beside him, slides a hand over his. "I'm so sorry." Her mom-magic works on James too, it seems, as tears roll down his cheeks. "You have the Rose?" he asks me.

I nod, opening my fingers which have been clasping the ruby so tightly, I have tiny indentations in my palm.

James wipes his eyes. "Can I borrow that for a minute?"

"Of course," I say, passing him the gem.

He clears his throat. "The Rose," he says sadly, "does more than shield against magic, it can steal it as well." The sun, burning brightly now that Julianne's clouds have vanished, shines through the ruby as James rotates it in his fingers, lighting it up to reveal a tiny, clear bubble in its center.

Rebecca sits up straighter, bracing herself since we're all looking at her now. Then she drops her head, her dark hair falling forward to curtain her face. "Do it," is all she says.

James leans toward Julianne and touches the ruby to her forehead. I hold my breath, waiting, but nothing happens at first. Then, slowly, tendrils of black mist rise from Julianne's skin where the ruby rests against it, making a cloud of shadows. For a moment, I can't see the Rose at all anymore, just black mist obscuring even James' hand. But then he lifts the Rose and the mist is sucked into the gem, converging inside that tiny bubble in its center.

"Will she die?" Rebecca's voice is a wisp.

"Eventually," says James. "Her immortality was part of her magic."

I can hear the breaths of everyone around me in the ensuing silence, a collective rising and falling of inhales and exhales.

"I guess it's my turn then." Rebecca's quiet voice whips my head around.

"Your turn for what?" I ask, but she's not looking at me. She's looking at James.

"Will it hurt? When you take my magic?"

James swivels toward me, then toward Mom, then he glances at Wally, Bridge, Jack, Fritz. "It's your call," he says, holding the ruby out for me to take.

So many emotions run through me all at once: anger, fear, sadness, rage, pity. I can't contain them all and they leak out of my eyes as I look at Mom, imploring her to make this decision for me. She grabs the Rose from James' hand.

"Rebecca," Mom says, her stern voice reminding me of every single time I got in trouble as a kid, "your actions nearly destroyed my family and for that, we would all be well within our rights to take your powers, and more."

Rebecca's shoulders plummet as she buries her face into her blackened arms and sobs.

Nobody else speaks, just Mom. Bridge and Jack hold each other as Fritz slides his hand into mine. Wally stands behind Mom, a hand resting on her shoulder. And I'm scared. I'm terrified Mom will do it, that she'll punish Rebecca. I know Rebecca deserves to be punished, but I also feel like she deserves a chance, a chance to figure out who she is, who she could be, without Julianne making all of her decisions for her.

"I'd do it, Rebecca. In a heartbeat, I would take your powers and never think twice about it. But you just so happened to have cursed my daughters, who are two of the most loving and forgiving people you'll ever care to meet. I know they'd want you to have a second chance."

"Speak for yourself," mutters Bridge, but as she nestles closer into Jack's arms, her lips curl into a smirk.

Rebecca raises her head. "I don't deserve it, your kindness, your forgiveness. I don't deserve any of it."

"You might be right," I say, trying to match Mom's sternness and not doing too badly, if I do say so myself. "But luckily for you, for once what happens up here isn't your decision."

Mom hands me the ruby and I put it back into my pocket. In the awkward silence that follows, a tiny rumbling reaches my ears.

"Nona!" It's Charlie. "Nona, come here!"

I stand, shielding my eyes with a hand over my brow, trying to find Charlie in the blinding white of sun-drenched snow. But when I spot him, it's not Charlie whose arm reaches up toward the sky.

"Larry!" I bellow, racing through the snow toward the bear I'd thought for certain was dead. I trip and fall face first into a mound of powder, fine crystals of snow sticking to my tear-soaked cheeks. "Larry!"

Charlie sits next to the massive bear, and I drop down beside him, helping him push Larry up to sitting.

"Larry, are you all right?" I hold one of his paws in my hands, stroking my other hand over his soft fur.

He shakes his bear head, left to right, then nods it up and down. Then he tilts it side to side. "Larry fine. That hurt, though. Bears hate lightning."

Charlie and I throw our arms around the bear and I kiss his furry forehead over and over.

"Enough." He swings his gaze into the trees, like he's checking to see who might be watching us. "Please stop. Larry has reputation."

Laughing hysterically because my heart is overflowing with relief and my brain is absolute mush incapable of anything else, I stand up and help Charlie get Larry to all fours. We walk beside him as he lumbers back toward the cabin.

Charlie pats the bear's head and scratches behind his ear. "It worked, sending Sam and Marge here. Smart thinking. Julianne never saw them coming. Thank you, Larry."

Larry grunts, accepting hugs from everyone, then lets himself back into the cabin, probably to find something to eat.

Charlie approaches James, who is still hovering over Julianne's limp body. "I'm sorry, Dad. I had no idea she had you under a spell. I would have tried harder to get us out if I'd known."

James says nothing, just pulls his son into a tight embrace, the shoulders of both men shaking as emotion overwhelms them.

I have to turn away, and that's when I notice Julianne stirring.

Fritz is at my side again, noticing the same thing. "We'd better get her inside and figure out what comes next."

～

MY CABIN IS FILLED with people, and a bear, more bodies than it's held quite possibly since it was built. The fire crackles and pops as Julianne sits dazed on the couch, Rebecca sitting across the room in the rocking chair, her expression shifting between anger and something like grief while she watches her mother come around. Charlie and James have started healing her arms which are pink and shining with five tiny buds where her fingers are growing back. I catch Rebecca, every now and then, staring at them, grimacing, biting her lip, blinking back tears, then glaring again at her mother.

I haven't stopped hugging my human family for the last thirty minutes. But now, secretly, I find Charlie and drag him down the hall into my room to ask him the question I've been dreading. Because as wonderful as everything feels right now, there is a deep dread gnawing at my insides.

I sit him down beside me on the bed. I can feel the hesitation radiating from him.

"Just tell me," I say. "The curse. It's not broken is it? I mean, it's not permanent, right?"

He takes my hands in his. "Well, nothing is permanent," he says evenly, running his thumb over my skin. "But it is broken, it's just not easy to keep it that way."

"What does that mean?" My voice cracks.

He blows out a breath. "All magic has a cost, Nona. For Julianne it was her humanity, for Rebecca her happiness. The magic used to break this curse has a cost too."

"What is it? What's the cost?" I'm trembling now, my eyes misting over because I know he's going to tell me we can't stay together, that the cost is us. And if it is, I refuse to pay it. "Is it… you and me?"

"Jesus, no." His hold on my hands tightens, his eyes meeting mine with a stark intensity. "No, it isn't us. I'd die before I'd lose you again."

"What is it, then? Tell me. Please, tell me."

He takes my face between his hands and lowers his mouth to mine. He kisses me fiercely, passionately, and for a very long time. Long enough that I forget why I'm panicking and just want more. More of his mouth, his tongue, his body.

He lets me go. "Sorry, but you were kind of freaking out."

My eyes are still closed, his lips still a whisper against mine. "Thank you. I feel much better now."

He laughs, low and soft. "The magic, the curse, it's incredibly powerful. The strength of magic required to break a curse this powerful needs an anchor to keep it stable."

"Go on," I encourage, while I also might be kissing a trail along his neck as I undo the top two buttons of his shirt.

He stiffens as I slide my hand into his shirt, placing his hand over mine to halt my progress. "Rebecca and I tried to anchor the curse to the Rose, and then to me. We even tried to use Larry. But it wasn't enough. The only thing that worked was to anchor the magic to the cabin."

"That doesn't sound so bad."

"And to you," he continues. "And me. And…Larry."

"Okay," I say apprehensively, trying to remove my hand from his chest. He doesn't let me. "What does that mean?"

"It means that no matter what, we will never be able to leave this cabin for very long. We will always have to come back. To fill the well of power keeping the curse at bay for you, for your family, for Fritz."

Now when I pull my hand away, he lets it go. "Huh," is all I can say.

Devastation deepens the lines between his brows. "I'm so sorry. If there was any other way, we would have found it. There is strong magic in these woods, maybe because of Lulu, maybe the Rose. But we tried to find another way. Please believe me, we tried everything. And we can keep trying. This could all just be temporary. I know you probably want nothing more than to leave this place and never come back, but—"

My lips interrupt him, taking their turn to kiss him until he stops talking. "You're wrong, Charlie," I eventually tell him. "It's okay. I love it up here."

"But your career," he says while I finish the task of unbuttoning his shirt. "The band. The music. It would be next to impossible to have the kind of fame you wanted while still having to come up here for months at a time."

I shrug, running my fingers over his shoulders after I slide off his shirt. "What if the kind of fame I wanted five years ago isn't what I want anymore? I don't want to be like Rebecca, exhausted, lonely, scrutinized day in and day out. I'm used to my freedom up here. I cherish it. I'm not sure I could give it up, whether I was or wasn't magically connected to the cabin."

Charlie blinks. He doesn't believe me. "Really? Are you sure? Because if I keep searching, I'm sure I'll be able to find some other way to stabilize the curse."

I cup his cheek in my hand. "I'm sure."

"I love you, Nona."

I yank my shirt off over my head and tell him, "You have five minutes to prove it." And then I pin him to the bed.

AFTER CHARLIE MAKES love to me silently and thoroughly, I finally realize, lying in his arms, what the curse being broken really means. Even if Charlie and I need to come back, we can leave the cabin. Everyone else can leave the cabin. My family, Fritz, they can leave for good. They can leave...me.

"Charlie," I whisper, clinging to him. "I'll have to say goodbye," I'm looking at my door, hearing their laughter streaming in through the space below it, "to them."

CHAPTER TWENTY-SIX

"Nona, sweetheart, you've got to get up."

I pull the blanket over my head, hiding underneath it like a child. "No. I can't. I can't do it."

I knew this day would come. Everyone has stayed up here for five months while Charlie and Larry poured magic into the cabin to stabilize the curse. Enough so Charlie and I can leave and go back to our lives for longer than a few days. They're close, they tell me, just another couple of weeks and then they'll have it.

I know they've all wanted to go, Fritz and my family, but they've stayed, for me. And now, apparently, they're ready. They say they want to give me and Charlie a couple weeks alone in the cabin. That we deserve it. Charlie was emphatic in his agreement. I completely faked mine.

"Just let them French exit, okay?"

Charlie yanks the covers all the way off the bed. "Get up!"

I sit up, glaring at him. "I can't do it!" I shout before falling onto my pillow and curling up fetal.

There's a rapping at the door. It creaks a little before it's flung open so hard that it bangs off the wall. "Nona, get your ass out of bed and come say goodbye to your family."

I groan. "Fine, Mom, but I will not be held accountable for any injuries incurred when I break down and command Larry not to let any of you leave until I can." It may seem silly to be this upset over a couple of weeks. But it's so much more than that. We're separating, moving apart, stretching the distance between us from mere feet to hundreds of miles. And it feels like my heart will break into jagged little pieces trying to stay with them all at the same time.

Charlie grabs my feet and slides me to the bottom of the bed, then he takes my hands and pulls me upright. I slump against him as he wraps his arm around my shoulders and shepherds me into the front room.

"Sam will be here any minute," says Wally, sitting on the couch, already wiping at his eyes.

Sam's bringing his truck down to drive everyone into Three Rivers, and away from me. I hate Sam.

Fritz comes to us first. Charlie hugs him tightly, whispering something into his ear. Then Fritz takes me in his arms, lifting me gently up off the ground. I nestle my face into his neck and press a kiss just under his ear. "We'll see you soon."

Fritz is going home for a while to see his mother. But he's still my manager and whatever shape my career takes over the next few months, he'll be by my side through it all.

Letting me go, he winks at me and says, "Have a fun couple of weeks."

I kiss him on the cheek, then whisper, "Won't be the same without you."

His laughter is low and sultry. "That's exactly what Charlie just said. Great minds."

I hug him again. "I love you, Fritzy."

"Love you too, baby. Always will." He picks up his bags and

walks out the front door, leaving me to say goodbye to everyone else.

Jack comes next, shaking Charlie's hand. He tries to shake mine too, but I attack him with a hug. "Go make a million babies," I tell him. "I want nieces and nephews."

He laughs, blushing a candy-apple red. "I'm on it."

Tears are streaming down my cheeks. I pull him to me and kiss him square on the mouth. Blushing even harder, he leaves to join Fritz on the porch.

Next Wally stands and my tears morph into gasping sobs. I can't say goodbye to him. I can't say goodbye to my dad. He and Mom will move to South Carolina. It might be months before I see them again. "Please," I say, holding a hand out to stop him from coming any closer. "I can't."

"Oh, Nona, you can. You're the strongest woman I know, aside from your momma." He pushes my arm out of the way and leans in for a hug, strong and solid and I crumble into his arms.

Then Charlie wraps his arms around both of us, and we all stand there, hugging and crying.

"No more tears, at least not for me," Wally says, wiping his eyes. He stands at attention, raises his hand to his forehead, and salutes us. We salute him back but before he heads to the porch, he turns around and gives the cabin a long, final look. One more tear slips down his round cheek. And then he's gone.

I glance out the window and see all three men standing together, staring out at the few blades of green grass shooting up between patches of melting snow in the yard, all wiping at wet eyes.

But then Bridge and Mom stand from the couch and I break, wheeling away from them, burying my face into my hands. Charlie turns me back around and leads me to the couch where Bridge and Mom sit down again, one on either side of me, just like they did that first night Charlie made them human again.

"I can't...live...without you guys," I gasp, my body racked by sobs.

Mom sniffles, running her hand up and down my back. "We'll be seeing you in a few months. Don't be so dramatic, Nona."

I laugh at this, but my laughter quickly morphs into a solid, gulping, ugly cry.

"That's right," says Bridge through her own tears. They're not nearly as outrageous as mine, but I have a hard time managing my emotions these days.

Bridge reaches a hand out to cradle the growing bump of my belly. "We wouldn't miss this one's debut for anything in the world."

Mom's hand joins Bridge's on my belly. "I'm going to be the best grandma you've ever seen in your life."

The moment is coming, the moment where they both stand up to go, and I have to let them. The moment rushes at me like a tidal wave when I hear the rumble of Sam's diesel coming up the road.

"No," I whisper, grasping their hands and keeping them on my stomach, "I'm not ready."

They both kiss me, Bridge on one cheek and Mom on the other. "We'll never be ready, honey," says Mom. "But it's time."

"A few months? You promise?" I'm shifting my eyes from one to the other, memorizing their faces, searing them into my brain.

Bridge shakes her head. "Oh hell, Nona. Who am I kidding? I'll be back up next weekend."

We all laugh, then cry, and then we stand.

∾

Charlie holds me, but I'm inconsolable while we watch Sam's truck disappear behind the trees. They're gone. They're all really gone.

"What'll we do without them?" I ask, my nose running.

Charlie hands me a handkerchief, then says through his own tears. "Have lots of loud sex."

I laugh into the hankie, wiping my nose, then I look to my right where a large bear rocks in my Poppop's rocking chair. "At least we still have Larry."

Charlie whips his head from side to side, like he's trying to shake off his sadness the way a dog shakes water from its coat, then he takes my hand. "Come on, sweetheart. I've got something I've been wanting to show you."

"Now?" I groan, wanting to do nothing but crawl back under the covers and cry for the next few days.

"Now."

He leads me out the door and up the trail leading north from the cabin. The snow is finally melting in the valley and tiny shooting stars and yellow bells hover over patches of bright green grass.

"Where are we going?" I ask.

"It's a surprise."

We hike to Sam and Marge's cabin, stopping in briefly to say hello, promising to stop by on our way back for some preserves. Then we carry on north.

"Aunt Lulu's?" I ask, still wondering what he's up to.

"Sort of," Charlie replies, cryptic.

We do end up at Lulu's cabin, but we hike past it, behind it, further on for about a half mile. The woods open up, revealing a beautiful, sparkling, mountain pond. It's a different time of year. Snow still lingers around the banks and the center of the pond is still frozen. But I know this pond.

I walk closer, kneeling by the edge to touch my fingers to the icy water. "This is the pond from the picture, isn't it? The one in Lulu's house?"

Charlie comes to my side. "The very same."

I stand up to face him and he hooks his pinky with mine. "I've been saving this one, just for us. Hang on tight, sweetheart."

The scenery before me shifts, swirling in front of my eyes. And then everything is so much bigger as I fall back into the memory.

"GRANDMA FISHES IN THIS POND," Charlie says, his voice sweet and high. "She says it's got magic fish in it."

I stare up at him. I have to because he's a little bit taller than me. "Magic fish? Seriously?"

"Seriously," he says. "Grandma wouldn't lie."

"Charlie Brown, if you're pulling my leg…"

"I'm not kidding. They taste like candy."

I laugh from my belly. "No fish in the history of ever has tasted like candy."

Charlie's laughing too, then he turns to face me. "Sing that song for me, Nona. That one about the clouds."

"Really, again?" It's a silly little song I came up with last night in the bathtub. Charlie's already asked me to sing it to him five times today. But he's grinning at me, so I sing for him once more.

> Have you ever seen the sky
> Without a cloud
> Maybe a perfect kind of blue
> But with no fun allowed
>
> Have you ever seen the sky

> With no clouds floating by
> And the sun's got no shade
> So you gotta drink lemonade
>
> I don't ever want to see
> A bird without a bee
> A circus without a crowd
> Or a sky without a cloud
>
> So next time you see the sky
> With clouds high above
> Fluffy white, gray, or pink
> That's a sky full of love

Charlie giggles. "That's the best song."

"You know something, Charlie?" I say, staring out over the water as dusk muddies the colors of the pond, the grass, and the trees until they all look the same shade of gray. "I miss fireflies."

"Fireflies?" he asks. "Oh yeah, they don't come up here do they?"

I shake my head. "Never. Not once."

"Not once, huh?" He squeezes my pinky a little tighter. "I don't know. Maybe we'll get lucky tonight."

"Oh, come on. It's like an animal fact. They can't survive this far north, Momma said so."

A breeze blows Charlie's shaggy hair out of his eyes. They're a pretty brown, like Momma's coffee.

"Well, you sang me a song, so maybe I can do something for you."

"Sure. Wanna make me ice cream or something? I'd rather have that than candy fish." My face scrunches as I stick out my tongue.

"I was thinking of something else. Look out there, Nona."

I squint at him, suspicious, then I turn toward the pond

again. "Charlie, is that? Is it?" Words fly away from me as I see one, then two, then hundreds of tiny yellow lights flickering on and off over the water. "Fireflies!"

~

"Open your eyes, Nona."

I'm smiling so wide my face hurts. "That was us? In the picture?"

Charlie nods. "Lulu must have taken it."

"I remember. I remember meeting you. I was what, six, seven?"

"Must have been around then. It was the year before my mom died. The last year I ever came up here." He looks at me. "I loved you, you know. Even then, I loved you. I was so pissed when you and Bridge didn't recognize or remember me when I joined your band." He smiles. "I remembered you."

My mouth falls open. "You did? Why didn't you say something?"

"I didn't want you to think I was a weirdo stalker or something." He scratches his head. "I don't know, it just never seemed like the right time."

"I totally did think you were a weirdo back when we were kids," I admit. "A very cute weirdo. Charlie, you brought me fireflies. It is the nicest thing anyone has ever done for me, aside from breaking a powerful magical curse on me and my family, of course." I want to kiss him, but just as I'm leaning in, right in front of my face, a tiny yellow butt blinks into existence.

I gasp, then squeal as fireflies hover all around us, blinking on and off in their slow and lovely mating dance. "How! How do you do it?"

He slides his arms around my waist and pulls me to him. "Magic," he says, then he kisses me. "Sing it for me?"

"The cloud song?"

"No," he laughs. "Sing me my song."
I turn back toward the water and sing.

> This morning I woke to a dark gray sky and an
>   empty bed
> You'd left in the night for an early flight with too
>   many things unsaid
> The driving rain on my windowpane sings a
>   bitter song
> Of a late-night fight where no one's right
> And still we played along
>
> I should've said goodbye
> I should've held you close to me
> I should've said I'm sorry, baby
> Now I'm missing Charlie
>
> When you look at me, you see all of me
> And when I look at you, my heart reaches through
> All the distance between where I stand and sing
> And where I want to be
> Where I want to be
>
> Later that night with the curtains pulled tight
> And my tears staining my pillow
> I don't hear you come in, but when you touch
>   my skin
> I grab your hand and don't let go
>
> I wish I'd said goodbye
> I wish I'd held you close to me
> And I'm so sorry, baby
> Don't ever leave me, Charlie

When you look at me, you see all of me
And when I look at you, my heart reaches through
All the distance between where I stand and sing
and where I want to be
Where I want to be
With you

"That's the one." He winks at me, and then I attack him.

We stumble into Lulu's cabin. Well, Charlie stumbles, I'm clinging to him, my legs wrapped tightly around his waist. We're kissing as he walks so it's got to be hard for him to see where he's going. Eyes closed and hands grasping at his shirt, I'm no help at all.

He pushes me into the door to Lulu's bedroom and it swings wide for us. Then he throws me onto the bed.

"We're taking that back with us," I say, pointing at our picture.

"Mmmhmm," he mutters, climbing on the bed and sliding my shirt up to kiss a trail along my swollen belly.

I'm sorry Aunt Lulu, but we are absolutely defiling your bed tonight. I hope you don't mind.

"Woah! What the hell?" blurts Charlie. He's sitting up and staring down at an object that's appeared out of nowhere in his hand. "What is this?"

I'm laughing. "Well, honey, that one looks like oatmeal raisin."

I guess Aunt Lulu doesn't mind.

MUCH, MUCH LATER

MUCH HAS HAPPENED since that day. Much has changed, and much has remained the same.

We gave Rebecca six months to fade from the spotlight so I could return to my career in her place. She and Fritz concocted a likely story—drugs, alcohol, moving to New Mexico to live with a self-proclaimed guru named Zol. She decided she liked New Mexico, and as far as I know, she's still there, making jewelry or something.

The last we'd heard of Julianne, she'd lived out the remainder of her magic-less days in a nursing home in Wyoming, never speaking another word. But sometimes—even after hearing she passed years ago—I still wake up and see her at the foot of my bed. Maybe I always will.

Charlie and I were married right before I gave birth to our first daughter. We had a short ceremony, officiated by a reluctant Larry because, evidently, when a couple is married by their totem it's a sign of good luck. That's what Charlie told me anyway, but honestly I think he just wanted to be married by a bear. The pictures are phenomenal.

We had two girls we named Janey and Lulu, and they had

eight kids between them. Last count we have fourteen great-grandkids. Everyone in the family inherited at least a little magic from Charlie, some more than others, and one, Lulu's youngest daughter Sophie, is downright amazing with her gift for earth magic.

My career never fully recovered from the move away from Rebecca's pop stardom. My triumphant return from rehab and back to my folk roots was the biggest story in music, for about a week. But everyone wanted to hear Rebecca's songs at every concert, and I never wanted to sing them. So Charlie and I played small clubs, recorded a few more albums. It wasn't bad. I loved the intimacy of smaller venues, the freedom to write whatever I wanted. And my last album even had a hit that won me a Grammy nomination.

But after our kids went off to school and my voice started changing, I hung up my guitar and Charlie and I moved, believe it or not, back up here. To the cabin. We both missed it, missed Larry, and it was just easier than having to come back up every few months to re-stabilize the magic that broke the curse.

James eventually moved up here too, into Lulu's cabin. Whatever bit of her remains in that cabin kept him company for years with cookies and card games. James had a dream one night that he could make pictures appear out of thin air, and when he woke up, he held that picture of me shooting cans in front of the cabin, the same picture given to Charlie that restored his memories. That's how we found out it was Aunt Lulu all along who led Charlie to my cabin, using her magic beyond the grave to send him that picture.

James and Charlie became as close as any father and son could. They spent days going through Aunt Lulu's letters, the ones from James telling her all about Charlie. When James died years later, we kept his ashes at Lulu's, hoping whatever magic linked her to the cabin might work on James too. But James might not have had that same sort of magic because, sadly, we haven't heard a word from him.

Bridge and Jack thrived after they left the cabin. They had a whole gaggle of kids and grandkids, and they still come up to visit us every summer. They used to visit more often, but it's harder now. Jack has bad hips and has to use a power scooter to get around, so the snow is too much for him. Sometimes Bridge comes up with the kids or grandkids without him, and sometimes she comes all by herself. Those visits I cherish above all others. We drink too much, eat until we're sick, and laugh until we cry.

Mom and Wally both lived well into their 90's, tearing it up in Charleston. They visited too, but never enough. When Mom died, for weeks I thought I'd die too. It was like this solid bit of my existence, this bedrock supporting me as I moved through the world, letting me know where I came from, who I was, and that no matter what, somebody out there loved me unconditionally, just vanished right out from under me.

We brought her ashes up here and now she lives with us again, her urn sitting on the mantle right next to Wally's, who passed six months before she did. I swear sometimes even now I can hear her laughing at my stupid jokes or telling me, "Oh, don't be so dramatic," when I'm too worked up about something.

Fritz stayed on as our manager until we stopped performing, even though he could have made a much better career for himself if he'd left us for one of the many offers he received from other artists. But he's as loyal as they come. And our best friend. But don't tell Larry I said that, he'd be devastated.

Fritz found his husband Joe, a photographer from Chicago during one of my photo shoots. After we moved back to the cabin, Fritz and Joe came up every fall until the travel got to be too hard for them. But when they came, we had more fun than should be legal. In fact, it probably wasn't legal in most states.

Summers are still rowdy up here, full of laughter and children screaming and begging me for ice cream and coffee cake and venison stew. But now winter is coming and I'm out chopping wood, the sun beating down while a storm brews to the south.

Not many people, I imagine, get to grow old twice. It's stranger this second time around. I've taken care of myself, kept my body strong and my skin moisturized to the point of obsession. But today, one week after my eighty-third birthday, I feel older than I did the last time I was this age.

I haul firewood into the cabin, armful after armful, the rough wood tearing my thin skin despite my layered shirts. After I'm finished, I stand at the sink and stare out the window, watching the sky darken, storm clouds rising over the tips of the pines. Another winter. Another six months of snow and cold, fires and tea, whiskey and cuddling. Each winter is a bit harder than the last, but each spring is more beautiful than the one before.

I wash my skin with my goat's milk soap, then I dry my arms with a dish towel before reaching for the gauze.

"Let me help with that." His voice, familiar as any I've ever known, tickles my ear as he leans down to press a kiss onto my neck.

I turn and hand him the gauze, then hold my arms out to him. "Where have you been all afternoon?"

"Oh, just hanging out with Larry." He starts wrapping my left arm.

"Is he coming for dinner?"

He moves onto my right arm. "No, not tonight."

"That's too bad. But we should leave the shed open for him in case he wants to come in from the storm."

"Already done."

There's a gleam in Charlie's eyes as he reaches behind me to flip on the radio.

"Hmm, I love this song," I say, winking at him. Somehow, he always knows when "Night Life" is playing on the radio. A curious yet surprisingly useful spark of magic.

"Dance with me, sweetheart."

I place my hand into his and he takes it, wrapping it around his neck before pulling me close.

"I love that move, too." I slide my other hand up his arm.

"I know."

Ray Price croons in our kitchen and I dance with my husband, my best friend, my soulmate who won my heart first with fireflies, later with music, and finally with a fake broken leg and a real talking bear. Charlie sings in my ear, his voice rumbling through my chest as he holds me close, just as it has for the last sixty years. I smile against his shoulder and sing along, letting him sway me side to side while outside our window, the snow begins to fall.

~THE END~

ABOUT THE AUTHOR

A Montana transplant hailing from the suburbs of Chicago and about twenty other places, Jess K Hardy is a lover of mountains and snow, long nights and fireplaces. She has been a sandwich artist, a student, a horse trainer, a physical therapist, a wife, a mother, and also a writer. She writes contemporary and speculative adult romance.

ALSO BY JESS K HARDY

COME AS YOU ARE: BLUEBIRD BASIN BOOK 1
LIPS LIKE SUGAR: BLUEBIRD BASIN BOOK 2
THE 7 RULES OF MOVING ON
The Ignisar series—Scifi romance:
LOVE IN THE TIME OF WORMHOLES
I, BIONIC.
THE PRINCESS AND THE BRUISER

Please join my MAILING LIST for book news!

ACKNOWLEDGMENTS

Thank you to my family, my friends, my readers, my dogs, and Montana.